The Cottage in Maple Hill

MICHELLE LEIGH MILLER

D1714677

Dedicated to my husband, Tim Miller

Prologue

Liza Blackburn hadn't realized she'd nearly stopped painting. Not until her grandmother strolled around her studio and studied the canvases stacked along the wall. She stopped, crossed her arms, and scowled at Liza. "Where are the new ones?"

Liza looked around the room—the small second bedroom of her apartment that had served as her studio for years—and back at her grandmother. "There are some new ones in here."

"No ma'am. Not one of these is new. I've seen them all."

Liza considered her grandmother's comment for a moment, trying to pinpoint the newest piece of artwork.

She landed on a painting of an elderly couple in the park. "There," she pointed, confident. "That one is new."

Her grandmother shook her head. "No, child. I saw that last year. Beautiful. Reminded me of your grandpa and me. Had he lived long enough to get old. But definitely not new."

Panicked, Liza searched the stacks of canvases again, mentally picturing herself painting them. Her eyes wandered to the table that held her paints, the splotches of color long dried, and thought back to the elderly couple in the park. She visualized herself, sitting on the park bench, sketching them in her pad as they smiled at each other. Their heads together as they talked. Her brain pieced together a timeline until the realization settled onto her like a heavy, wet blanket. She'd stopped by that park after her niece Chloe's second birthday party, in need of a few moments of quiet to offset the chaos of screaming kids she'd just survived. Chloe was now nearly five.

Had she gone almost three years without painting? Three years without finishing a piece? She had sketches in her pad. She knew that. It's what she did when she was bored or if something inspiring caught her eye. Always safely tucked in her bag, just in case inspiration struck. But when was the last time she bought a new one? She couldn't remember.

While Liza was lost in her own thoughts, her grandmother continued around the studio. She stopped in front of a painting of a red fox in snow Liza had completed after a late-night binge of nature shows. "This one. I want to buy this one. It will look good in my living room."

"Grandma, you can just have it," Liza started but was cut off by an irritated tsk, tsk.

"I said I'll buy it, child. And I intend to do just that." A warm, brittle hand rested on Liza's shoulder. "Come on. I need some tea."

Liza followed her to the kitchen and sat on the bar stool while her grandmother pulled the tea kettle from the cupboard, filled it and put it on the stove. While it was heating, she pulled out two mugs and the box of tea bags, opened two bags and put one in each mug. "You know, if you would visit me at the cottage, there are all kinds of things you can paint there."

Liza laughed. "I can't help it you decided to winter in Ohio. No offense, Grandma, but who does that?"

Her grandmother turned to her and leaned her back against the counter. "Me, I guess. I like the cold and snow. Reminds me of my childhood. Though I must admit, these old bones are revolting against me."

"And I like warm and sunny."

"Well, the offer always stands."

A little quiver of guilt set in. It wasn't like they didn't spend a lot of time together. Her grandmother was in Florida nearly as much as she was in Ohio. But still. "I'll try to get some time off next winter. I promise," Liza said.

That seemed to please her grandmother, who switched topics. "When's the last time you left this place? Went on a walk in the park? Went out with friends? Painted?"

"It's been a while, I guess. Things have been busy at work. By the time I get home, I just kind of collapse. Weekends, I don't know. I just..." Her grandmother waited while Liza processed her thoughts. "I don't know. I guess I just haven't felt much like painting lately. It's really a hobby now, anyway. It's not like anyone sees them but you."

A short, irritated huff escaped her grandmother. "And whose fault is that?"

Liza braced herself for the lecture, one she'd heard countless times. Over the years, her grandmother had needled her, sent her information on galleries looking for artwork, pushed her to put it out there. And she'd listened politely and nodded in agreement when needed. But she knew something her grandmother didn't—her art wasn't good enough. As loud as her grandmother's voice was, her former art professor's voice was louder. Constantly criticizing. Constantly condescending. Where her grandmother looked at those pieces and gushed over them, she saw the mistakes, the areas she could improve.

She was saved by the high-pitched whistle of the tea kettle. Her grandmother turned back to her original task, poured the boiling water over the tea bags, and placed the steaming cup and saucer in front of Liza. While Liza dunked the tea bag in the water and watched it turn from murky to brown, her grandmother sat down next to her and did the same.

"Inspiration doesn't always come to you, child. Sometimes, you have to go out and find it."

"I know, Grandma."

"I mean, you're not getting any younger."

Liza gasped. "Grandma! I'm only thirty-three."

Her grandmother shrugged. "Time moves faster the older you get. Trust me on that." After taking a sip of her tea, she reached over and gently placed her hand on Liza's chin, turning her head until their eyes connected. "You are an amazing artist."

Liza tried to shake her head, but her grandmother's grip on her chin held firm. "You are. And I'm not saying it just because I'm your grandmother. You could spend your life being afraid, my dear. Just existing. Or you can go out there, take a chance and maybe really live. The choice is yours. But I think it's a sad thing for all those pieces to be hidden away in a room. That's all."

With that, she released Liza's chin, and Liza quickly turned away to hide the tears forming.

"Now that we're done with all that nonsense, where are you taking me to dinner?"

Liza laughed and wiped her eyes before turning back to her grandmother. "Charlie's?"

"Charlie's it is."

As they walked out the door, Liza didn't know that she would never get to visit her grandmother in Ohio or have another dinner with her. Just four months later, she was gone.

Chapter One

Liza stood outside the church doors and considered her mother might actually kill her this time. From the moment her eyes had sprung open with the realization she'd slept through her alarm to recklessly speeding through downtown St. Petersburg, Florida, her phone had buzzed relentlessly.

She had sent a text that she was on her way, long before she was actually on her way, but hadn't read the subsequent text messages. Thirty by last count. Or listened to the five voicemails. They would all be a version of the same thing: Who the hell is late for their grandmother's funeral?

If she was smart, she'd turn around and go back home. Feign an illness. Maybe go to the emergency room. Would she be too terribly hurt if she wrecked her car doing ten miles an hour?

Except she wouldn't. Regardless of the aftermath, her grandmother deserved better than that. Taking a deep breath, Liza ran her hands down the front of her dress, then pulled at the material to stretch it. Apparently, she'd put on a few pounds in the last five years, something she would have known had she tried on the dress early as her mother had recommended. Shaking that off, too, she adjusted her purse and took hold of the church door handle.

Flecks of dried paint covering her fingers caught her eye. She snatched her hand back and self-consciously rubbed it against her dress. When she grasped the door handle again, they were still there.

"Nothing you can do about it now, Liza. Get it over with," she said aloud and then pulled.

The squeal of the door hinges reverberated into the high rafters of the small church. Mourners packed into the wooden pews pivoted and craned to look as she used her back to let the heavy door close softly behind her. Heat rising in her cheeks and her eyes trained on the faded and tattered carpet under her feet, Liza scurried along the back row to the main aisle. Pastor McCarty, who everyone knew left his hearing aids turned down at the pulpit, continued his sermon, oblivious to the interruption.

As she rounded the corner to the aisle, pain shot through her foot when her toe connected with the thick, wooden base of the back pew. One minute she was walking, and the next, she was landing face-first on that tattered carpet with a bone-shuddering thud, hearing the back of her dress rip as she went down.

For a moment, she lay there unmoving, trying to catch her breath, pushing down the string of curse words threatening to escape. Her muscles and bones, initially shocked at the sudden impact, made themselves known one-by-one with sharp, shooting pains.

Under Pastor McCarty's escalating sermon, gasps and mutterings erupted all around her. She raised her head and gingerly placed her hands on the carpet, feeling the back of her dress let loose as she pushed herself to her knees. She reached back, feeling bare skin where the zipper used to be. A fresh wave of embarrassment washed over her as she struggled to find her footing while pulling the ripped seam closed.

She startled when large hands met hers and then took over the job of closing the gap in her dress, evident by the way it tightened around her waist. Craning her neck, she looked up at the man, and faint recognition sparked. She didn't have time to analyze it, as his other hand had already encircled her upper arm and was helping her to her feet.

Silently, he removed his simple, dark blue suit jacket one arm at a time, his grip on her dress changing as needed, and then draped it over her shoulders. As he let go of the ripped fabric for good, she felt the tension on her dress release underneath the jacket.

Then he was gone, leaving her to make the rest of the trip up the aisle alone. Clutching the suit jacket around her shoulders, head still down, she made her way to the front pew where her mother and sister, Anna, sat. She'd almost made it when past and present collided and faint recognition morphed into a mortifying realization that her rescuer was Derrick Lowe. Her grandmother's neighbor. And for two weeks out of the year, for three years, the love of her pre-teen life. A memory flashed of him riding his dirt bike past her grandmother's driveway while she stood at the end pretending to be interested in whatever was on the ground that day. The memory was so overwhelming she could almost smell the exhaust. Then it vanished, leaving just an empty feeling in the pit of her stomach and a little extra heat in her cheeks.

By the time she slipped into the empty space in the front pew, the weight of the moment had settled on her shoulders. Her eyes focused on the closed casket in front of her, as she felt Anna's hand slip onto hers and squeeze. Behind her, she heard her niece, Chloe, start to say her name and being gently shushed by her father. Part of her wanted to turn around, but she couldn't remove her gaze from the casket. A lump formed in her throat, and then tears welled in her eyes, making the white and yellow carnations blanketing the casket swim. She pushed the tears back down as she battled a wave of guilt and grief.

Guilt over being late. Guilt over making a scene. Guilt over not visiting her grandmother in Ohio. Guilt over not following her advice. Grief over losing the one person who would have found her fall funny. The person who would have given her a hug and a kiss on the cheek and told her an embarrassing story of her own. She was gone, her body prone in the casket at the front of the church. There would be no more lunches or strolls along the beach. No more giggling in the corner at a family function over something neither should have been doing. No one to care about the artwork hiding in her makeshift studio. No one to gently—and sometimes not so gently—nudge her to do something with the pieces, to follow her dreams.

The tears returned, refusing to be pushed back, and cascaded down her cheeks. Anna's hand disappeared and reappeared holding a tissue. She took it, dabbing away the tears as they fell. Then Anna's arms slipped around her shoulder and squeezed. She leaned into the hug, her gaze resting on her mother's face on the other side of her sister.

Her jaw tight, the muscles contracting as she worked to contain her anger, Deborah Blackburn's back was ramrod straight against the wooden pew, her eyes trained on Pastor McCarty. Then her head slowly turned toward Liza, her eyes shooting daggers at her youngest daughter before returning to the front.

Liza looked up at Anna, who gave her a wink that squeezed tears from her red-rimmed eyes. Straightening her spine, Liza turned her attention to Pastor McCarty's sermon. She couldn't do anything about her mother. That battle would come later. All she could do was spend the rest of the time doing what she'd planned to do and that was to say goodbye to Dorothy Elizabeth McDonald, Dot to her friends, Grandma to her, and the one person who had understood her.

Chapter Two

Alone in the guest room, which had once been her childhood bedroom, Liza unhooked the clasp at the base of her neck and the dress fell into a heap at her feet. Stepping out of it, she scooped it up and held it in front of her, examining the ripped zipper. Then she tossed it onto the bed next to the neatly folded suit jacket.

Despite the tension between her and her mother, the rest of the funeral and the burial had gone smoothly. Deborah had invited everyone at the graveside back to her house for a meal. Seeing the way her dress had given way after unclasping the top, Liza was glad she hadn't found the right time to return the jacket.

When they'd arrived at their mother's house, Anna had retrieved a skirt and blouse she'd worn to the viewing the evening before and handed them to Liza. While it wasn't black, it was dark enough not to draw attention. As Liza slipped the blouse over her head, she breathed a sigh of relief that it fit.

She was just finishing up when someone tapped on the door, and Anna entered without waiting. Liza thought she looked exhausted as she walked across and flopped down on the bed. Moving the coat to the armchair, Liza dropped her dress on the floor and lay down beside Anna, both staring up at the ceiling.

"Today sucked," said Anna.

"Yep."

"So, why were you late anyway?" Anna asked, turning her head to face Liza.

"I just overslept." Liza saw no point in telling Anna why she overslept any more than she planned to tell her mother. Neither would understand.

"Sorry."

Liza let her cheek fall to the bed to face her sister. Her lips pulled into a thin line. "It is what it is."

Anna flipped on her side and propped her head on her hand. "Hey, who was the guy who helped you in the aisle?"

Liza followed, propping her own head up and smiled. "That was Derrick Lowe."

Anna stared blankly, and then her eyes lit up. "Derrick? You mean grandma's neighbor, Derrick?"

"Yep."

Anna's eyes widened, then wiggled. "He grew up a bit, didn't he?"

Liza adjusted her cheek against her hand. "Yes, he did."

"You were so obsessed with him. I remember you used to beg Grandma to ask him over to fix things. Sometimes she did, if memory serves."

"Yeah. I was like twelve. I think he was seventeen or eighteen. Something like that. Whatever he was, he was completely not interested," Liza said with a laugh. "In me, anyway."

"And I had no interest in him," Anna said. "Though, if I weren't happily married with a kid, I could be persuaded now. Whoa." With dramatic flair, she fanned her face with her hand.

Liza smacked Anna's arm with her free hand, and the two women playfully slapped at each other before falling into a fit of giggles. Then it slowed, and they stared at each other. "That felt wrong," Liza said.

"Nah. It's okay. Grandma would want us to laugh," Anna said, reaching over and resting her palm on Liza's cheek. Liza leaned into the touch, and they both stayed that way for a moment, sharing their grief with one another.

Ever the responsible one, Anna sighed, slapped the bed, and sat up. "We should get downstairs. Mom is going to start wondering where we are."

Liza groaned and pulled herself to a sitting position, eyeing the jacket as she did. Anna followed her gaze. "You think he'll be here?"

Liza shrugged and stood up. "I hope so. I'd rather just give that to him now, so I don't have to remember to ship it."

Standing up, Anna draped her arm over Liza's shoulder and gave it a squeeze. "Come on. On the bright side, you know mom is entirely too classy to let loose on you with others around, so at least you know nothing is going to happen right now."

"True, but man, can that woman still give some withering looks."

Anna let go of her grip and walked toward the door, shooting a glance over her shoulder. "Yep, you and her both darling." Then she grinned and walked out. Outside, she heard Anna yell for Chloe to hurry and then her footsteps thudded on the stairs.

At the mirror, Liza inspected herself one more time, smiled and checked her teeth, straightened her shoulders, and walked out.

Except for the black attire, one would have thought Deborah was hosting a party as opposed to an after-funeral reception, the way she flitted from the living room to the family room to the dining room where people were settled. Ever the dutiful daughter, Anna tried to keep up, keeping Chloe on a short leash for instances when someone wanted to see the "baby."

Liza had stuck close to the outer edges, moving from one corner to the next. It didn't stop people from coming up to her, though they were few. Mostly those she recognized from her grandmother's mobile home park where Liza typically spent a great deal of time during the summer. Liza couldn't help but wonder if people just didn't know her or if everyone else was avoiding the topic of her embarrassing entrance like she was.

A few times she made eye contact with her brother-in-law, Scott, who looked equally uncomfortable. They would smile at each other and then move, trying to avoid drawing attention to their lack of involvement. Eventually, Liza landed next to the kitchen, which provided a peaceful escape, even if for only a few minutes. It also allowed her to keep a close eye on the door in case Derrick appeared.

"How are you holding up?" Liza turned to find Scott standing next to her, his arms folded against his chest leaning against the wall.

Liza shrugged. "Okay, I guess. You?"

He gave a thumbs up and returned his arm to its previous folded position. Liza flashed him a smile, knowing it was a lie. On an introverted scale of one to ten, Scott was a solid twenty. As a matter of fact, it had taken a good month after they'd met before Liza had decided to like him.

That moment had only come after a house party Anna had thrown in her college apartment and multiple shots of tequila Anna hadn't known she'd consumed. They'd stood in the kitchen, bonding over art history. So much so, Anna finally had to interrupt and pull him back to the party. To this day, Liza thought maybe he'd kept her in the kitchen so she would sober up before her sister caught on.

Over eighteen years later, he was the quiet, big brother she'd never known she needed.

He started to speak, but then looked over Liza's shoulder, straightened and held his hands out. Liza turned to find Anna headed their way, carrying Chloe. The hand-off was seamless and without words, as Anna gently pried Chloe's hands from around her neck and passed her to Scott. Exhausted, Chloe's cheek planted on Scott's shoulder, and her eyes closed.

"Aww." Liza rubbed Chloe's back lightly.

"She's exhausted, Scott. Would you mind taking her upstairs for a little nap?"

"I don't need a nap. I'm a big girl," Chloe slurred, then promptly closed her eyes.

All three chuckled, and Liza rubbed her back again. "It's okay, Chloe. Even big girls need naps sometimes." But Liza realized she was already out.

Scott pecked Anna on the cheek, then winked at Liza. "Hang in there, sis."

"I will," Liza said, watching them go.

Anna took his spot. "You've done a pretty good job at hiding in plain sight."

Liza laughed. "That's the point."

"It's a good turnout."

"Yeah. It is. Grandma would have been happy."

"Yep. I mean, she would have complained about all the people, but she would have been happy."

"True, that," Liza said.

"By the way, I think I saw Derrick come in." Anna slid past Liza into the kitchen. "Also, shields up. Mom is headed this way."

Liza, who'd been momentarily excited over Derrick's appearance, steeled herself just as her mother arrived.

"Liza, have you been hiding out here the whole time?" snapped her mother as she passed.

"No," she lied, glancing through the opening at Anna. "I just came over to get something to drink." Realizing she didn't have a drink in her hand, she stepped into the kitchen and took the drink Anna was thankfully already handing her. Taking a sip, she said, "I was just getting ready to go back out and find Derrick."

Deborah opened the refrigerator, pulled out a glass bottle of water, closed the door, and took a drink. "Derrick?

Who's Derrick?" Then she realized. "The nice young man who lives next to your grandmother? How do you know him?"

"He was the man who lent me his coat at the funeral."

Her mother nodded and as she walked toward the door said, "You mean when the dress ripped that you clearly didn't try on?"

There it was. Liza has been waiting for a comment about the dress. As usual, her mother had just been waiting for the perfect moment. Before Liza could say anything, Deborah had already sauntered out of the kitchen.

"Chin up, li'l sis," Anna said as she walked by her, giving Liza a light punch on the arm. "It could be worse."

"How?"

Anna shrugged. "Don't know. But it can always be worse."

When the coast was clear, Liza slipped from the kitchen and darted upstairs to retrieve the jacket. As she descended, she scanned the crowd for Derrick.

Off in the corner, she finally spotted him weaving through the mourners hovering near the back door, then slip out. Picking up her pace, she managed to greet people and thank them for their condolences while still making steady progress toward her destination. Finally, she reached it, turned the knob, and stepped out, blinking against the bright Florida sun.

At first, she'd thought she'd missed him. As far as she could tell, no one was around. Her shoulders hunching, she pulled the coat to her chest and turned to go back into the house when a male voice caught her attention. It was coming from behind the tropically landscaped section at the corner of the house.

Trusting her instincts that it had to be Derrick, she walked toward the voice. The closer she got, the clearer the words were. Slowly, she stopped walking and stood instead, unsure if interrupting him or eavesdropping was worse.

"My flight leaves at six, so I'll be back in town by one, hopefully."

Silence.

"It was very nice. Well, nice except for the granddaughter's entrance."

Every muscle in Liza's body froze and dread washed through her. She should turn around and leave. She knew that. But she couldn't move.

"Yeah, it was bad. First, she was late. I mean, super late. Then when she came in, she looked like she'd just rolled out of bed. Then she fell. I mean, face-planted right there in the aisle. And her dress was so tight that it ripped right down her back."

Silence.

"The family has to be horrified. I was horrified. I jumped up and covered her with my jacket. The worst part was, she didn't even act bothered by it. Embarrassed or anything. Just took my jacket and headed to the front. It's why I came to this. To get my jacket back. Otherwise, I'd already be at the airport."

Shock first, then anger swept through Liza. Not bothered by it? Really? How would he know?

"Dot used to talk about Liza all of the time. I mean, all of the time. Like she was the best thing since sliced bread. I couldn't believe it. That woman is not the woman I pictured. Not someone I want to get to know, that's for sure."

And that was it. Liza, her body tense and her knuckles white on the hand clenching the jacket, strode toward the clearing and stepped into it.

A small amount of satisfaction slid through the raging anger at the look on his face when he saw her. She stood there, one hand on her hip, the other thrust toward him with the jacket. He sputtered a few times then told the person on the other end of the call he needed to go. Disconnecting the call, he slid the phone into his pocket, then started to take a step forward. The look on her face must have stopped him because he halted, then took a step back.

"Liza," he said. She could tell by his tone, the niceness of it spread across uncertainty, that he was trying to figure out how much she had heard.

"Here," she said, shaking the jacket dangling in front of her. "I brought your jacket."

Her original intention had been to thank him profusely for saving her and maybe even explain a little why she'd been late. Not now. Now, she'd die right there before showing him any gratitude.

Refusing to move toward him, she cocked her head to the side as if to say, "Well?"

In one big step, he closed the distance between them, took the jacket, and returned to his spot.

She hadn't planned to say anything else, to just turn and walk away. But her plans to not speak rarely worked out. As she turned, she looked over her shoulder at him, "You can go now. Since that jacket is the only reason you came. And you don't know anything about me. And you sure as hell don't know anything about me and my grandmother."

Before he could respond, she turned on her heel and marched back to the house.

As Liza stepped back inside, she started for the stairs with every intention of hiding away, at least until the boiling anger subsided. She'd almost made it to the bottom of the staircase when Anna appeared in front of her and grabbed her hand.

"Come on. You've left me hanging long enough tonight. Your turn."

Resigned and knowing Anna was speaking the truth, Liza followed her into the sea of only slightly familiar faces. Throughout the rest of the reception, Liza orbited her mother and Anna as they chatted with various people. Occasionally, the guests would speak to her. Telling a story of how they'd met her when she was a little girl, talking about how much they'd miss her grandmother at bridge club. A few were extended family. Anna even had some high school friends attend.

Her mother kept a pleasant smile throughout, though she'd avoided eye contact with Liza. There was a glimmer of hope that Deborah would let Liza's transgression go without further comment. It was rare, but it happened occasionally.

Finally, it was over, and the crowd thinned. As Deborah ushered out the last of the guests, Liza marveled at how quickly the gracious hostess act dropped from her mother's face, revealing the brewing thunderstorm underneath.

As soon as the door latched, Deborah spun around on Liza. "Now. Do you mind explaining to me how you could be late for your grandmother's funeral?"

Take whatever is coming, Liza thought as she looked down at her feet. Words escaped her. Of only one thing was she certain—the truth that she'd been up all night painting wouldn't make things better. At the same time, she was entirely too drained to lie. So, what came out was, "I know. I'm sorry."

Silence filled the space between them and stretched out so long Liza finally looked at her mother.

Deborah was just staring at Liza, her hands on her hips, fury etched into her face. "I didn't ask if you were sorry, Elizabeth Ann Blackburn. I asked why."

Immediately, Liza felt the surge simmer at the use of her full name. Like she was a child, being scolded for not eating all of her dinner. The little voice sounded. *Just take it.* And she pushed it back down. "I just overslept, Mom. I'm sorry. I don't know what you want me to say."

Deborah's arms flung into the air in frustration. "Of course you don't, Liza." The volume of her voice steadily increased. "Do you have any idea how mortifying your little display was this morning? Late. Falling. The ripping dress! Do you? Do you have any idea?"

"Yes, Mom!" Liza's volume rose to match her mother's. "I know how mortifying it was. It was me who fell!"

"Well, great! At least you appear to have the decency to be embarrassed. Finally!"

"Finally? What does that mean? Finally?" she asked, hearing the way her words clipped in her growing anger. Her plans to just take it had evaporated.

"Exactly what I said! You go around just doing what you want without any regard for anyone else! Just me, me, me!"

"Well, maybe I pay attention to ME because I'm the only one who does!" Liza screamed back.

"Oh, here we go again. Poor Liza, who had everything she wanted growing up. Poor Liza, who squandered everything away for a worthless art degree. That she doesn't even use. I have no idea where I went wrong with you! If it wasn't for your sister, I would think I was just a horrible mother!"

Liza physically recoiled at the verbal slap, her voice lowering. "And if it wasn't for Grandma, I would think you're a horrible mother, too."

Anna stepped in between them, "Hey! Whoa! That's enough."

Deborah started to speak just as Chloe's cries interrupted them. They all looked to the stairs, where Scott stood. His mouth was hanging open in shock, his hand firmly holding Chloe's who was sobbing. Anna looked between the two of them—"Nice, you two"—then walked over and scooped up Chloe.

Deborah immediately crossed to Chloe, opened her arms, and took the crying child. "It's okay, Chloe. Aunt Liza and I were just having a little argument. It's over now." She said the last part as she glared over her shoulder at Liza, then disappeared into the kitchen.

Deflated, Liza moved to the stairs, brushing past Scott, who reached out and patted her back.

In the room, she grabbed her purse then returned to the stairs. Anna was waiting on her at the bottom. "Don't go. Mom is just stressed. It'll blow over."

"Maybe," Liza said. "But it'll blow over faster if I'm not here."

She kissed Anna on the cheek then walked to the front door. Thankfully, Anna didn't stop her as she slipped out and rushed to her car. On the drive to her apartment, she cranked rock music in the hopes it would keep the tears at bay. It didn't.

Just as she pulled into her parking lot, her phone dinged with a text message from Anna. *Since you and Mom aren't speaking right now, wanted to let you know to expect a letter of some kind from Grandma.*

Liza pulled her phone out of the holder and texted back: *What kind of letter?*

Anna sent back a shrugging emoji, then: *No clue. Mom just said the attorney called and said there would be letters.*

Liza responded with a thumbs-up emoji and *Thanks.*

Anna ended with a heart emoji and *Love you,* and Liza responded with *Same.*

With the text conversation over, Liza sat in silence, playing the day over in her head. Too many mistakes for one day. She glanced back down at her phone, the text thread still visible. Letters from her grandmother? For each of them? Why? Then she realized the why didn't matter. At least she could look forward to it. Again, grief settled on her chest when she realized waiting for the letter would be the last time she could look forward to something from her grandmother. She sat in the grief for a minute, letting the fresh waves roll through her. Then, with a sigh, she stepped out of her car and slammed the door behind her.

Chapter Three

On the drive home from work, Liza turned up the radio, flipped it to a rock station and pulled the clasp in her hair free. The drive to and from work was like a switch for her and something she'd learned she needed to survive. On the way to work, she listened to softer music and got her head ready for a day of mundane tasks. On the way home, she cranked the rock station and loosened any tight hair or clothing.

At her apartment, she went straight to the mailbox and opened it, as she'd done every day for the last week. Usually, she'd go a day or two without checking it. She rarely had anything of interest in there. A few unopened bills she kept forgetting to put on email delivery and sales flyers were the sum total of her weekly mail. Knowing whatever was coming her way would be the last wishes of her grandmother left her with both sadness and excited anticipation.

Still, she paused in surprise when she swung open the mailbox door and saw a shipping envelope crammed inside. Pulling it out, she held it to her chest and hurried up the flight of stairs to her second-story apartment. Inside, she dropped her keys on the side table, her purse on the couch, and headed to the small bar that encircled the kitchenette. Sliding onto the stool, she placed the envelope in front of her and stared at it while she worked up the courage to open it.

It wasn't exactly what she expected. The outside of it bore her name and address typed in the center and at the top left, William C. Mason, Esq. with his office address in Maple Hill, Ohio. Running her hands across it, she felt the outline of another envelope inside, then flipped it over and ripped off the white strip. As she turned the package over, a letter-sized envelope slipped out and landed upside down on the counter.

When she flipped it over, her grandmother's elegant cursive penmanship greeted her. *To My Dearest Liza.*

Her hands shook as she turned the envelope back over, gently opened the sealed flap, and pulled out the folded stationery paper. She let the envelope fall back to the counter, as she unfolded the two-page letter and propped her elbows on the countertop.

As she read, tears welled and dripped onto the letter.

The first page detailed how much her grandmother loved her. How proud she was of her; how she hoped she'd carry the memories they made together in her heart.

And then the last lines gave her pause.

My dearest Liza, you've let your fear and insecurities take hold and shape your life. And I know, somewhere in there, is the fiery, young woman who snubbed her nose at what was expected of her and set off to live her life as she saw fit. What you're about to read will probably make you angry. I know it would me. Even as I sit here and write this, I cringe that I can't be there to offset the hurt and anger you will feel. But know, it is done out of love.

Letter outstretched, Liza let her hands fall to the counter while she considered her next move. Those last words rang ominously in her mind, warning her that what was about to come she wouldn't like. More than that, her grandmother's words stung as the realization that this, all along, was what her grandmother had thought of her. That she was failing at her own life.

Pulling the letter back up to view, she slipped the first page off and tucked it underneath. With a deep breath, she started to read. Anger sparked as her eyes scanned the words on the page. Then she read it again, just to be certain, the second look only fanning her rage. When she reached the last line, she threw the letter into the kitchen, watching it sway back and forth to the floor until it dropped out of sight. Then she shoved herself off of the stool.

Marching to her purse, she pulled out her cellphone and called Anna, her toe tapping on the bit of linoleum at the entrance while it rang.

"Hello?" Anna said, and Liza launched into furious pacing around her small apartment.

"Did you get the letter?" Liza's voice near shouting. Anna was quiet for a moment then said, "Well, I did.

But something is telling me I didn't get the same type of letter you did."

Liza broke down.

Over the phone, Liza heard doors close as Anna moved to another room. As Liza's tears slowed, Anna asked, "What in the world?"

Liza's breath caught. "I'm sorry. I..." She paused and sniffed, wiping her cheeks with her collar before taking a deep breath and letting it out through trembling lips. "Sorry. I don't know where that came from. Sorry."

"Stop apologizing, and tell me what is going on." "Apparently, Grandma thought I was a loser after all."

"What? No, she didn't. What makes you say that? What did her letter say to you?"

Standing up, Liza walked to the kitchen and picked up the tossed letter, then moved to the couch. Reading over the second page again, she pushed back the tears that threatened to start all over again. Then she pulled out the first page and read the last sentences to Anna.

When she finished and the silence on the other end stretched out too long, Liza's heart sank. Anna always went silent when she was figuring out a way to tell Liza a hard truth. "So, what is the rest of it?"

Liza flipped back to the second page, wiping her eyes again with her hand. "She's leaving me the cottage in Ohio and a nice trust fund." Liza said the last part hesitantly, hoping Anna had been left the same.

"Okay? She left me the mobile home and also a trust fund. Again, not seeing the big deal here."

"I get both if I live in the cottage for a year and complete a list of things. Otherwise, nothing."

"Oh. Hold on. Let me get my letter." Liza listened while Anna moved around the room, opened a drawer, then returned to what she assumed was the bed. There was the sound of rustling papers, then a quiet, "I don't have a list. What kind of things?"

Liza stiffened. Why wouldn't her grandmother make Anna jump through hoops, too? Why just her? This was ridiculous. All her life, her grandmother had been the only one Liza thought understood her. The only one who appeared to support her, no matter what. And while Liza would have taken her grandmother over her grandmother's money any day, the offer had been made. And it was a lot of money. Sixty thousand dollars, plus the cottage and her grandmother's car. Not to mention, she would receive a four-thousand dollar a month stipend during her year stay.

It was enough to finish paying off her student loans and her two credit cards. She could sell her beater car and still have a little leftover for savings. For once, she would be able to breathe a little with her finances. On the flip side, she had a job—one she was good at. She had worked hard to climb that ladder, and it wouldn't wait a year for her.

"Liza?"

"I'm still here."

"Sorry. Maybe it won't be that bad. Ohio. I mean, Grandma loved it. Maybe you will, too."

"I didn't say I'm going yet."

Anna laughed. "If you don't, then what happens?"

"You get all the money."

There was silence, and then Anna laughed again. "Well, then, by all means, flake out and don't go. I will totally take that money. What about the cottage?"

"Mom."

"Oh, she'll love that. It might be entertaining just to watch her reaction."

Liza stood up, walked to the kitchen, and pulled a wineglass from the cabinet. "This is so ridiculous," she said as she retrieved a bottle of wine from the refrigerator and filled the glass to the rim.

"All joking aside, Liza, just do it. It's one year. You can always find another job when you come back. You'd be crazy not to do it."

"Maybe I don't want another job," Liza snapped. When Anna went quiet, she rubbed at her temples. "I'm going to get off here. I'm tired and have a headache."

"Are you okay?"

"No," she said and pulled at the back of her neck. "No, I'm not. But I will be. Night."

"Night, hon. Call me when you know what you're going to do."

Liza disconnected the call and returned to the couch where she flopped down and let her head fall back against the cushion. Deep down, she already knew she was going. There was no way she could let herself give up that much money without giving it a try. The older she got, the harder it was getting to exist on her stubbornness.

Downing the contents of her wineglass, she returned to the kitchen and refilled, ignoring the voice in her head telling her a hangover would not help matters. Then straight back to the couch, where she promptly stretched out, pulled the blanket from the back of the couch, and turned on the television. Tomorrow, she'd deal with the life-altering decision. Tonight, she was getting drunk.

Chapter Four

The next day during her lunch break, Liza sat in her car and punched the phone number from the letter into her phone. It rang only once before a pleasant woman with a well-seasoned customer relations voice answered. "William C. Mason, Attorney at Law. How may I help you?"

"Hello. I'm calling for Mr. Mason. My name is Liza Blackburn."

"Oh! Ms. Blackburn. I'm very sorry about your grandmother. We all loved her. Can you hold for a few minutes? He's on the other line, but I'll slip him a message. I suspect he'll wrap it up quick."

"Yes. I am on my lunch break, though, so I only have about twenty minutes."

"Understood. I'll be back with you in a jiff." The line went silent while she was placed on hold and then soft classical music played. Was that Mozart? Beethoven? She really should have paid more attention in music class.

"Liza?" A man's voice broke through the calming music.

"Hi. Yes. This is Liza Blackburn."

"How are you?"

"I'm fine." Glancing at the clock, she cut through the niceties. "I'm calling about my grandmother's will. To get more details."

"Of course. Of course. The details are fairly simple. Stay at the cottage for one year and it, the car, and sixty thousand dollars are all yours. Oh, and complete whatever tasks she listed in the letter you'll receive your first day."

"And the monthly stipend?"

"Four thousand dollars each month at the beginning of the month. You can choose direct deposit or a check."

"Are you able to tell me the average monthly bills?"

"She said you'd ask that." Liza could hear the smile in his voice. "Water and electric run about one hundred dollars a month. Given your grandmother didn't own a lot of electronics, that might go up some. But I should warn you, it's a remote area. I'm not sure what services you will have available. There is a landline."

Liza let that sink in while she ran her palm around the steering wheel. Not only did her grandmother expect her to pack up and move her life for a year, but she was also expected to do it 1980s style? Great! The recent past due bill on her cellphone surfaced in her mind, and she sighed.

He cleared his throat. "I have all of this detailed in writing. If you like, I can have Edith email it to you."

"Yes, please do." She gave him her email address, patiently spelling it out for him while he no doubt scribbled it down somewhere. "My lunch break is nearly over. I will look over everything this evening and email you back my decision, if that's okay?"

"That would be fine. There will be some documents to sign if you decide to move forward. Your grandmother had everything done in a legal fashion. But your decision is all that is needed right now. Once I receive that, then your grandmother has given you six months to start, to give you time to make any arrangements."

"How kind of her."

If he caught her sarcasm, he didn't let on.

"Mr. Mason. Did my grandmother mention why she did this?"

"I'm sorry. She didn't." He cleared his throat again. "If it helps, she talked about you often. She loved you very much."

Liza knew her grandmother had loved her, but the fact that she'd attached stipulations to her inheritance and not to Anna's still stung. She hadn't talked to her mother yet, wanting to wait until she'd decided before attacking that discussion. Except for a brief apology phone call a few days after the funeral, they hadn't spoken.

"Thank you, Mr. Mason."

"Please, call me Bill."

"Bill. I'll get back to you soon."

"I look forward to hearing from you."

Disconnecting the call, she leaned back and stared out the window and tried to plan her exit in her head. She couldn't stomach giving just a two-week notice, not with the number of projects currently in progress. A month? Would her boss be upset or understanding? Her lease on her apartment was up soon, so that wouldn't be a problem. But where would she store all of her stuff for the year? Or would she need to move everything to Ohio with her?

Rubbing at her temples, Liza glanced at her phone and saw the email notification pop up. Her thumb hovered over the notification as the alarm on her phone sounded, signaling her lunch break was nearly over. Clearing the message, she stepped out of the car and walked back to her building.

Chapter Five

Tantrum came to mind as her mother stomped around the living room in a full tirade about her own mother. Liza just listened, occasionally rubbing at her temples, hoping to rub out the massive wine hangover. She'd spent the entire evening researching Maple Hill and the results hadn't made her decision any more exciting.

With a population of fewer than twelve hundred people, the little village was miles away from anything that resembled a city. Middle of nowhere was an appropriate description. Because it was off of a major highway, it had a chain hotel, which was a plus. It would mean Liza wouldn't be forced to stay in the cottage her first night. In the winter, average temperatures plummeted to the teens, which made Liza shiver just thinking about it. Summer brought temperatures in the high nineties. Sometimes the hundreds. As far as fun, Liza found very little. It was going to be a long year.

Deborah stopped in the middle of the room, her hands planted firmly on her hips. "Do you need money? Is that why you're considering this ridiculousness? Because if you needed money, all you had to do was ask."

And allow you to get knee deep in every aspect of my life? No thanks. "Mom. It'll be fine."

"It will not be fine. What about Thanksgiving and Christmas?"

"You know Mom, kids have been moving away from home since forever. And they make it work."

"But what if you get hurt, and no one knows to check on you?"

Liza may have been touched by her mother's concern if it hadn't been so condescending at the same time.

When Liza didn't comment, Deborah's arms dropped to her side, and her shoulders slumped. "You've already made up your mind about this?"

Liza nodded as her mother dropped, defeated, into the armchair. "When?"

"I don't know yet. I'm talking to my boss tomorrow."

"And your apartment?"

"My lease is up in four months. Speaking of, if I need to, can I store some of my stuff here?"

Deborah pursed her lips. "I suppose that would be fine."

It was as close as she would get. Her mother never answered with a simple yes or no. The next hour, they talked about anything but her impending move. Well, mostly her mother talked about herself and all the projects she had going, their fight after the funeral pushed to the back burner along with their other arguments.

That was okay with Liza. Anything to keep the topic as far away from her grandmother's wishes as possible, to avoid stirring up the hornet's nest again. When she headed back to her apartment, she found she was a little lighter, having finally gotten it over with.

While she hadn't voiced it to her mother, not wanting to give her an opening, Liza wondered how her mother would get on without her there. Despite their consistently volatile relationship, she was still living in the same city. More than once, she'd called Liza for some last-minute help with this issue or that problem.

It's only a year, she thought. The notion she might actually like Maple Hill and decide to stay didn't even cross her mind.

"So, how bad was it?"

Anna's voice filtered through the car's speaker system as Liza merged onto the highway.

"It was fine. We parted on speaking terms, at least."

Anna let out a sigh of relief. "That's good. When you two fight, I get stuck in the middle and I don't like it."

It was true. On the occasions when she and her mother were not speaking, Anna was left to fill the gaps.

"So, it's official? You're going?"

"Looks that way. It's a year. I can do this."

In the background, Liza heard Chloe summon Anna. "I'll have to call you later. Chloe is cleaning her room. We are on hour three of reasons why she shouldn't pick up her toys."

Liza chuckled. "So, in other words, you'll end up doing it?"

"Oh no, I'm not. She's currently in a full-on breakdown because she might lose her favorite teddy bear shirt if it's in her drawer. So, I'm just sitting in there watching her lose it."

"Says the woman whose bedroom floor was so covered she had to create a path."

"You shush."

Liza laughed.

"Call me tomorrow after the boss talk."

"I will. Night."

"Night."

After disconnecting, Liza finished the trip to her apartment in silence while her brain played out different scenarios with her boss.

Chapter Six

Of all the scenarios she had gone through, being immediately released from her duties had not been one of them.

Liza entered the building, dropped her things on the desk, and walked straight to Dr. Leach's office, ready to get it over with. It was open, which was a good sign. Rapping on the door frame, she waited patiently while Dr. Leach finished scribbling something in her notepad. Then she turned, giving Liza a warm yet questioning smile at the atypical interruption.

"Morning, Liza."

Taking that as an invitation, Liza stepped in to the office, hands clasped at her waist. "Dr. Leach. I was wondering if you have a few minutes."

Pushing back from the desk, Dr. Leach swiveled her office chair all the way around and motioned to the wooden chair across from her. "Sure. Have a seat."

Liza glanced back at the open door, considered closing it, then realized she really didn't care if anyone walked in. She hoped the conversation would be short. Announce her resignation, give several months' notice and then head back to her desk. Sitting, she adjusted in the hard chair, then forced herself to match Dr. Leach's intense gaze.

"I want to thank you for the last few years. Serving as your executive assistant has been a great experience, and I've learned a lot."

Dr. Leach nodded, but Liza saw her smile falter.

"Something came up recently, and I will be moving to Ohio for a year, so I will need to resign from my position. I am, however, able to stay on for a few months until we get through the renovation project and to give you time to find a replacement."

With it all out, Liza waited while Dr. Leach processed the information. Liza thought she saw a flash of irritation when Dr. Leach's lips tightened, but then they slipped back into a smile, albeit a much tighter and thinner one. "Well, I can't say this isn't a surprise, but life is what it is. I appreciate your willingness to stay on through the project, but I have a pretty strict rule when it comes to these things. I, of course, will be happy to give you a glowing recommendation wherever you land, but your services will no longer be needed. We will, of course, pay you for the two-week notice you are required to give under the personnel policy guidelines."

It was Dr. Leach's turn to wait while Liza processed what she said. Shock coursed through her. Liza knew Dr. Leach was a hardliner, not one to suffer excuses, and she'd seen others enter that office to turn in a resignation, only to exit, clean out their desks, and be escorted from the property.

But she honestly hadn't thought it would happen to her. Embarrassment crept in under the current of shock. Embarrassment over her own ego, considering herself more valuable than those other people who had walked through the doors. All the thoughts started hammering her brain. Her apartment lease. Her car payment. She thought she'd have more time to get accustomed to the idea of moving. She locked the thoughts down. There would be plenty of time to process it all later. Right then, she just needed to get out of that office with as much of her dignity intact as possible.

She stood, and Dr. Leach followed, extending her hand. Liza took it, shaking it gently. "Liza, it really has been a pleasure and I wish you luck in whatever is next for you."

"Thank you." It was all Liza could muster. She knew she should return the niceties, especially since Dr. Leach had indicated she'd give a good reference. But she could not bring herself to do it. She managed a weak smile then turned and walked out of the office to her desk.

At eight in the morning, she'd walked into work like she'd done every workday for twelve years—nine as a receptionist and three as an executive assistant—and just a mere one hour later, she was walking out of the building for the last time, all of her belongings stuffed into a banker's box. At least they had been nice enough to provide her one.

Dropping it all in the trunk, Liza sat down in her car and dropped her forehead to the wheel. This turn of events had messed up her entire plan. She'd had a plan: work through her remaining lease and then move to Ohio. Now, she didn't know what she would do. With four months still on her lease, she couldn't afford the rent without her job. She would need to make this move now and use the stipend money to help pay the rent. The thought of paying for a place she didn't live in physically hurt her.

Her phone buzzed in her purse. With a sigh, she dug through it, pulled it out, and answered without looking at the name.

"Ms. Blackburn? It's Bill Mason. Just checking to make sure you received the documents and to see if you have any questions."

Liza cleared her throat. "Please call me Liza. I planned on calling you this evening. I'll be in Ohio next week."

He was silent at first, then said, "Your grandmother would be so happy. She wasn't sure if you'd do it."

"Well, I'm not sure I want to."

"Maple Hill is a beautiful place to live, Ms. Blackburn."

"I'm sure it is," she said, hearing the dejection in her own voice. "I'll see you next week."

They said their goodbyes, and when she tapped the end call icon, she dropped the phone in her lap and cried.

Chapter Seven

The nearest airport to Maple Hill was three hours away. By the time Liza saw the sign welcoming her, it had been over eighteen hours since she'd left her apartment in Florida. What should have been a three-hour flight had turned into a fifteen-hour ordeal of sitting in uncomfortable terminal chairs, boarding and disembarking planes, and finally being crammed into the window seat next to a very talkative woman who knits. Then, an hour into her road trip in the car she'd rented, she'd taken the wrong exit and driven an hour in the wrong direction before she'd realized she had somehow paused her GPS app.

Her intention of visiting the cottage first was the collateral damage. Ignoring the electronic female voice telling her to turn left, she drove right past, her eyes locked on the curvy two-lane, tree-lined road ahead of her. Liza assumed, once daylight appeared, those trees would multiply into a dense forest and whatever scary creatures inhabited them.

Rows of trees finally gave way to rows of houses, and Liza released the death grip she had on the steering wheel and stretched her hands. All the pep talks she'd given herself about the move being an adventure had long ago worn off, leaving just exhaustion and a severe case of regret. Slowing her speed at the city limits, Liza glanced on either side of her at the businesses along Main Street. All housed in buildings that looked to be hundreds of years old, she saw a pizza shop nestled against an insurance agency. Attorney, attorney, old movie theater converted into a museum of some sort, diner, attorney, insurance agent, dress shop. Thank the good lord, a coffee shop!

She stopped at a red light and took the time to stretch the muscles in her neck and look around her. To her left was a tree-filled park, the outline of various structures— monuments maybe, multiple benches, possibly a splash pad—barely visible under the lights of the vintage streetlamps strategically placed around the perimeter. To her right, more businesses. On the upside, it looked like the community had put some work into revitalizing the downtown. On the downside, nearly all the businesses appeared closed already, and it was only ten. Except for a car behind her and one also waiting at the light ahead of her, the streets were virtually empty.

As she continued forward, the small business district morphed into the residential district, full of large, beautiful homes and large front porches where no doubt the residents sat and watched or visited. It was a small town right out of the movies. Lights lit up nearly all the homes and occasionally she glimpsed families inside winding down from the day.

The entire trip through the town took less than fifteen minutes, and when she finally saw the hotel which took up residence on the far end of the city near the only major highway, she hoped there would be more to see in daylight.

Pulling up to the hotel doors, Liza put the car in park and grabbed her purse from the passenger seat. Her stomach growled in protest when she moved, and she realized she'd barely eaten all day. Check-in. Find food. Sleep. Those were the three things on her immediate list. Everything else could wait until morning.

"Welcome to Maple Hill!" Liza had barely crossed the threshold when the bubbly receptionist on the other side of the counter shouted the greeting. Small in stature, she sported a dress shirt and vest with the hotel's logo on the upper left. Her blonde hair was styled in a pixie cut and if she was wearing make-up, it was just enough to highlight her large, round blue eyes.

"Hello," Liza said, hearing the exhaustion in her voice. "I have a reservation."

Liza glanced at the woman's name tag while her fingers flew across the keyboard. Christy. Liza briefly wondered if it was short for Christine. "Name?"

"Liza Blackburn."

Christy let out a squeal that made Liza take a step backward. "Liza? Ms. Dot's Liza! I heard you were coming into town."

For a second, Liza thought Christy might come around the counter and hug her. Thankfully, she didn't. "Yes."

"This is so exciting!" Then her face fell. "We were all so sorry to hear about Ms. Dot. We all loved her."

"Thank you," Liza said, moving back to the counter.

"You know, she was like a grandmother to so many people in town, including me. She was always doing something. Every time you turned around, there was Ms. Dot. She talked about you all the time. Her Liza, she'd say. And Anna? That's your sister, right?"

Uneasiness stiffened Liza's spine at this stranger knowing so much about her. "Christy, right?" Christy lit up and nodded like an excited two-year-old. "I don't mean to be rude, but it's been a really long day."

The light in her eyes dimmed, and Liza inexplicably felt bad. Whether or not she meant to be rude to her, she heard the clip in her words. There was no doubt her grandmother would not have approved. "Yes. Yes. Sorry about that." Christy slipped back into customer service mode and looked at the computer. "I have you staying two nights?"

"Maybe," Liza said, thankful the check-in process had started. If there were ruffled feathers to smooth, she'd do that later. "It might just be one. When would I need to cancel the room tomorrow?"

"Well," she said. "Typically, you need to cancel twenty-four hours in advance. How about we just cancel the second night's reservation? Then if you decide to stay, I don't see that being a problem. There's nothing going on in town, so we aren't anywhere close to full."

"That will work," Liza said.

"Are you paying with the credit card you reserved the room with?"

"Yes, please."

Christy pulled key cards from behind the counter, ran them through a machine, stuck them in a holder, then wrote the room number on the sleeve before she handed it to Liza. She pointed toward the hallway. "You are on the second floor, room two twelve. If you follow that hallway, you'll find the elevators. Just take them to the second floor and turn right. Your room will be on the left. Our fitness center and business center are open twenty-four hours. The pool is open until ten p.m. every evening. No lifeguard on duty. Our complimentary breakfast is served from six a.m. to ten a.m. every morning."

Liza's stomach growled again, reminding her it required attention. "Do you have dinner service available?"

Christy grimaced. "No. Sorry. Most of our pizza places will deliver to the hotel, though."

It was Liza's turn to grimace. Not that she didn't like pizza, but she was hoping for something a little less greasy. "Are there any restaurants nearby? With real food? Not fast food."

"You should try Hank's Pub on Third. It has great food. Full disclosure, my brother owns it, but despite that, it is fantastic."

"Do you have a menu?"

Excited to help, Christy disappeared behind the counter. Liza heard rustling, and then she popped back up and handed her a menu. "Most of our restaurants are up that way, so if nothing on this menu sounds good to you, there's a full list in your room. Pizza places are the only ones that deliver, though. Sorry."

"Thank you, Christy. And I'm sorry if I sounded rude earlier. It really has been a long day."

Christy waved her off. "It's okay. I kind of hit you with all of that, anyway. We've heard so much about you, I forgot we're all strangers to ya. Must be weird having someone you don't know talk to you like they do."

Liza chuckled. "Weird is a good word for it. Thanks again."

"You're welcome. And if you need anything at all, you let me know."

With a nod, Liza walked toward the exit to retrieve her bags.

Twenty minutes later she was in her room, freshened up and looking through the Hank's Pub menu. She wasn't sure what she had been expecting, but it definitely hadn't been salmon and steaks. Better than greasy pizza and overheated chicken nuggets. Hank's Pub it was, she thought as she grabbed her purse.

It was literally the only place on the block that still had its lights on. Set back from the road, Hank's Pub was a tiny little hole that didn't look promising. But the packed gravel parking lot in front told a different story. Liza found parking on the street, which thankfully wasn't too difficult or too far of a walk.

When she stepped in, she was greeted with loud music, louder conversations, and the smell of cooking food that set her stomach to growling again. If anyone noticed her entering, they didn't make a scene. She scanned the small dining area, looking for a place to sit, but came up short. Which was fine, as she planned to order to go, anyway.

Moving through the crowd, she finally reached the bar in the corner and peered up at the chalkboard behind the bartender, a list of craft beers written on it in scrawling yellow chalk. In the corner, the evening's special—garlic butter baked salmon with rice and broccoli. Perfect.

She spotted an empty bar stool at the far end of the bar and worked her way to it. Before sitting, she glanced at the man sitting next to the open stool. He sported a well-faded ball cap, a sweat stain circling above the bill. He hunched over the bar, sipping on the bottle of beer clasped in his weathered and cracked hands. She took notice of his faded jeans and work boots that he'd kicked mud off of a few times.

"Excuse me?" she said, knowing her volume was too low. She cleared her throat. "Excuse me, but is anyone sitting here?"

The man turned to look at her, and she watched in fascination as his eyes turned from disinterest in life to full interest in her. "Nope. No. Have a seat."

He shifted to give her more room. Placing her purse on the bar, she turned to him. "Thank you."

"No problem. I don't think I've seen you before. Name is Eddie." He stuck his hand out, and she took it, giving it a gentle pump. The callouses on his hand rubbed against her soft skin when they released.

"Liza."

"Well, that's a pretty name, Liza."

"Lay off, Eddie. That's Ms. Dot's granddaughter."

The voice came from behind the bar, and Liza glanced up to find Derrick staring at her, an unreadable smile on his face as he dried a beer glass. Immediately, the surge of anger she'd felt at the funeral reception reopened, fueled by a long day of traveling and hunger.

"You have got to be kidding me," she muttered, not realizing she'd said it out loud until his eyebrows raised.

Derrick knew there were two ways he could handle it—give it back to her or let it go. His pride raised its hand in favor of giving it back to her, but something stopped him. Guilt, maybe. Christy had given him a good dressing down over the whole incident after the funeral. Plus, Dot had been good to him. A grandmother he hadn't known he needed. From the look of Liza, she'd had a long day already. No point in adding to someone's misery. Even if they were rude and probably deserved it.

"Welcome to Hank's Pub," Derrick said, forcing his best customer service smile.

Her mouth opened to speak, but Eddie beat her to it. "Ms. Dot's granddaughter, huh? Great lady, there. She was. How about another one, Derrick?" He held up his empty beer bottle and gave it a shake for effect.

Derrick nodded, rolled back the cooler doors at his waist, then shut it again. "I have to get more from the back." His attention turned to Liza. "Did you want to place an order?"

"Please. The special is fine," she said and then added a clipped, "to go."

With a nod, he disappeared through the swinging saloon doors. As he did, he looked over and saw Eddie lean closer to her. "So, are you the artist, then?"

In the back, his cook, Maryanne, had her head stuck inside the large commercial refrigerator. "One special, Maryanne!" he yelled, making her jump. She spun around on him, brandishing a knife.

"I swear, Derrick. Stop that!"

Derrick chuckled before saying, "To go."

Maryanne answered with a nod and started preparing the special while Derrick walked to the cooler. There, he pulled out a couple of cases of beer, exited, and shut the heavy cooler door with his hip.

As he pushed open the swinging doors, he heard a loud, "Don't touch me," and turned to find Eddie pulling his arm from around Liza's shoulder. It was at that moment he realized the look she'd given him earlier was not as venomous as he'd originally thought. When compared with the rage-filled stare she was giving Eddie, her earlier look could be described as simply irritated.

Eddie leaned back and held his hands up in surrender and then he removed himself from the bar stool. "I don't think I need that beer after all, Derrick."

Liza turned her gaze back to the chalkboard—her jaws clenched, her hands balled into a fist over her purse—as Eddie dropped a wad of bills on the bar. "Suddenly got a little frigid in here," he snapped, then vanished into the crowd.

As his presence disappeared, Liza deflated, the redness in her face drifting away as adrenaline seeped into her hands, making them tremble. "I'm sorry. I...," she started, then stopped. "I'm not a big fan of men I don't know putting their arm around me."

His first instinct was to place his hand on top of hers to steady them, but he resisted and instead just set the cases on the bar and moved in front of her. "Nor should you be." He grinned. "I will say, I've never seen Eddie move that fast away from a woman in my life." Then he held out his fist to her. She looked confused at first, then a smile pulled at her lips, and she reached out and bumped his fist. He gave her a wink. Another laugh released the tension in her shoulders just as a young couple moved up to the bar.

"I'll be back in a minute," he said. "Do you want a beer or something while you wait?"

Liza shook her head. "No, thank you. The last thing I need after the day I've had—and on an empty stomach—is alcohol. I'll just grab a water at the hotel."

With a nod, he waited on the couple, sneaking a glance at Liza occasionally as he mixed up a margarita and pulled a beer from the cooler. Another customer walked up, and then another. A good fifteen minutes passed before Derrick made it back to Liza, a full water glass in hand. "Just in case," he said as he slid it across the bar.

"Thanks," she said and took a drink. They stared at each other briefly before Liza said, "Christy at the hotel sent me here. She said her brother owns it? I'm assuming his name is Hank?"

That she was trying to make small talk caught him off guard. "Actually, Hank is my dog."

He waited while it sank in, watching as confusion, then understanding washed across her face. "Wait. You own this place? You're Christy's brother?" Her memory sparked again of the little girl who used to tag along with him occasionally to her grandmother's house. She'd been quite a bit younger than Liza.

Nodding, he pulled beers from the cases and filled the cooler. "I'll go check on your order."

"Thank you," she said.

"No problem."

As he entered the back room, Maryanne held a bagged order out to him. "To go order is done," she said without looking up. He took it and headed back out to the floor and stopped short when he was greeted with an empty stool.

Scanning the room, he spotted her standing next to the wall, looking at one of the paintings. It dawned on him then that he should have pointed her toward them. In truth, he often forgot they were there.

As he came out from behind the bar, he made his way through the small crowd, greeting customers as he went. Then he stepped up beside her. "Order's ready."

She turned to him, and his heart clenched. Tears welled in her eyes, glistening under the lighting above. Liza turned back to the painting, a watercolor depicting a spring day at their local City Park. Kids frolicked on the splash pad. An elderly couple sat hand-in-hand on a bench. A man and woman picnicked on a blanket in the center. She pointed at the placard underneath the painting and read it out loud. "Spring Has Sprung. Artist, Dorothy McDonald."

Then she silently moved to the next painting on the wall, another watercolor featuring a dense forest with a stream running through it. A deer and a fox drank at the water's edge. She didn't point at that one's placard, but Derrick knew it bore the same artist's name.

She finally turned to him. "Did my grandmother paint these?"

"She did. Good, aren't they?" he asked.

"Are you sure she painted them?"

A flashing red sign of danger appeared in Derrick's mind as he took a step back. This conversation didn't appear to be going the way he'd expected it to go based on her wide eyes and snappy tone. What had he gotten himself into? "Yes," he said cautiously. "I'm sure. Why?"

She turned back to the painting, her voice almost a whisper under the jukebox music. "I didn't know."

"That she painted? You're the artist, right? Your grandmother never told you she painted?" The moment the words left his lips, he wished he could snatch them back. Not only because he was heading into family drama territory that he wanted no part of, but also because of the way Liza's frown deepened. She started to speak, then just shook her head.

Scrambling for words to fix it, he finally said, "Maybe she was planning to surprise you someday? She's only been painting for about four years or so."

Liza spun toward him. "Four years?"

Nope. Wrong thing to say, apparently. He should have gone with his original thought of keeping his mouth shut. Which he did, resulting in the two of them just standing and staring at each other. Then her shoulders straightened, and one hand wiped angrily across her eyes. Internally, he breathed a sigh of relief when she asked, "Is that my food?"

He handed it to her. "Yes."

"How much do I owe you?" she asked. The edge in her voice had returned, signaling the interaction was over.

"No charge. Call it a welcome gift. And an apology."

Her eyes narrowed with suspicion. "For?"

"For whatever you need an apology for." Then he turned on the grin. That boyishly charming grin that always worked with women.

"Thanks," she said, then turned on her heel and stalked to the door.

Well, most women, anyway.

As she disappeared into the night, Derrick took a deep breath. He was glad he'd already reached a decision regarding Dot's letter to him. While he would help Liza as much as he could because he owed Dot that, there was no way he was going to be contractually tied to that hot mess. No way in hell.

Chapter Eight

Despite falling asleep quickly, the general hotel noise had woken Liza multiple times throughout the night. Instead of waking rested and ready to conquer the day, she felt only slightly better than she had the day before.

Using the GPS on her phone as a guide, she traveled down the winding gravel road to what she hoped would be the cottage. When she pulled into the driveway, she got her first glimpse of what would soon be her new home and was pleasantly surprised to find it in relatively good shape. It could probably do with a new paint job on the slightly faded white exterior, but all-in-all it was actually quite cute. She scanned the lawn as she walked to the door and noted the flower beds strategically placed throughout. Off to the side of the house was her grandmother's red and white Buick.

Not a car she'd pick for herself, but it would do. Key already in hand, Liza walked up the three stairs to the front porch, stood at the door, and took a deep breath.

"Please don't let there be flowered wallpaper. Please don't let there be flowered wallpaper," she chanted as she unlocked the door, stepped inside, and nearly did a dance at the absence of wallpaper on the walls. They were painted a light yellow from what she could tell in the dim light.

Walking over to the bay window, she grabbed the closed curtains, flung them open and back-pedaled as a cloud of dust exploded around her. Covering her nose and mouth with her hand, she waved at the air until it dissipated. Turning around with her hands on her hips, she surveyed the room under the rays of sunlight.

Where the walls lacked floral pizzaz, the couch made up for it. Dark brown and deep red, covered in floral print, Liza was certain she'd seen pictures of her mother as a child sitting on that same couch. To each side were ornate wooden end tables. A coffee table ran the length of the couch, a match to the end tables. On either side of the room were two armchairs that matched the couch.

Her eyes landed on the fox in snow painting hanging on the wall above the couch, and a lump rose in her throat. Fearing another tearful moment, she quickly turned away to explore the rest of the cottage.

The living room opened into a kitchen with a two-bowl stainless steel sink, a white refrigerator that looked older than her, and a stove that looked about the same age. The counterspace filled the gaps, which weren't very big. A kitchen table, also covered in flowers, sat in a small nook with four brown upholstered chairs surrounding it.

Turning out of the kitchen, she walked through the living room to the other door and stepped into the tiny bedroom. More flowers greeted her on the bedside table lamps to either side of a queen-sized bed. A quilt served as the bedspread.

Stepping back out of the bedroom, she peeked into the bathroom. A claw-foot tub with a shower, a toilet, and a one basin sink filled the small space. Continuing past, she returned to the living room, and stood in the middle, and turned in a slow circle. *It's only a year*, she thought. *One year.*

The sound of crunching gravel under tires drifted through the open door. Liza walked onto the porch as Derrick turned his truck off and stepped out.

"Hey," he said, slamming the door behind him, causing Liza to flinch, half expecting the beat-up old truck to collapse under the force.

She crossed her arms as he approached. "Hi?"

"Was that a question or a statement?" He took the three wooden steps to the porch in one step.

Surprised by his directness, she let her arms drop. "Both, I guess."

"Christy called. Said you'd be out here this morning and might need help finding some things."

"I think I found everything. It's not very big. Thanks, though."

"The breaker box?"

Of course, she hadn't found the breaker box. She hadn't even looked, figuring the lack of electricity just meant it had been turned off.

"And the main water shutoff? You'll want to know where that is this winter."

She hadn't found that either, not that she knew exactly what it was. She could deduce that it would shut the water off to the house, but she had no idea why she would need it. "No. I didn't find either of those."

He smirked. An honest-to-goodness smirk that sliced through her nerves like a fiery sword. She almost told him to forget it, that she'd find them herself, even if that meant looking up things online. But he was already in the door and walking through the living room. She followed with her arms again wrapped tightly around her chest.

He worked his way through the small kitchen to a door she had assumed led to a pantry. Turning the knob, he pulled it open, slipped his phone from his back pocket and turned on the light. Then he disappeared.

Intrigued, she made her way to the door, then stopped at the sight of a rickety wood staircase leading into a dark abyss. A musty, dirt smell filled the air. "You coming?" he yelled from below. She said a silent prayer that he and Christy weren't sibling serial killers, tapped the light icon on her own phone, and descended.

A dirt floor greeted her at the bottom. Above her, the floor joists looked just as ancient and were being held up by posts strategically wedged between the dirt floor and the floor joists above. The whole aesthetic gave off a severe horror film vibe. With a shiver, she turned her attention to the glow of his light and followed it around the corner, noting a big bin in the corner as she moved next to him.

"They used to keep potatoes there. This was a one- room cabin. Dates back to the 1800s or something," he said as he popped open the front of the breaker box. "Part of a bigger farm. Your grandma bought it and renovated it."

He paused while he flipped the big breaker at the top of the box. He pointed around the corner. "Light switch is at the bottom of the stairs."

Liza walked to it, flipped it, and three bulbs hanging from wires glowed to life. It didn't make the basement any more appealing. The stairs looked even worse, and Liza tried to imagine her grandmother slowly ambling down them. How had she not fallen all those years? She made her way back to Derrick, who had moved to the other wall. He had his hand on a metal valve.

"Main water shutoff. Righty tighty. Lefty loosey." He turned it to the left, and the pipes overhead creaked and groaned as water rushed through them. "And that over there is your furnace. You may not need it for the rest of the year, depending on how cold it gets. You'll want to change the filter, though, before you start back up in the winter."

Liza nodded as she continued to scan the room, murder scenarios still playing out in her head. She could have gone the whole year without knowing the basement existed. "Creepy, huh?"

Liza laughed. "Just a bit."

"If it makes you feel any better, there's never been a serial killer in Maple Hill."

"That you know of."

He chuckled and moved past her, headed back to the stairs. "True. That I know of."

Stopping at the bottom, he pointed to a door in the corner. "That's a cellar door. Leads to the outside."

Great! She thought. So, someone could get into the basement from the outside? She studied the bolt lock at the top, and she noticed it was unlocked. Walking over to it, she tried to force it into the lock.

"Lean into it to lock it," Derrick said.

She pressed her body against it and felt the door creak under her, but the bolt slid into place.

Wiping her hands on her jeans, she joined him on the stairs.

He turned his light on again. "Flip the switch."

She did, and the cellar plunged back into darkness save the light from his phone and the light filtering down from the top of the stairs.

As they emerged from the cellar, he continued. "You have city water and sewer. They ran lines out here about fifteen years ago, thinking it would help with development of the area. It didn't. Electric stove. Electric water heater. Your grandmother would have preferred gas, but they didn't run that out this way. That's about it. Any questions?"

It took her a second to realize he'd asked her a question. "What? Oh, no. Thank you."

"Welcome. Anything else?"

She shook her head.

"Okay, then. I should get going." He pulled out his wallet and slipped a business card from one of the pockets. He handed it to her. "My cell and landline are on there if something happens. Or you can try the pub. I'm usually there most afternoons and evenings."

Taking the card from him, she glanced at it, then slipped it into her back pocket, making a mental note to add his phone numbers to her phone.

He stood there for a moment, as if waiting for her to speak. Then said, "Well, if that's it, I'd better get going."

He turned on his heel and strode toward the door, then stopped and turned again. "Oh, and you'll probably meet Hank soon. Don't be scared. He's a big baby. But I'll try to bring him down first. He had a thing for Ms. Dot. I'm fairly certain she let him sleep here at night, but she would never tell. You afraid of dogs?"

"I don't think so," Liza said, trying to imagine what type of dog would warrant such a warning.

His head cocked to one side. "Don't think so? You haven't been around dogs before?"

"I've seen them, obviously. But not really. My father was allergic. One of my childhood friends had a little dog. Mean, snappy, little thing. They usually kept him up while I was around. I never really thought about it, but no, I haven't been around many dogs."

"Well, when he comes around, you won't be able to miss him. If he becomes a pest, just let me know. He knows better than to go off the property, but to him, this is part of the property."

Great, she thought. Now she was going to have to take care of someone else's dog? One more thing to mark on her list of items she planned to talk to her grandmother about in the afterlife. She wanted to tell him just to teach Hank not to come on the property, but instead, she just nodded. "Thanks again."

With an answering nod, he left. She resisted following him out on the porch and waited until the truck started and the crunching gravel indicated he was pulling out before turning back to the cottage. Cabin, really, she realized. A really old cabin with some paint on it. Surveying the room, now fully lit with sunlight and the overhead lighting, she noticed the bookshelf for the first time. Walking over to it, she lightly ran her fingers over the titles of the neatly bound books. Some she recognized, like Jane Eyre and Wuthering Heights. Others she didn't. She'd have to come back to those later.

Pulling her phone from her pocket, she opened up the Notes app and started at the front door . She had some serious shopping to do, she thought as she started making a list.

Chapter Nine

As she locked her car door, she hoped everything inside would be okay in the parking lot. Her original plan had been to take everything back to the cottage before her appointment with Mr. Mason, but she'd gotten a little carried away with the shopping trip. Instead of the few needed items she'd planned to get, like toilet paper and paper towels, she'd ended up with two carts full of stuff and three hours of shopping. Tack on the forty-minute drive back to Maple Hill, and she'd pulled into the parking lot with just a few moments to spare.

Inside, she was greeted enthusiastically by Edith. At least Liza assumed it was Edith. She hadn't told Liza her name. But her voice sounded familiar, and she'd known Liza on sight. "Have a seat over there, and Mr. Mason will be out soon. Candy?" Edith shoved a bowl toward Liza full of hard candies.

"What? Oh. No. Thank you," Liza stammered as she made her way to the couch in the corner.

It had the feel of a doctor's waiting room, with its leather furniture, magazines spread across the tables, and generic artwork on the walls. Picking up a magazine, she flipped through it without really reading. Putting it back down, she pulled out her phone and checked the time. Then she opened her social media app and scrolled. Liking a couple of photos, she closed it and opened a game.

"Liza!" Mr. Mason's baritone voice boomed through the office, making Liza jump. Shoving her phone back into her purse, she stood and faced the attorney. For some reason, when she'd envisioned him, Liza had thought of an elderly man. To her surprise, that wasn't the case. Guessing he was closer to her age than her grandmother's, Mr. Mason was fit and lean under his well-tailored suit, his wire-rimmed glasses bringing attention to his stark blue eyes and away from his thinning hairline. His smile was warm, like they were old high school friends as opposed to complete strangers.

She crossed the waiting room, her hand extended. "Mr. Mason."

He took her hand, pumping it enthusiastically. "Bill, remember? Come in. Come in."

Closing the door behind her as she crossed the threshold, he waved his hand at the two seats on the other side of his desk. "Have a seat," he said as he settled into his own chair behind his desk. Sitting, she placed her purse on the empty chair while he rifled through a drawer in his desk. "Your grandmother would be so happy you decided to come here."

Liza forced a thin smile. As much as she loved her grandmother, she was still angry at being forced into the situation.

He apparently caught it. "She also said you would be...how did she put it? Less than enthused about the arrangement."

"Less than enthused is an appropriate description."

Pulling a large file folder from the drawer, he opened it, pulled out a stack of papers and two letter envelopes, then closed the folder. Placing the papers in front of her, he turned them so she could read them. "This is the agreement I sent you. Feel free to look over it again before signing."

"I don't need to," she said, as she grabbed a pen from the holder, flipped to the signature page, and scrawled her name.

Bill pulled the papers back and stuck them in the file. "When do you plan to spend your first night?"

"Tonight. I just went shopping for things I needed."

He nodded. "You already saw the place?"

"I did."

"Any questions?"

She shook her head, and Bill returned to sifting through the papers.

"Now, for your monthly stipend, do you want a paper check or direct deposit?"

"Direct deposit." He slid a direct deposit form across the desk to her. She pulled out her phone, opened her banking app, and filled out the information, then slid it back.

"We will get this all set up today. It might take a little time. Would you prefer your first stipend be in check form, or do you want to wait?"

"I'll wait. There aren't any branches of my bank around here, anyway."

"Okay. Then we'll get that started. Next month's stipend will be deposited on the first, and it will be the first of each month from this point on. Any questions?"

Liza shook her head, and he grinned again as he filed the folder away in his drawer. "Now that the business stuff is done, how are you doing?"

"I don't know yet. I've been here for less than twenty- four hours."

He nodded. "It really is a nice place, and your grandmother was adored. I hope your year is not as painful as you're assuming it will be."

"I'm sure it will be fine."

His phone rang, interrupting whatever he was about to say. He answered it, listened, and then said, "Okay. Thank you." Liza thought he looked uncomfortable, but she discarded it. She didn't know him well enough to know if he was uncomfortable or not.

As he hung up, he smiled again and handed her the two envelopes. "These are from your grandmother. They go over the other stipulations."

Liza took the letters and dropped them in her purse without looking at them.

"That's all for now," he said as he stood.

She followed, taking his extended hand and giving it a gentle pump.

"If you have any questions, don't hesitate to call me."

As he opened the door, she saw Derrick standing in the corner of the waiting room. When he saw her, his eyes widened and then shot behind her. She looked over her shoulder at Bill, whose eyes were locked on Derrick's. When he realized she was looking at him, he glanced at her and gave a thin smile. Derrick did the same.

"Thank you for helping me this morning," Liza said, unease creeping up her spine. Something felt off in the room, weird, like she'd inadvertently walked in on something she shouldn't have.

Derrick nodded his head once. "You're welcome."

"Derrick, come on in," Bill said and waved him toward his office door.

Derrick crossed the waiting room, skirting around her, and disappeared into the office.

"It was nice finally meeting you in person, Liza."

"You, too, Bill."

He closed the door behind him.

As Liza passed Edith's desk, the secretary gave her a stunted wave. Just like Derrick and Bill, Edith seemed on edge, too. By the time she reached her car she decided it was none of her business. Whatever was causing all the weirdness in the office couldn't have anything to do with her. She'd only been in town for a day. She had real things to worry about.

Chapter Ten

U pon arriving at the cottage, she unpacked first and threw the new bed sheets and towels in the washer. Then she pulled out the cleaning supplies and wiped down the sinks and the toilet. Back in the kitchen, she turned on the oven to preheat, then grabbed the new cookie sheet she'd bought and washed it, before throwing a frozen pizza in. While it cooked, she finished unpacking everything she'd purchased and found places for them.

Finally, pizza and a glass of wine in hand, she collapsed on the couch. If she'd been at the hotel, she would have called Anna. But a glance at the lack of bars on her phone told her that would not happen at the cottage. She made a mental note to have the landline turned on the next day.

Pressing the music icon on her phone, she tapped shuffle and set it on the table. Nineties Grunge filled the silence. She made a mental note to also pick up a Bluetooth speaker.

Letting her head fall back on the couch, she soaked in the music and tried to make the muscles in her neck and back relax. She was wound tight. She knew that. But after the month she'd had, who wouldn't be?

Sitting up, she leaned over and pulled her sketchbook from her bag. Settling back on the couch, she started to draw. It felt foreign at first as she focused on the kitchen and nook area, letting her eyes adjust to the lines and shading of the two rooms. The way the shadows played along the wall, the subtle differences in color along the edges of the countertop.

She felt like she was in school again, sketching out a bowl of fruit on a table or the intricacies of the human body. As her pencil moved across the sketch paper, she felt the last few days release from her shoulders. The hyper-focus on lines, shapes and shadows calming the whir in her brain. She felt at home again. Something she hadn't felt for a very long time.

A knock at the door made her jump, sending a straight line across the page where she'd been shadowing in the kitchen counter. She grimaced at it, then flipped the sketchbook shut, dropped her pencils in their bag, and deposited both onto the side table.

She was almost to the door when she stopped. Living alone didn't bother her. She'd been doing it for much of her adult life. While she had always been cautious when walking alone, when unlocking her apartment, when unfamiliar noises woke her in the middle of the night, she'd never been afraid. But now, stuck in the middle of nowhere with no phone, no connection to the outside world, she realized she could die, and no one would know.

"Who is it?" she yelled.

"Christy!"

Torn between relief and annoyance, Liza crossed the living room and opened the door. Christy didn't wait for an invitation, barreling past Liza, her arms laden with shopping bags and a large box.

"Hey," Christy said, walking to the dining room table, where she dumped the load she was carrying.

"Come in," Liza muttered under her breath, then plastered on a smile.

"I brought some food for you," she said as she pulled aluminum foil dishes from the box. "That's a casserole. Something chicken. I don't know, but I'm sure it's good. Mac and cheese. Meatloaf in this one. These chocolate chip cookies. I made those, so I know they're good. Green beans." She held up the grocery bag and wiggled it. "Also, bread and butter. You're not a vegetarian, are you?"

Shocked and now feeling guilty over her original reaction, Liza took a step toward the table. "What? No. What is all this?"

"Welcome to Maple Hill!" Christy said with a grin. "I know. Seems kind of cliche, but if it's not broke, don't fix it, right? Some of the women in my book club, they like to do this stuff. I'm not a big cook, but I can make a mean cookie. Anywho, I told them about you and that you were Ms. Dot's granddaughter and they wanted to do this. So, here ya go."

She scanned the table. It was so much food. Way more than she could ever eat on her own. Her stomach growled loudly, and she laughed as her hand slapped over it.

"Thank you," Liza said. "Apparently, I'm hungry."

Christy laughed. "Yeah, I heard that. Well, speaking of, I need to get going. And you're welcome."

"Would you like to stay and eat?" Liza shocked herself by asking.

Christy beamed. "You sure?"

"I'm sure. There's a lot of food here, and I can't eat it all. Not that I'm not grateful," she added quickly.

"Well, thank you. I'll totally take you up on that. Heath is out with friends, so I'm eating solo tonight. Will totally take the company. And Alice's meatloaf is da bomb. It took everything in me not to break into that dish on the way over here," Christy said, shedding her jacket and heading to the table.

As they unpacked the paper plates and silverware and uncovered the dishes, Liza found it was all still hot. "Heath your husband?"

Christy laughed as she plopped a piece of meatloaf on her plate and then spooned on macaroni and cheese. "Son." She waggled her ring finger at Liza. "Not currently taken. Not that I don't want to be one day, but the pickings are slim around here at my age. Heath keeps me hopping though, so...," she ended with a shrug.

"All I have is water and wine to drink," Liza said.

"I'll take water. I'm a beer girl."

Liza retrieved a water bottle from the refrigerator and handed it to Christy then filled her own plate. As they sat, Liza asked, "So, how old is your son?"

"Fifteen. One more year and he can drive, thank the good lord." Christy screwed off the lid of the water and took a drink, then said, "Yes, I was young when I had him. Seventeen, actually."

Liza didn't know what to say to that, so instead shoved food in her mouth. Her focus shifted from Christy to the savory goodness in the form of a meatloaf now exploding with flavor in her mouth. She chewed slowly, then swallowed.

"Told you. It's awesome, isn't it?" Christy asked and took a bite herself.

"Yes. Yes, it is."

"Anyway, pregnant at sixteen, mom at seventeen, the father took off. Older than dirt story."

"That must have been hard," Liza said, thinking back to when she was seventeen all those years ago. She could barely do her own laundry, much less raise a kid.

"At times, but I had a lot of support. Just had to change the picture in my head a little. I wouldn't change him for the world, though. Even when he's being a brat."

Liza smiled, and they ate in silence for a moment. "So, what's your story?"

Liza thought for a moment. "Rebellious teenager goes to art school. Then starts working and forgets about her art. Older than dirt story."

Christy grins. "You're an artist, then?"

"I used to be."

Christy dismissed her statement with a wave of her hand. "Don't think I didn't notice that sketchbook on the table."

Heat crept into Liza's cheeks as she glanced at the sketchbook on the side table. Christy took a drink of her water then pointed the bottle at Liza. "You're still an artist. Just like I'm still a singer."

"Really? Are you any good?"

"I am. At least by Maple Hill standards. I had my eyes set on music school and then, well. Baby. Dreams." She made a crashing and explosion sound and took another drink. "But if I hadn't gotten pregnant, I wouldn't have Heath. By the way, that's a mother thing. You're not allowed to regret things in your past without also mentioning how happy you are with your child. Unwritten rule."

Liza laughed and took a drink. "Good to know."

"So? What about you? What slowed your roll?"

Liza shrugged. "Life. I funded my own college. When I got out, I had loans to pay and rent. A car payment. Insurance. I don't know. I still did quite a bit when I moved in, but as the years passed, it just got easier not to."

A dog bark at the door made them both jump. "What was that?" Liza asked, scooting back her chair.

The dog barked again, a deep, loud bark that could only come from an extremely large animal. Christy grinned. "That would be Hank. You afraid of dogs?"

Another bark. "In theory, no."

Christy stood up and walked to the door. Liza cautiously followed, torn between Christy's calmness and the nervousness bubbling up inside her. Based on what Derrick had told her, Hank would expect to see her grandmother, not her. What would happen if he took offense at her presence? Could Christy control him?

"Maybe we should call Derrick," she started, but it was too late. Christy has already opened the door.

He strolled in like he owned the place, his massive frame taking up most of the doorway's width. A long, red tongue hung from his brown block-shaped head. The muscles under his short coat rippled when he walked. And his tail, long and thin, whipped back and forth, bouncing off the door frame as he entered.

Excitedly, he greeted Christy first, nuzzling into her with enthusiastic yips, and then he turned to Liza. She froze, foreseeing her death as he attacked. "It's okay. Just put your hand out and let him sniff you."

He seemed hesitant at first, head low, the wag of his tail more cautious. Stretching his nose forward to her hand, he sniffed it a few times. And then his body pressed against her legs as he begged her to pet him. She obliged.

Then he was off, walking through the house, sniffing at the air. Christy's face fell. "He's looking for Dot."

The sound of a truck pulling into the driveway caught their attention, and they were both nearly bowled over as Hank rocketed past them through the open door.

He stopped just short of the driveway, his feet leaving the ground with each bark, his tail wagging furiously as Derrick put the truck in park and stepped out.

Christy and Liza walked out on the porch to greet Derrick as he strolled toward them, Hank bouncing and running next to him.

"Hey," he said, giving Hank a pat. "I see you met Hank."

Liza nodded. "It's a good thing Christy was here. I'm thinking Hank would have sat outside all night."

"Yeah, sorry about that. My intentions were to bring him down and let you meet him, but he had other plans."

As he climbed the stairs, he automatically reached over and gave his sister a side squeeze. "So, what are you two ladies up to?"

"The food brigade made her some welcome dishes."

His eyes lit up. "Alice's meatloaf?"

Christy's mouth screwed into a pout. "And my cookies."

"Of course. And your cookies."

"You want some?" Liza asked. "There's plenty. I can't eat it all."

"I'll never turn down Alice's meatloaf."

They made their way inside, and Liza fought off the feeling of claustrophobia. She thought back to her younger years, when she and her friends had crammed into little apartments and dorm rooms to party.

There had been blasting music and smoke, bodies pressed up against each other in various corners of the rooms. It had been deafeningly loud and always hot. And not once could she recall feeling claustrophobic.

Then eventually, those friends had moved away, married, had families, and her social life had slowly dwindled into non-existence. Save her grandmother and the occasional reluctant visit from her mother, other people rarely graced her doorstep. Even Anna's visits were few. If she was in town, they typically met at their mother's. She'd grown accustomed to the solitude of her apartment and its safety. Hosting was now a foreign concept to her, the realization tightening the knot in her stomach even further.

"Hey," Christy said, waving her hand in front of Liza's face. "You good?"

Brought back, Liza smiled. "Yes. Sorry. Tired, I guess." They were standing around the table while Derrick fixed his plate. He looked up, then past her, his crooked grin spreading across his face as he gave a sharp nod for them to look. Christy and Liza's heads swiveled around to find Hank curled up on the couch.

"Guess that answers the question about Dot letting him sleep here," he said with a chuckle. "Want me to tell him to get off?"

Liza shook her head. "No. He was obviously here before me. As long as he doesn't go all Cujo on me, he's welcome to stay as long as he wants." Truth be told, it wouldn't hurt her feelings at all if he hung out for the evening. The quiet in the unfamiliar space was unsettling in the daylight. She had a feeling it was going to be worse at night. She wasn't used to her surroundings being devoid of noise.

They all sat at the table as Liza and Christy finished their dinners and Derrick worked on his. Their conversation was light, and as soon as Derrick finished eating and Liza insisted on cleaning up, the siblings headed for the door.

"You're sure you want him to stay?" Derrick asked again.

Liza looked over at Hank, who was now eyeing his departing master from his curled body. "Positive. He's fine." "Okay, then. If he gets to be a pain, just open the door and tell him to go. He should listen. And thanks for feeding us."

Christy stepped up and gave Liza a hug, who tentatively returned it. "We need to hang out while you're here. I think we're going to be friends," she said with a grin and then bounced away to her car.

Derrick smiled lovingly at her, then turned to Liza. "Okay, then. Good night."

"Night," Liza said and waited for them to pull out before waving at them.

Liza took a beat to admire the orange glow of the setting sun as their vehicles disappeared down the dirt road, then closed the door and locked it. Returning to the couch, she pulled out her sketchbook and started to sketch again. Then her eyes roamed to her purse where the letters were stashed. There was a part of her that didn't want to read them, didn't want to know what else her grandmother had planned for her. But another part of her, the bigger part, wanted to hear from her grandmother one more time.

With a sigh, she stood up, walked across the room, retrieved the envelopes, and returned to the couch.

"Well, Hank. Here goes nothing," she said and opened the first letter.

Chapter Eleven

H er mother used to call it rage cleaning, and Liza realized she was in the midst of such an episode as the rising sun drifted through the kitchen window onto the freshly scrubbed floors. From her vantage point on her knees, scrub brush in hand, she could see the light wash over the tips of the tree leaves.

Hank had tapped out around 3 a.m., the vacuum cleaner being the last straw. He'd side-eyed her and slid from the couch, padding to the front door. There he whined until she opened it so he could escape.

As flurried as she'd been all night, wiping down walls and trim, scrubbing floors, sinks, and the toilet, the music app on her phone blasting, the moment the first rays of sun hit, she deflated. Tossing the sponge in the bucket of soapy water, she stood up and stretched out her back and moved to the couch. She eyed the open letters tossed carelessly on the table.

The first one had been sweet, a long love letter in her grandmother's neat cursive handwriting telling her youngest granddaughter how much she loved her. She told of her history with Maple Hill, the little town where she'd grown up. How she'd met Liza's grandfather at nineteen, a Navy man, and had fallen deeply and hopelessly in love. She'd followed him through their adult lives until they'd landed in Florida. There they had stayed and raised their family. Liza had few actual memories of her grandfather. Sitting on his knee while he watched television. A memory of him taking her out on a boat.

Her grandmother wrote that he'd always promised they'd move back to Maple Hill one day. But he'd passed before that could happen. So, she'd done it herself. Winters in Ohio because she loved the snow and cold. Summers in Florida with her family. It was a three-page letter full of history and love and very few regrets. When Liza had finished the letter, she'd held it to her chest and let the tears fall freely.

Then she'd opened the second letter marked *Inspiration*. It lacked the niceties in the first letter. Just a list. She'd scanned down it when "hold an art show" caught her eye. Dread, years of pent-up anxiety and anger exploded through her as she read and reread the letter multiple times. Mentally, she catalogued her finished pieces, all still sitting in her studio in Florida, and none jumped out as being show-worthy. Not to mention this would mean properly packing them and moving them back to Ohio instead of storing them at her mother's as she'd originally planned.

Until that moment, she hadn't been furious at her grandmother. Hurt? Yes. A little angry? Sure. But flat out furious? Not really. Now though, as her grandmother tried to force her will from beyond the grave, Liza considered just giving up and moving on with her life.

She looked at the list again. Attend the annual Snow Ball Dance. Go sleigh riding. Watch the sunrise from the front porch. Landscape the cottage. Volunteer with at least one organization. All things she could stomach, though none made her particularly happy.

Then, at the very bottom, the two items that gave her pause jumped out at her again. Hold an art show and finish six pieces.

Six. She hadn't finished a piece in years, and now her grandmother expected six? And the art show? Why would she do that to her? She knew how she felt about it.

As she tossed the letters onto the table, her head fell back on the couch. Squeezing her eyes closed, she let her brain mull over the thought of just quitting now. Except she couldn't. And she knew it. She'd have to find a job first. "Suck it up, Buttercup." Her grandmother's voice was loud and clear. So clear, her head snapped up, and her eyes flew open to glance around the room. But she was alone. "I need sleep," she said out loud as she rubbed her face.

With a groan, she lifted herself from the couch and plodded toward the bedroom. There she fell face-first on the quilt. Within moments, her breath evened, and she was out cold.

It was well into the afternoon when she finally rolled off the bed, mostly at the behest of her bladder. For good measure, her stomach growled to ensure she stayed awake. To get it out of the way, she showered, then slipped on a pair of worn jeans and a t-shirt. Her moussed hair wrapped in a towel on top of her head, she headed to the kitchen. A warmed-up plate of leftovers in hand with a bottled water, Liza flopped down at the kitchen table and ate.

The first thing she noticed was the quiet. Not complete silence. Outside birds chirped, but other than that, it was just quiet. She hadn't realized how noisy her apartment complex had been. Slamming doors. Voices yammering on the other side of her door. Honking horns outside. The steady bouncing of a basketball on the road. Sometimes sirens or screaming. The occasional gunshot.

Even with her television cranked, the outside noises of city life had always filtered through. Now, none of that interrupted her thoughts. Just the birds, a chorus of short tweets and excited chattering through the closed windows.

It was unsettling, really.

She finished eating as quickly as possible, then moved to the couch. There, the letters still waited on her. Picking up the second one, she leaned back and read it again. It didn't have quite the same punch, but anxiety still nagged her. She dropped it on the coffee table and leaned back with her eyes closed.

As she saw it, she had two choices. Follow through with her grandmother's plan, stick out the year, finish the list and walk away from it in a much better place than she had been. Or tuck tail and run. The image of her slinking away didn't settle well. Neither did a flash of her grandmother's face, pursed in disappointment.

She opened her eyes and stared at the ceiling, letting her inner thoughts do battle. Then, with a deep sigh, she sat up straight.

Liza picked the letter up again and looked over the tasks, landing on "landscape the cottage." She shook her head. She knew nothing about landscaping. The only plant she'd ever had in her house was a cactus, which she had killed. Apparently, even cactus plants need water occasionally. She didn't even know if she should plant yet, but she decided she was going to do it anyway.

"List doesn't say they have to survive," she said aloud with a shrug. "Be careful what you ask for Grandma."

Chapter Twelve

Liza stood in the middle of the outdoor plant area, staring at the vast array of flowers and wanting to die. She'd been there for the better part of the hour, reading the little signs stabbed into the potting soil of each flat. Bright sun. Partly shade. Perennial. Annual. All words that on the surface, she understood but had no clue how to put in action. On the bright side, she knew what a flat was.

And then there was the mulch. Black mulch. Red mulch. Hardwood mulch. Bark nuggets. What the hell were bark nuggets?

She was so lost in her own thoughts, she didn't hear someone approaching until he spoke.

"Need some help?" Jumping, she spun around to find Derrick, who laughed and took a step back. "Sorry. Didn't mean to scare you."

"It's fine. I'm jumpy anyway."

"Need some help?" he repeated.

She laughed. "That obvious, huh?"

"Just a bit."

"What are you looking for?"

Liza let out an exasperated sigh. "Absolutely no clue. It's for the cottage."

"Outside or inside?"

"Definitely outside. I can't be trusted with inside plants."

He chuckled. "Black thumb, eh?"

"The blackest of black thumbs. If it were up to me, I wouldn't have plants at all."

His head cocked to the side. "And it's not up to you?"

"Not yet. Not much of anything right now is my idea."

As they talked, he strolled down the aisles of floral displays, stopping and studying them along the way. She followed with her cart. "I kind of figured that."

"How so?"

"Let's just say, you haven't really given off the happy-to-be-here vibe." He picked up a flat of flowers and put them in her cart.

She gave a half-hearted smile. "Yeah. Probably not." They continued down the aisle.

"What's your budget?" he asked.

She considered. She hadn't really thought about a budget. Budgets mean expensive. It hadn't occurred to her it would be expensive. "I don't know. What is normal?"

"It depends on how big you want to go with this. Couple hundred would probably do it for what you're wanting."

She grimaced. "That's fine."

He continued meandering down the aisle. "So back to not wanting to be here."

Surprisingly, the entire story tumbled from her lips. He listened, occasionally depositing a flat of flowers into her cart, then laughed. "That sounds like Dot. She had a way of getting what she wanted."

"Yes. Yes, she did."

"So, what's on this list? If you don't mind me asking."

Pulling the list from her purse, she handed it to him.

He looked over it and handed it back to her. "That doesn't look so bad."

"It's all perspective, I guess."

They continued past the flowers and into the mulch section. He reached down, grabbed several bags, and deposited them in her cart. He stepped back to look at his handiwork. "That should do you."

She assessed the contents of the cart. Different types of flowers of varied colors, some in full bloom, others that looked to her like weeds. A couple of other flowerless plants. A fern, maybe? She didn't know. The mulch he'd chosen was black.

"Thanks. I really appreciate it."

"You're welcome. Your grandma kept all the tools in the shed out back. You should find everything you need out there."

The thought of planting all the flowers in her cart was almost as overwhelming as choosing them had been. She had no idea where and how. Typically, she would have just watched some how-to videos, but without internet service, that was out. She was just going to have to wing it.

He watched her closely and as if he read her thoughts, said, "Would you like some help?"

Relief escaped her in one long breath. "Typically, I'd say I've got this. But I don't got this. Not in the least. I'm happy to pay you," she added quickly.

He waved her off. "No payment necessary. I can swing by tomorrow morning about ten and we can knock it out. I would do it today, but it's going to be a busy night at the pub, and I have to get these supplies over."

Liza craned her neck to see his cart, still parked on the other side of the garden center. From a distance, she could tell it was packed full of supplies like toilet paper, paper towels and cleaning supplies. On top, a flat of flowers balanced precariously. "If you're busy, you really don't have to. I can manage."

"I'm fine. Seriously, it's no problem."

Liza nodded. "Okay, then. Thank you."

He walked away, then stopped. "Oh, by the way, I noticed Hank was on the porch early this morning. Was he a problem?"

"He wasn't a problem for me at all. I was a problem for him," she said with a laugh. "I may have gone on a little cleaning binge last night. He'd had it with the vacuum around three, I think."

Derrick nodded. "That'll do it. For some reason, he thinks vacuums are Satan's work. Just let me know if he is a bother."

Liza gave a quick nod. "I will. Promise."

With a wave, he walked back to his cart, and she headed for the checkout. By the time she made it back to the cottage, the time was inching into evening, despite the daylight still shining. Liza unloaded the flowers, knowing enough that leaving them sit in a car overnight was probably not the best environment for them. She'd spent a lot of money on those flowers. She fully intended to make them last until they were at least planted. After that, it was in nature's hands.

She made herself dinner, feeling the chill creep through the house as the sun set. Briefly, she considered kick-starting the furnace, but immediately dismissed it when she realized she didn't know how to change the filter, instead opting for a blanket and thick socks. Her Southern blood would just need to adjust.

Finally, she curled into the corner of the couch and called Anna from her newly connected landline.

"So? How is it in the sticks?" Anna asked over a cacophony of dishes clanking against each other.

"If you're busy, I can call you back," Liza said, wincing as a clatter of metal on metal sounded through the receiver.

"It's fine. Just putting away the dishes," she paused. "The pots go in the bottom cabinet, Scott!" More rattling pans, then silence. "I swear. It's not that hard. One day, when we get divorced, it's gonna be over the kitchen."

Liza laughed. "Give him a break. It could be worse. He could fold the towels wrong."

Anna let out a gasp. "Don't you even put that out in the universe. Enough about my issues. Let's talk about yours. How is it going?"

"It's going. I got grandma's list of things."

"Oh, yeah? What kind of things?"

Liza retrieved the letter from the table and read it.

"That doesn't sound near as awful as your tone of voice is relaying. I mean, except for the whole landscaping thing. Makes me think she doesn't know you at all."

"Stop. I will have you know, I picked everything out today, and it's ready to be planted tomorrow, thank you very much."

"Oh, yeah? With whose help?"

"Who said I had help?"

"I'm waiting."

"Fine. Derrick."

Anna's voice moved into a high pitch, reserved for when she was picking on Liza. "Oh, Derrick. Well, now."

Liza could see Anna's eyebrows waggling as she stretched out Derrick's name.

"Stop it. He happened to be there, is all."

"You two are playing nice now, huh? You no longer want to beat him over the head with that suit jacket?"

Liza chuckled, then took a sip of her wine. "Not at the moment, no. Though it's still there, just brewing under the surface."

"In his defense, you were kind of ridiculous."

"Hey! Supportive sister, not judgmental sister, moment here."

It was Anna's turn to laugh. "You are right. He deserves a beating over the head for calling you out on your ridiculousness. Better?"

Liza groaned. "No. But point taken. I need to let it go."

In the background, Liza heard Chloe yell, "Mom!"

It was Anna's turn to groan. "I swear that child is like a bloodhound. I'm in here, honey! You want to say hello to Aunt Liza?"

An excited squeal warmed Liza's heart. A rustle followed as Anna handed off the phone to Chloe. "Hi, Aunt Liza."

"Hi, Bug. What are you doing?"

"Getting ready to take a bath. I need my fish."

Anna broke in. "Your fish are in the drawer under the sink."

There was a thump of the phone dropping, followed by Chloe's voice as she disappeared from the room. "Daddy! I know where my fish are!"

Anna came back on the line laughing. "Well, I guess that conversation is over. I should probably get back to cleaning up the kitchen."

"Understood. I should probably start planning out this list of things. Love you."

"Same. Oh, and call Mom and fill her in this week. Or she'll be asking me about it."

Liza wrinkled her nose. "Can't you just fill her in?"

"Liza," Anna said, her tone shifting to that of an authoritative older sister.

"Ugh. Fine."

They said their goodbyes and when Liza hung up, then looked around the cottage, the emptiness of it set in. Just as she looked over at the door, a scratch and whine from the other side made her jump from the couch.

She opened the door and grinned at Hank, who ambled inside, rubbing against her leg as he entered. "Didn't run you off then?" she asked, giving him a scratch behind the ears.

Beelining for the couch, Hank crawled onto it, turned around twice and then curled into a ball in the corner. Retrieving her sketchbook and pens from the side table, she sat next to him and started to sketch.

Chapter Thirteen

"Grandma did more than let Hank sleep in the house," Liza told Derrick as they carried the flats of flowers off the front porch and into the yard. As promised, he'd pulled in precisely at ten, climbed out of his truck and was now surveying the flower beds scattered throughout the yard and lining the sidewalk.

After he finished plotting their next steps, he'd simply started unloading the mulch from the car. She'd pitched in, dropping the mulch where he pointed.

"Do tell," he said, dropping a flat of flowers and returning to the porch.

Liza did the same. "She let him sleep with her, which I found out when he crawled into bed with me."

He laughed. "And did you let him?"

With a grin, she picked up the last flat and followed him back to the sidewalk where he sat his flat down and pointed for her to take the other one farther down the line. "I couldn't help it. Have you seen that face?" She paused to wipe sweat from her forehead with her arm.

"I have. It's dangerous."

"Yes, it is."

"You ready?"

"Let's do this," Liza said, trying to pump herself up for the project. She'd never been a fan of dirt. As kids, it had been Anna who dug out worms, dangled them in front of her, and laughed when she screamed. She hadn't wanted to jump in mud puddles or pick weeds from the flower beds, which only existed at her grandmother's. Her mother didn't really like flowers either, and any landscaping done on their home consisted of bushes and non-flowering plants that required minimal attention.

Now, looking at the multi-colored spread of flowers, Liza was surprised she hadn't argued against buying them. Maybe she was channeling her grandmother? Or maybe, deep down, she just knew it was what her grandmother would have wanted. Regardless, she was ready to get this job over with and mark one thing off that list.

As they worked across the yard, digging holes, planting flowers, spreading mulch, Liza lost track of time. They labored in virtual silence, the only spoken words coming from Derrick when he directed her to the next part of the project. She followed along, not at all interested in having her own ideas. She trusted him, and that revelation caught her off guard.

Trust didn't come easy for Liza, but here she was, allowing this virtual stranger to map out and control something she would have to look at for months. But her grandmother obviously trusted him. She remembered her telling stories about Derrick, how he helped her when she was in town. How funny he was. How he was like the grandson she never had.

Part of her was jealous that this man had such a relationship with her grandmother. Part of her was glad she'd had someone to help her. Then a small twinge of guilt for never having visited reared up. She stuffed it down. Later, she thought.

When they reached the last flower bed and spread the last of the mulch, Derrick stepped back to survey, his hands resting on the upright hoe handle. "What do you think?"

Liza looked around, her breath catching in amazement. The front yard of the little cottage had been completely transformed. Instead of depressing weeds and empty spots, there was now a multitude of colored flowers, all seemingly in the perfect spot. "This is amazing. I couldn't see it when you were dropping all those flowers in my cart, but this is beautiful. How did you learn to do all of this?"

Letting the hoe rest against the front porch, Derrick stretched his back out. "I worked for a landscaper in the summers through high school."

"Well, as we've established, I don't know anything about landscaping, but as far as I'm concerned, you're really good at it."

His grin stretched wide, and she was struck by how boyish he looked in that moment. She had a feeling he'd broken a lot of hearts in his lifetime.

Wiping her hands on her shorts, she motioned toward the porch. "You want an iced tea or water or something?"

"Iced tea would be good."

Nodding, she disappeared into the cottage, filled two glasses with ice and sweet tea, and returned to the porch. He was sitting on the stoop. She handed him his glass then maneuvered beside him, aware of how the narrow opening pushed them close to each other. She hoped she didn't smell too bad.

Leaning over, he extended his glass toward her. She smiled and tapped it with her own. "Cheers to a job getting done."

Silently, they both sipped on their drinks and surveyed the property. "Those trees could probably be trimmed back some this year before they get into the power lines. I'll bring my trimmer over sometime."

"Thanks. So, do you think she would have liked what we did?"

He nodded, then smiled at her. That charming smile again. The flutter in the pit of her stomach took her by surprise.

"I have a confession to make," he said, bringing her out of that momentary attraction and back to their sweaty, exhausted reality.

"Really? And what would that be?"

"I did all the landscaping for your grandma, so I chose things I knew she would like."

Her drink paused at her lips, then dropped back down. "What?"

Leaning to the side, he pulled his wallet from his back pocket, flipped it open, and pulled a card out. He handed it to her and took a drink while she read. "Marvin's Landscaping. Derrick Lowe. Owner. Are you serious? She didn't even do any of this herself?"

He took another drink, then laughed and shook his head.

"Then why would she make me do it?"

"If memory serves, the letter doesn't say anything against hiring someone."

Standing up, she stomped into the house, pulled the letter from her purse, and read it again. Her lips screwed into a pout as she returned to the front porch and dropped dejectedly next to him.

"It wasn't that bad, was it?" he asked.

"Not the point. Let's just say, playing in dirt is not my favorite thing."

She expected a snide remark, but he just nodded. Several sips later, the silence reached an uncomfortable level as Liza searched for something to say. Finally, she landed on, "I do appreciate you doing this. And stopping by that first morning. In case it wasn't obvious, just wanted to say it."

Again, he nodded. "Your grandma was very important to me."

"It seems like she was important to a lot of people."

"She was." Silence again, then he shifted to look at her. "While we're at it, if it wasn't obvious, I'm sorry that you overheard my conversation with Christy at the funeral."

"Sorry you said it? Or sorry I overheard it?" When he stammered, she laughed. "I'm just messing with you. I probably deserved it. As my sister said, I was a little ridiculous. Apology accepted."

"You think maybe we can start over?" he asked, then wiped the palm of his hand on his jeans and stuck it out to her. "Hi. I'm Derrick."

With a grin, she did the same. "Liza. It's nice to meet you." Their eyes locked as his hand enveloped hers, and she tried to ignore the little spark his touch set off through her body. What in the world was wrong with her?

"Likewise," he said, then released her hand, pulled his phone from his pocket, and checked the time. As he downed the rest of the tea, he stood, then put his empty glass on the stoop. "I probably should start cleaning up and get going."

"Don't worry about it. Seriously. I'll clean up." When he started to argue, she stood, her position on the steps making her eyes level with his. "I'm not kidding. You go. I've got the clean-up covered." He checked his phone again, and she could tell he was torn between leaving it for her and the call of whatever he had next on his agenda. She laughed. "Oh my gosh, seriously. I promise I can handle throwing away some trash and putting up some tools on my own. Go."

With a smile, he nodded. "Okay, then. Just let me know if there's anything else you need. I'll see you around?"

"I'd like that." The quizzical look on his face made her revisit her statement. "I mean, this was fun. Minus the dirt and worms and all."

He smiled. "It was. See you."

Flustered now, she just waved and waited for him to drive away before heading back inside. To call her mother. As promised.

"You're sure you're okay there?" Deborah asked after a surprisingly stunted tirade about the ridiculousness of the whole situation.

"I'm fine. Or at least I will be. Some people I've met are really nice and helpful. Grandma was apparently quite the social butterfly."

That pulled a chuckle from her mother. "She always was. I remember, we'd be at a store or someplace, and she would just randomly start talking to people like they were her best friends. It irritated Dad so much."

"And you?"

There was silence, then with a sad weight to her voice, she said, "Sometimes. But sometimes, I wished I could be like that, too." Before Liza could say anything, she continued, "Anyway, what's on this list again?"

Liza picked the list up from the kitchen table and read through it again, leaving out anything art-related.

"That doesn't sound too bad."

Why did everyone keep saying that? Liza dropped the letter back on the table and walked to her bedroom. "I think

I was just mad about the whole deal. I'm getting over it. Not much I can do about it."

"True. Okay, then," her mother said, signaling the conversation was coming to an end. "You take care of yourself and call if you need something."

"I will."

"Love you."

"Love you, too."

As soon as the word "too" came out of her mouth, she heard the line go dead. Deborah wasn't one for long goodbyes, so it didn't take Liza by surprise. What did take her by surprise was the sadness that washed over her at the disconnection. If she didn't know better, she would have thought she might be a little homesick.

Chapter Fourteen

Sipping her cappuccino, Liza sat at the outside table of the little coffee shop, people-watching. Some continued past her, on to their next destination. Others swung into the shop and either reappeared shortly after, armed with their morning dose of adrenaline, or stayed inside and emerged looking a little more energized than they had when they entered.

It was hard to believe she'd already been in town for several weeks. She'd settled into the remoteness of the cottage, but the 1970s décor had not grown on her. New curtains had already been hung, and she planned to bring her furniture back with her when she went to Florida. Paint samples had already been collected for a complete overhaul, since a paint job was not deemed a major renovation. She had other plans but decided to hold off until at least her lease ran out. The list hung on her refrigerator, and while the only thing she'd checked off was landscaping, she'd started plans for the rest.

Which reminded her of her day's task, and that was to do some recon on the little art gallery in town before making her presence known. According to the letter, they would expect her, and if she was being truthful with herself, it was simply fear prodding her to do research before setting foot in the door. But who wanted honesty before the first cup of coffee, anyway?

Opening her laptop, she typed in "art gallery near me" and waited for it to load. Only one result returned: The Maple Leaf Art Center. *Someone hadn't put much thought into that name*, she thought as she clicked on it. What loaded was a website that could have easily been created at the beginning of the Internet days. She wrinkled her nose at the one-page site that simply listed upcoming events at the bottom and had one very outdated picture.

The volunteer task came to mind, and she smiled, check-marking that box. She would help the Art Center build its digital presence. If they let her, anyway. Maybe she could also volunteer there fulltime. Suddenly, an idea of art classes for children formed and maybe even some offerings for adults. What about other classes? She hadn't even seen the place yet, and her mind was already working in overdrive.

"Liza?" A voice behind her pulled her out of her mental rabbit hole and back to reality where the clock was ticking on her stay in Maple Hill. Closing her laptop, she turned her head to find Christy and a sulking teenager at her side.

She shifted her entire body, finding she was truly excited to see Christy. "Christy, hi!"

"You look busy. I just saw you and wanted to say hi."

Liza pushed her laptop to the side. "It's fine. I was just doing some research on the town. You want to join me?"

While Christy beamed at the invitation, the teenager didn't appear impressed. Liza even caught the stunted eye roll. Christy was unaffected as she rounded the table and took a seat, shooting her son an order with her eyes to sit. He did, flopping down next to her. Regardless of his initial reaction, he forced an amiable face now that he was in full view of his mother.

"Heath, this is Dot's granddaughter I was telling you about. Liza, this is my son Heath."

Liza put her hand out to him, and he seemed a little surprised by this. She watched him straighten, then extend his hand. "Nice to meet you, Heath."

His handshake was firm. "You too, ma'am."

"So, how is it going? I'm sorry I haven't been around much. Between work and baseball season, it's been kind of hectic," Christy said.

"It's fine. It's going well, I think. I'm starting to get settled in and work through my grandmother's list. You play baseball, Heath?"

He nodded. "Shortstop."

"I played softball all through high school. I played shortstop, too. Maybe we can toss a ball some time, if I can find a glove, that is."

Before he could answer, Christy piped up. "What do you say, Heath?"

"I was, Mom," he said, returning to the sullen teenager in an instant. "Thank you."

"You're welcome."

While Liza sipped her coffee, Christy removed one of the breakfast sandwiches from the tray and slid it to Heath, then handed him a drink. She unwrapped her own sandwich, then settled back into the chair and nibbled while Heath lit into his like a starving dog. A side-eye from his mom slowed him down, but not by much.

"Derrick mentioned he helped you get the landscaping part of your list done."

"I don't know how much help I was. He did most of the work. But yes. One thing down. I was just researching the Art Center actually, hoping to check off a couple of other things. Do you know if they offer classes or anything?"

"I know they did at one point, but I don't know about now. The executive director retired about six months ago. I've heard rumblings that there is some internal fighting going on, but how much of that is true and how much is small town gossip, I can't say. I've been there a few times, but the whole scene is really outside of my paygrade, if you get my drift." She grinned and took another bite of her sandwich.

Liza didn't need further explanation, being fully aware of who typically bankrolled those types of facilities. Her mother was often one of those people. "I plan to go check it out. I thought about maybe volunteering to teach some art classes."

From the corner of her eye, she caught Heath perk up at the mention of her plans. He looked like he was going to speak but then thought better of it and went back to scarfing down the rest of his breakfast.

Christy pulled her phone out of her pocket and looked at the screen. "Heath, we should get hopping. We're going to be late."

They both stood in unison, and as Heath turned to the side, she saw Christy's features in his face. Heath cleaned up their trash from the table and carried it to the cans. "We should meet up like this every once in a while," Christy said.

"That would be nice." Liza looked up at Heath, giving him a wave, which he returned. Then Christy waved, too, and walked away.

Downing her coffee, Liza packed up her laptop and her purse then took her coffee cup inside and deposited it with the other dirty dishes on top of the trash can. She'd done all the recon she needed. Now it was time to put things in motion.

Chapter Fifteen

When Liza walked in the front door, she paused, momentarily fearing she'd just walked into someone's home. Located in one of the historic houses along the main street that paralleled the river, the only thing showing she was in the correct place was a small plaque to the left of the door. Even though she'd seen it and checked it, stepping in made her want to step back outside and check again.

The foyer looked like any other foyer one might expect in such a home. Nothing about it felt like an Art Center past the other doors, and it was eerily silent inside. Once the initial panic passed and she'd told herself she was in the right place, she gently closed the heavy wooden door behind her and listened for any movement inside.

"Hello?" she finally said, taking a tentative step inside.

A scooting chair and rustling papers sounded from an opening ahead. "Be right with you!" a voice called, and Liza took a step back onto the carpeted mat in front of the door.

"Hello," the owner of the voice said as she stepped into view. She was a petite woman, either naturally or as a result of age, Liza didn't know. Definitely up in years, she used a cane to keep balance as she carefully walked into the light. Upon seeing her three-piece suit up close—it smelled like cedar and screamed money—Liza wondered if she should have put a little more effort into her appearance and self-consciously smoothed her jeans. The once-over she received before the woman removed her thick glasses to let them hang from a chain around her neck didn't help.

The woman extended her hand, and Liza took it, feeling the frail bones in her palm and holding back the typical firm handshake she would have given. "Welcome to the Maple Leaf Art Center. I'm Margaret Leach, volunteer and president of the board."

Liza cleared her throat, letting go of Margaret's hand. "My name is Liza Blackburn."

The professional and slightly judgmental look on Margaret's face softened and her eyes lit up. "Liza? Dot's Liza!"

She stepped forward, reaching up and cupping Liza's face. "I've been waiting for you to visit me, dear. Come in, come in."

Margaret beckoned for her to follow as she ambled away. As they rounded the corner, she stopped at the view of the gallery, a sharp intake of her breath her immediate reaction. It was a gorgeous space with two ornate doors opening onto a patio overlooking the river. At one time in its life, the space had probably served as a ballroom or formal dining room. And while the décor had been kept, the walls were bare, and a large centerpiece sat in the middle, no doubt to display artwork like pottery. Crates were piled around the space, waiting to be unpacked.

"I'm sorry I didn't hear you come in earlier. I'm in the middle of hanging a show. Come on in. What do you think of our gallery?"

"It's beautiful," Liza said, stepping up to the double doors and looking through the glass at the river. "Gorgeous, actually."

Margaret pulled a painting from a crate, struggling with the weight but managing it in the end. Breath held, Liza watched as the painting dipped from her hand, then righted again before making it safely to the floor. "Would you like some help?"

With a laugh, Margaret moved to the next crate. "Help is always appreciated. Do you know how to hang art?"

"I do."

"Well then, help is definitely appreciated."

It hadn't been in her plans, but without hesitation, Liza dropped her purse in the corner and went to work.

Several hours later, they stood at the end of the gallery and surveyed the room, both smiling. Liza had been impressed with the paintings—watercolors of nature scenes, most likely of the local area. As they were unpacking literature, she read the bio. An amateur painter who had started with a class at the Center ten years prior and just kept at it. There was one painting she already planned to buy of a Snowy Owl that would pair nicely with her own fox painting. It also answered the question about whether the Art Center held classes.

"Come on," Margaret said, waving at her to follow again. "Let's go get a water and have a seat."

Grabbing her purse and taking one last look at the gallery, she followed Margaret through the hall and into another room near the back, which looked set up for a reception.

"The reception is this weekend," Margaret said and swiped a handout from a table in the corner, then handed it to her. "You're welcome to attend."

"I'd like that." Liza stuffed the handout in her purse and continued with Margaret through the reception room and into a small kitchen.

"Would you mind getting two waters from the refrigerator? I need to sit down for a moment," Margaret said as she eased into a chair in the room's corner. Liza did as she was asked, then took the seat next to Margaret, opened their bottles and handed one over.

Her hands trembling just enough to notice, Margaret lifted the bottle to her lips, took a long drink and then let out a satisfied, "Ah! That's better. It's already starting to get hot out there, isn't it?"

Liza shrugged. "I'm from Florida, so it's a little different for me. I'm more worried about the cold."

"No worries, dear. Your body will adjust. I'm a Georgia girl myself. Your grandmother told me a lot about you. You're an artist, right?"

Liza nodded. "I am."

"Good! I always worry I'm confusing people. Old age is a bitch."

Liza's hand flew to her mouth to stop the spray of water that threatened to come out with the laugh. So much for first impressions.

Margaret grinned and winked. "Gotcha with that, didn't I? Don't let these wrinkles and this shrinking body fool ya, honey. I still have some spunk left in me."

"I see that."

"So, not that I don't enjoy the company, but what brings you here today?"

"When my grandmother passed away, she left some tasks for me. One of the items on the list is to have an art show, so I wanted to check with you about availability. I'm happy to provide a portfolio."

Margaret took another drink of her water and waved her hand at her. "No need. Your grandmother has already shown us some pictures of your works. Beautiful. She also told me you would be visiting me if anything happened to her. Or at least, she hoped you would."

Pushing herself from the chair, Margaret took a second to balance herself, then ambled toward the door. She turned and waved for Liza to follow again. They made their way to the office just off of the main hallway where Margaret eased into an office chair and pulled a large binder from the desk.

She flipped it open to a schedule. "We have September or October open for a show. Which would you prefer?"

Immediately, anxiety washed over her at the realization that the show was going to happen. Deep down, she'd hoped the gallery would be booked beyond the year, certain she could argue her case with Bill. It was the only gallery in town. Certainly, she couldn't be held responsible if it wasn't available.

That, however, wasn't the case. She could lie. Tell Margaret she couldn't take either and hope they filled up, but something told her in such a small town, it wouldn't be long before Bill found out the truth. And was it worth doing all this, only to have a lie bite her in the end?

"Might as well get it over with." Margaret glanced at her, telling her she'd said that out loud. Clearing her throat, she forced a smile, "September. I'll take the September one."

Margaret picked up a nubby pencil from the desk, scribbled in the book, then turned and smiled at Liza. "Perfect. You just tell me the name of your show, and we will handle the rest. I'll get with you the end of July to schedule drop-off, hanging, and the reception."

Liza nodded, unable to bring herself to smile. "Sounds good. Thank you, Margaret."

"You're welcome, dear."

"One more thing. Do you by chance need any volunteers? I would be happy to help with your online presence or maybe even teach some art classes. Whatever you need."

With that, Margaret's eyes lit up, and she clapped her hands together. "Do we need volunteers? Oh, yes, we do. This place wouldn't be able to survive without volunteers."

Digging through a stack of papers, Margaret produced a single sheet and handed it to Liza. "Here. Just fill this out and drop it back off to me."

Liza glanced at the paper. Just a simple name and address sheet, plus a few questions. "Mind if I just fill it out now?"

Margaret pulled a pen from a cup at the corner of the desk and handed it to Liza. "Sure."

While Liza filled out her name, number and answered the three questions about her experience, Margaret busied herself stuffing envelopes. When Liza finished, she handed the sheet back to Margaret, who took it, looked it over, then put it in a blue folder on the desk.

"I'll present you to the board of directors next Wednesday, then I'll call you to set up some hours. If you're interested in working with kids, you'll need a background check."

"Might as well get one."

"Good. Just go down to the Sheriff's office, and they'll take care of you. We don't pay for it. Wish we could, but we can't. If that changes your mind, I understand."

Liza shook her head. She'd had background checks before when she'd worked in the schools while in college. It couldn't be that expensive. "It'll be fine. Well, I hate to cut this short, but I should get going."

Margaret stood and extended her hand again. When Liza took it, Margaret covered their clasped hands with her other hand and looked her in the eye. "We loved your grandmother very much. She is deeply missed."

The honest seriousness of her statement washed over Liza, and tears formed. She smiled and squeezed Margaret's hand gently. "Thank you. She is very deeply missed."

Releasing hands, Liza turned and walked out, excited to be one step closer to completing the list.

Chapter Sixteen

From a distance, Derrick caught sight of Liza headed for one of the food vendors. He checked his watch. The dinner rush, if there was one at all, wouldn't start for another hour. Rushes were few during the July 4th weekend. The annual event, while good for the overall economy, always put a hurting on his business, especially when it fell on the weekend.

So much so, every year, he considered closing for the three days. He never did. There were always a few stragglers looking for something other than greasy festival food or a place to have a few beers in the evening, but he typically lost money.

He'd only wandered the three blocks over to talk with a knife dealer who set up every year. They were finishing up the haggling process when Derrick spotted Liza.

"I think that'll do me this year, Mark," Derrick said as he handed over his credit card to pay for the knives.

Mark, whose white hair, white beard, and crinkly eyes fit his age, took the card and swiped it through a reader plugged into his phone. "My granddaughter set this up for me. Still boggles my mind what this little piece of machinery will do."

Glancing up to keep tabs on Liza, he saw her order at the window then step to the side to wait. "I know. Crazy." Mark let the payment run through, then handed his phone to Derrick. A quick scribble with his fingertip and the deal was done. He handed the phone back to Mark.

"You'll drop them off on your way out of town?"

"Yes, sir." He stuck out his hand, and Derrick clasped it, feeling the protruding bones underneath. "Thanks for another year of business, Derrick."

"Thanks for the knives. It was good working with you again."

"Same. Same." Before Derrick cleared the tent, Mark was already focused on another customer.

By the time he made it to the midway, Liza had moved off to the side, her back to him. He couldn't help but notice how the tank top she wore rested just at the top of her fitted jeans.

His eyes kept traveling down, over the curve of her butt, then back up again at the thin silver necklace resting on her slim neck. Her hair, piled on her head with a clasp, little tendrils snaking down her neck, shone in the sunlight.

"Liza," he said, and she turned, her eyes wide in shock and powdered fingers between her lips. She pulled them free and covered her mouth with her hand while she finished chewing, letting out an embarrassed laugh after she swallowed.

"Derrick. Hi."

He pointed at the funnel cake. "Can't go wrong with one of those."

She looked down at the greasy paper plate, the contents half gone already, and smiled. Then she thrust it toward him. "Want some?"

Holding up a hand, he shook his head. "No, thanks." Then he grinned. "You have a little powdered sugar on your cheek."

Unconsciously, he reached out and brushed the white dust from her skin. She froze at his touch. Then his hand shot back down to his side, and hers went up to her steadily reddening cheek.

"Sorry," he said, not exactly sure why he was apologizing, but felt he should anyway.

"Is it gone?" She brushed a couple of more times, and Derrick laughed as she redeposited more powdered sugar in the same spot.

Reaching over to the napkin dispenser, he pulled out a handful and handed them to her. "Try this."

"I forgot how messy these are." She took the napkins, gave her cheek a couple of wipes and then presented it to him. "Better?"

He nodded once. "All good."

The conversation stalled as they both looked around. What was he doing? He'd walked all the way over here to what? Stand around and look like a fool?

"Was the funnel cake part of your list? I can't remember."

"No. Just a perk."

"How's the list coming?"

"Good. I started volunteering at the Art Center, and I have a show planned for September. I need to go back home and clean out my apartment by the end of this month. Speaking of, do you know where I can rent a moving truck?"

Liza started walking, and Derrick followed. "I do, actually." As they moved toward a large oak tree with an empty bench underneath, he said. "From me."

She sat down and looked up at him. "Seriously?"

He eased down on the bench and shifted to face her. She sat facing forward, the plate now balanced on her thighs. "Seriously." Then he realized she'd stopped eating.

Figuring it was because he wasn't eating, he said, "If the offer still stands, I think I would like a small piece of that."

"Sure." Leaning back, she pointed at the plate. "Help yourself."

He reached down and pulled a chunk away, then leaned back and took a bite. He held back a smirk as she tore a small piece off and popped it in her mouth.

They were silent while they chewed, giving Derrick entirely too much time to study her profile. The way her neck dipped into her throat and the slopes down to the small mounds protruding from her chest. Stop it! The voice crushed the next round of images that started, and he turned to face front again.

"When do you need the truck?"

Her hand shot to her mouth again while she finished chewing, then dropped when she finished. "Sometime in the next couple of weeks."

"How big?"

She shrugged. "Not sure. I have to bring back all my artwork, but I think I'm going to bring back some furniture, too."

"I'll take a look at the schedule when I get back to the pub and let you know what I have. Are you staying for the fireworks tonight?"

"No, I don't think so. I've been told it draws a crowd, and crowds really aren't my thing."

"That it does." She offered the plate again, and he obliged, taking a smaller piece this time. Again, she followed his lead. "I watch them every year from the pub roof."

Eyes wide, she finished chewing again before speaking. "You can see them from there?"

"Yeah, it's a pretty big show. You're welcome to come to watch it if you'd like. We can get the truck rented, too." His own surprise at the invite matched the look on her face. Watching the fireworks had always been a kickback moment for him. Close the pub early, get everyone on their way and then relax in a lawn chair with a beer and enjoy the show. It had been that way since he'd bought the place eight years prior. Not once had he invited anyone to watch with him, not even Christy and Heath, who both preferred the view from the park, anyway.

He watched as her bottom lip curled in between her teeth, followed by a thin smile. "Thank you for the invitation. We'll see."

Taking that as a friendly way of turning down his offer, he just nodded. Scanning the midway, he checked his phone for the time. "I should get going."

"Would you like some more?" Again, she pushed the plate toward him, but he shook his head.

"Better not. My system doesn't handle a bunch of sugar like it used to."

"Oh, I understand that. I'll probably pay for this later. Getting old sucks."

He raised an eyebrow as he stood. "Who said anything about getting old? I'll see you later. Take care of yourself."

"You, too."

Halfway across the park, he realized he was walking straighter with his chest puffed out, just in case she was watching him walk away. Why? What was the sudden attraction? They'd only seen each other maybe a handful of times since the day he'd helped her with the landscaping. She hadn't even been in the pub. If she were interested in him, wouldn't she have stopped in? It had been so long since he'd found anyone attractive—at least anyone he wanted to pursue—he was having a hard time wrapping his head around it. It was just a passing attraction, he thought, as he continued up the street toward the pub. It would subside. And if it didn't, she'd be gone in a year, anyway.

As he rounded the corner, he realized he might have miscalculated his staffing for the night. It looked like there was a line of people standing outside the door. *What in the hell?* he thought as he stepped up his pace.

Derrick only had a split second to notice Liza had stepped up to the bar before he was yelled for by customers on opposite ends. He acknowledged her with a nod, then moved to one end of the bar, took the order, filled it, then moved to the opposite end.

A woman stepped up and waved her hand at him. He slowed his steps enough to listen to her. "I'm sorry. We've been waiting for thirty minutes for our food. Any idea when it'll be done?"

"Sorry about that, ma'am. I'll check for you."

"Hey! Bartender!" A man called from the opposite end, and he picked up the pace again, ignoring the customers waving empty bottles at him.

As he turned, he stopped short at the sight of Liza, a summer dress clinging to all the right places of her body, twisting her hair up as she stepped behind the counter. It also wasn't lost on him that she'd gone home to change before coming back to the pub. *Interesting*, he thought, as he moved behind her to grab a bottle of tequila from the display shelf and asked, "What are you doing?"

"Helping. Go check on that customer's food."

Lining up two shot glasses, he filled both, grabbed lemon and salt, and delivered them to the customer. On his way back, he picked up three more orders. When he reached Liza, she was already in full bartender mode. Pulling beers for this couple. Mixing a drink for that customer.

He held his tongue and watched her as she expertly moved around the back of the bar, talking and laughing with customers as she went. Any thoughts of telling her he didn't need the help evaporated as he felt his stress level deflate, if only slightly. He still had the kitchen to contend with.

As they passed each other, she whispered in his ear, "Go. I said I've got this."

He grinned at her. "I can see that. This is definitely a conversation for later."

Liza answered with a wink as he exited through the swinging saloon doors to the kitchen. And the chaos was exactly what he'd expected, with Maryanne feverishly trying to keep up with the stack of orders. When she looked up at Derrick, she threw her hands up in frustration. "What in the Sam Hill brought this on? This is crazy, Derrick."

"No clue, Maryanne," he said as he donned an apron and moved next to her. "But I'm not going to question it. How about we get this done and worry about the why later?"

"What about the bar?"

"Taken care of. I think, anyway. Where do you want me?"

She pointed at the fryer, and he got to work. The rest of the evening slipped by as all three kept their heads down and focused on the next thing. With Derrick's help, the food orders were filled. As he carried plates out, he glanced at Liza, who gave him a thumbs up and kept working. After smoothing a few ruffled feathers at the tables, even comping a few of the meals, he moved back to the bar and did a quick inventory.

With Liza expertly handling customers, he restocked the bar, then stepped up to help her. The two of them working together made quick work of any waiting customers, moving around each other seamlessly in what appeared to be a choreographed dance.

In the years he'd owned the pub, he couldn't remember being so relieved to yell "Last call!" There was a small rush of the bar, and then the crowd thinned. As the last person walked out, Derrick and Liza glanced at each other, then laughed.

"Well, that was a fun jog down memory lane," Liza said as she ran her forearm across her head. Then she glanced down at the floor and grimaced at her sticky, wet feet. "Though I don't recommend wearing flip-flops."

"Flip flops or not, you saved me tonight. I owe you."

She waved him off as she moved to the dining room to clear tables. "You do not owe me. I owed you. Now we're even."

Derrick worked on organizing the back of the bar. "I'm absolutely certain me planting some flowers and you saving my business are not even close to being on the same level. I still owe you."

At that, she turned, empty beer bottles hanging from in between her fingers and sporting a wide grin. "Fine. I enjoy being owed. It's the owing I can't stand."

He chuckled. "Same."

She turned around and continued cleaning, which he should have been doing, too. Except he wasn't. He was watching the way she moved around the bar, totally focused on her job. Determined, yet, and the thought took him by surprise, sexy as hell.

"Well, Derrick," Maryanne said as she exited the kitchen, her voice making Liza look his way. Quickly, he turned his head, pretending to wipe down the bar as Maryanne finished pushing through the swinging doors, purse in hand. "Kitchen is as clean as it's gonna get tonight. This old lady is tired. I'll come in a little early tomorrow and finish up."

Derrick patted her shoulder, trying to avoid eye contact with Liza until his earlier thought evaporated. "Don't worry about it, Maryanne. Thank you."

As Maryanne kept moving to the door, she said, "Don't thank me. Thank her. Good job, honey."

"Thanks," Liza said with a smile, barely getting it out before Maryanne disappeared through the door.

Derrick checked his watch, then pulled a beer from the cooler. "Hey. Fireworks are soon. Want to join me?"

As she dropped another bunch of empty bottles in the bin, she wiped her hands on the towel draped across her shoulder and nodded.

"Great. What's your poison?"

"Whatever you're having."

He cocked his head to the side, then shrugged as he pulled out another beer. "I was under the impression you didn't like beer."

As he unscrewed the lid, she moved behind the bar and up to him. "It's been a while since I've had a beer. Figure I'll give it a try."

He handed her the bottle, trying to ignore the feel of her fingers brushing against his during the handoff. And how did she smell that good after the night they'd had? Clearing his throat, he nodded his head toward the kitchen and walked away.

As Derrick disappeared through the swinging doors, Liza stopped in front of the mirror. Grimacing, she tried to smooth down the flyaways sticking up from the top of her head, then reached up and removed the clip. Her hair fell down around her shoulders, and she used her fingers to straighten it.

"You coming?" Derrick yelled from the back room. "Yep!" she yelled back, took one last look, rolled her eyes, and entered the kitchen. He was waiting for her in the back hallway. When she reached him, she saw him look at her hair, then he turned and continued down the narrow hallway. She noticed the camping chair hanging from his shoulder.

At first, she couldn't see their destination until Derrick ascended the set of rickety wooden stairs at the end of the hallway. Liza stalled. The stairs didn't look like they'd hold Derrick, much less both of them. They even creaked under his weight.

"You good?" She looked up to find him paused halfway up, his head angled to look over his shoulder. "They're safe. I promise."

As if that should have been enough, he continued up and then through a door at the top, which he propped open for her. A deep breath and a prayer later, she was moving up toward the night sky, a faint breeze carried on stifling heat drifting down to her. Despite the creaks, Liza could feel the solidness of the stairs under her feet, and by the time she'd reached the top, she'd released the death grip on the wooden railing.

Remarkably, the night air was cool on top of the roof, a stark difference to the sweltering heat she'd felt all day. Small goosebumps rose on her arms, and she wondered if she should have brought a jacket. Derrick was off to the right side of the door, standing next to two chairs bookending a small, plastic table. One of the chairs matched the brown table, while the other was the bag chair he'd been carrying.

"Your choice," he said, nodding to the chairs.

Her gut telling her the matching chair was his, she settled into the bag chair and adjusted to make sure her dress was still in place over her thighs. Once he sat down, she scanned the view of the town from her vantage point. She had to admit the town was beautiful from this height. Blooming trees rose over top of vintage streetlights, and the lights peppering the businesses and residents added to the homey feeling below her.

Off in the distance, she saw the top of the Ferris wheel, lit and turning above the buildings. What was absent was the overwhelming noise of the rides she'd heard earlier. It was there, a steady hum in the night's background, but not so loud to take away from the stillness.

"It's beautiful up here," Liza said, the awkwardness of the silence between them weighing on her.

"It's my favorite place." He took a pull of his beer and rested it between his legs, leaning back enough in the chair to show he was nice and relaxed. "How are your flowers holding up?"

Liza hoped the embarrassment she felt wasn't too noticeable. "Okay, I guess." That wasn't the truth. She'd nearly killed them all. But, given how much work he'd put into it, she hated to admit it.

"You've murdered them, haven't you?"

At first, she looked shocked, and then she laughed as she took a drink of her beer. "I don't know what you're talking about."

"Don't lie."

"I can't help it." Her voice rose to a high-pitched whine usually reserved for teenagers. "I told you I have a black thumb. I don't know what I did. They're all wilty. I just thought it was the heat."

"Have you watered them?"

Her eyes shifting away, she took another drink, then pressed her lips together. That prompted a laugh from Derrick. "I'll take that as a no. Would you like me to stop by and take a look at them?"

"Would you? I don't know if they can be saved or not, but I would like them to at least last the summer. Even if it means I have to water them."

"I don't mind."

"Thanks."

"How are you liking Maple Hill so far?"

She thought about that question for a moment before answering. "As much as I hate to admit it, it's starting to grow on me. I know now why grandma liked it so much. It's just, well, peaceful."

"It can be."

"This is the longest I've been away from home, so it took some getting used to."

"You didn't go to college?"

"I did, but it was in the same town, so I still went home a lot."

"What did you study?"

"Art," she said. "Did you go to college?"

He shook his head. "Only a couple of years. Long story, but probably for the best, anyway. I never did like school."

An image of him riding up the dusty road on his dirt bike, his long hair flying out from under a stained ball cap, made her chuckle.

"What?"

"Nothing. I was just remembering you riding up and down the road on that dirt bike."

"Oh man, that was a long time ago."

"Yes, it was. Do you still ride?"

"Nah. Had a nasty spill on one when I was in my early twenties. Nearly killed me. Just lost the taste for it after that." He took a drink, then asked, "You still play the trumpet?"

She nearly spat out her beer at that, having forgotten all about the two years during her fifth and sixth-grade years when she'd attempted the trumpet. Both years she'd stayed with her grandmother, who had forced her to practice. "Um, no. I never got any better, in case you're wondering. It's hard to believe how young we were then."

"You more than me. You were what, twelve?"

She nodded. "Something like that."

"I think I was seventeen or eighteen. You have an older sister, right? Anna?"

"Yeah. Anna. She would have been a year or so younger than you. It always surprised me you two didn't hang out more."

He shrugged. "I was busy being a soon-to-be new adult, I guess." He paused, then asked. "If you don't mind me asking, why did you all stop coming around?"

The mood dampened ever so slightly. "My Dad passed unexpectedly."

"I'm sorry."

"It's okay. Grandma said she didn't want to take us away from mom for so long around the holidays after that, especially since she came down every summer. But I think it was Mom who had an issue with it. It was a rough time."

"I understand that."

Liza glanced over at him, and under the moonlight, she could see the way his jaws clenched. She waited, but when he didn't offer more information, she decided the conversation was getting entirely too heavy for such a night and changed the subject. "So, what made you decide to buy a pub?"

That made him smile and immediately lightened the mood again.

"I don't know, really. I just thought it would be cool."

"And?"

"Oh, yes, it's cool. Most days, anyway. What about you? Why art?"

Oh, how she hated that question. It was always so hard to explain to people why she chose art, especially since she wasn't making a living at it. "I don't know. Can I say something without you laughing at me?"

"I will do my best but make no promises."

"I didn't really choose art. It kind of chose me. I don't know, really. When I'm painting, the world just goes away, and I see it in a whole new light. It's when I'm happiest."

She expected a laugh, but when she looked at him, he was nodding. "I get that, believe it or not. It's how I feel about landscaping, honestly. It was just hard to make a good living at it around here. So, I found other things I enjoyed to make money, and I do landscaping when I can."

As they slipped into easy conversation about their love of art and landscaping, segueing into talking about the jobs that paid the bills, Liza noticed the ease with which they interacted. It was the first time in a long time, especially with someone of the opposite sex, she'd felt at peace with herself.

As he took sips of his beer, her eyes wandered over the slope of his neck and the way his biceps pushed out from under his short sleeves. It wasn't in that body builder way, so tight the fabric looked like it could rip at any time. Just subtly there, announcing the strength underneath that thin piece of cloth without overt intimidation. When the overwhelming need to reach out and touch that bicep washed over her, she ripped her eyes away and back to the view, taking another drink of her beer.

The first pop of a firework made them both jump. Pushing himself from the chair, he walked to the edge of the rooftop, the beer in his hand nearly empty.

Liza, her beer only half empty, sidled up next to him and watched as colored lights exploded over the tree line. "Wow." It was little more than a whisper, but he heard it.

"Yeah. They do a good job."

For the rest of the show, they were silent, though each took turns glancing at the other under the colored splashes that lit up the sky every few seconds.

When it was over, he turned to her. "You ready to get that truck scheduled?"

She nodded, trying to ignore her disappointment that the night was over.

Chapter Seventeen

The paintbrush slid across the canvas, leaving a streak of baby blue where the white had been. Sitting on a stool, Liza stared past the canvas at the sky overhead as she dipped the brush in white and painted fluffy clouds. Sweat dripped from her forehead. She wiped it away with her arm and continued, lost in the process of creation.

This painting would be the second one she'd finished since arriving, more than she'd finished in the prior five years. It was funny how much time she had now without the distractions of her phone and the internet. Since the fourth of July, Derrick had been a near-constant in her thoughts. And it had thrown her off guard. There was something about that night, sitting alone with him on the roof, watching the fireworks explode in the distance, that set her body on a path that had been overgrown for years.

When she forced herself to think about it, she realized she'd lost track of the last time she'd been attracted to a man. A real one anyway, not some fictional hottie on her television. It had taken her by surprise, mostly because their first few interactions had made her feel like that annoying twelve-year-old all over again. But that night on the rooftop, she'd felt like a woman and, it had felt incredibly close to a date.

But it wasn't. Or at least, it couldn't be. While she wasn't opposed to a little flirting here and there, the last thing she needed or wanted was an added complication to the already complicated situation she was in. And a fling was out of the question. She'd tried that once, and it had gone horribly wrong.

The ringing telephone inside broke her away from the painting. She checked her watch and realized she'd already been at it for nearly two hours. Hopping down from the stool, she grabbed the phone from inside and answered as she stepped back out onto the front porch and looked at the piece from a distance.

Not too bad, she thought, though she'd noticed the way the tree was just a little off scale against the backdrop of the fence and field. Making a mental note to fix it as she said, "Hello."

"Heya. Whatcha doin'?" Christy asked.

Grinning, Liza stepped inside and shut the door, moving closer to the window air conditioner to cool her steaming body. "Painting. What are you doing?"

"I'm calling you to invite you over tonight for a cookout."

Liza's first instinct was to decline, but she pushed it aside. "That sounds like fun. What time?"

"Just come by anytime."

"Do I need to bring anything?"

"Just whatever you're drinking. We have the food covered. It'll just be me, Heath, you, and Derrick. That okay?"

Stepping away from the air conditioner, her initial reluctance was replaced with a strong desire to see Derrick again. It had been two weeks already, not that she was counting. Not that she couldn't have seen him whenever she wanted, considering he lived just up the road. And then there was the pub. It wouldn't have been unbelievable that there would be one night she wouldn't want to cook. And, as a matter of fact, there had been several nights like that. But she'd always steered clear of the pub, trying not to appear too interested in seeing him again.

"That's fine. See you in a while."

"See ya," Christy said and hung up.

Liza hung up and dropped the phone back in the charger. Then she headed to her bedroom to find something to wear.

"You look so cute," Christy exclaimed as she opened the screen door of the single-wide to let Liza inside. Adjusting the bag of water bottles and a six-pack of beer she held in each hand, Liza slipped inside, and Christy closed the door behind them.

"It's not much, but it's mine," Christy said, almost apologetically as she moved past Liza toward the kitchen.

"I was just thinking about how beautiful your home is," Liza said and didn't miss Christy's beaming smile. She meant every word. When she'd pulled into the driveway, the first thing she'd noticed was the gorgeous flower beds wrapping around the built-on wooden porch.

When she entered, she was also struck by Christy's interior decorating and the way picture frames and rustic wall decorations popped against the simple leather furniture inside. The kitchen was no different, carrying along with the rustic feel.

Liza set the beer and bag of waters down on the bar separating the kitchen and living room. On the other side, Christy was patting out hamburgers, seasoning each with salt and pepper before stacking them on a plate.

"Can I help you with something?" Liza asked.

"After I get these patted out, if you want to take them out to Derrick, that would be great. I can get the toppings done."

Shifting back a step, Liza looked out the window overlooking the backyard and saw Derrick lift a gloved hand just as a baseball slammed into it. He let the ball drop from the glove, took a step back, and his arm swung back, then forward, the small ball releasing so fast it disappeared from her view almost immediately.

Stepping a little to the right, she caught sight of Heath across from him, preparing to throw the ball back at Derrick. She watched them throw the ball back and forth for several moments. It wasn't until Christy stepped up beside her and said, "That makes me smile, too," that she realized she was grinning like an idiot.

Covering, she stepped away and dropped the grin, "Yeah. I've always liked watching adults and children interact. It makes for some great photography."

"Yeah, that's it," Christy said with a wink, then before Liza could comment, she shoved the plate full of hamburgers toward her chest.

Deciding to let the comment go, at least for now, Liza grabbed the plate and headed to the back door. Christy beat her there, holding it open for Liza. Catching the movement out of the corner of his eye, Derrick looked toward the door, held up a finger to Heath, and jogged over. Liza thought she noticed his step falter a little when they made eye contact, but he recovered too quickly for her brain to analyze it.

Reaching up, he grasped the door to hold it open while Liza cautiously took the small wooden steps to the ground. That's when she noticed the above ground pool off to the side, a wooden deck wrapping around it. Other than that, it was nothing but an open field on all sides for at least a football field and then trees. If there were neighbors anywhere in the vicinity, Liza couldn't see them. When she thought about it, she realized the entire stretch of dirt road she'd traveled was devoid of mailboxes.

"Hey," Derrick said, relieving her of the plate when she reached the last step.

"Hey," Liza answered, her voice entirely too shy and quiet for her own liking. "Hi," she said again, putting more force behind the words. Then felt like an idiot.

"Liza!" Heath jogged toward her, grinning wildly. It warmed Liza's heart that the teenager seemed so happy to see her, considering they'd only actually met a handful of times and usually while one or the other was on the go. It was also a welcome distraction from Derrick walking away.

As Heath reached her, Derrick had already moved to the smoking grill on a small concrete slab off to the side. Next to it, a picnic table also sat on a concrete slab under a large oak tree.

"Do you want to pass a baseball with me?" Heath asked.

Liza shrugged. "Sure." She turned to Derrick. "If Derrick doesn't mind if I borrow his glove."

He nodded to the place he'd dropped it in the grass. "Knock yourself out. Probably sweaty, though."

As she picked up the glove and stuck her hand inside, she couldn't stop the scrunch of her nose at the dampness.

"Yep," Liza said.

Derrick just laughed and dropped the burgers on the grill.

Shaking off the nastiness of the glove, she put her fist on the inside. It was way too big for her, but for a game of catch, it would do. "Take it easy on me. It's been a while," Liza said, holding her glove out to Heath, who'd closed the gap between them.

With a two-finger salute from his forehead, Heath dropped the ball from his glove into his open palm, then stepped back and threw it.

The ball arced lazily, telling Liza he had indeed taken some of the power away, but his aim was still true, and the ball hit the leather of her glove with a satisfying thwap. Nostalgia washed over her, standing under the scorching sun at the shortstop position, the crack of the bat, the feel of the softball hitting her glove. The smell of the dirt and leather and sweat. Chanting players in the boxes. Scraped legs and arms and the impact of the dirt when she slid into a base or dove for a ball.

With a smile, she dropped the ball into her palm. It felt odd. Smaller than her kinetic memory was accustomed to. When she stepped back and cocked back her arm, bringing it forward, she knew the moment it released she'd misjudged, and the ball soared over Heath's head far into the field.

Heath turned to look at it, then back at her, his eyes wide.

"Sorry!" she yelled.

A low whistle sounded behind her, and Liza turned to find Derrick paused over the grill, the spatula raised above the burgers. "Take it you played a little ball, huh?"

"A little," she said. "All through high school."

"No college?"

She shook her head. "Hindsight, I would have. But, by then, let's just say, I had a way of letting my stubbornness get in my way."

"Ready?" Heath yelled, having retrieved the ball and returned to his spot.

Liza turned to him and nodded. Again, the ball sailed into her mitt. "I'll try not to make you run for it again."

"It's fine!" Heath said, evidently more interested in having someone throw with him than how good they might be.

This time, Liza let the ball sit in her hand for a moment, before cocking back her arm. She adjusted the force and released. It arced and fell just short of his glove, but he managed to snag it.

"I'll get it eventually," she yelled.

Heath threw the ball. She caught it. Threw it back, this time landing her mark. He threw it. She threw it. Back and forth, back and forth, the steady impact of glove and ball got faster and harder as they both found their rhythm. They continued, both lost in the act of throwing the ball, until the sound of the screen door opening caught both their attention.

"Heath! Come help me carry this stuff out."

Stuffing his glove under his arm, he lazily tossed the ball to Liza and jogged to the door then disappeared inside. Stretching out her arm, Liza peeled off the glove and carried both over to the picnic table. Derrick flipped the burgers, then closed the lid. "There are drinks in that cooler if you want something."

"Oh, my drinks!" she said, realizing she'd left them sitting on the counter.

"You can have one of mine. We can put yours in the cooler when you're ready."

Walking over to the cooler, she pulled out a bottled water, twisted the top off, then half-sat on the top of the picnic table. Taking a drink, she rotated her arm, feeling the overuse in her muscles. She was going to be sore, of that much she was certain. "Thanks for that," he said.

"What? Throwing the ball? I'm glad he asked. I haven't done that in years."

"Can you bat, too?"

"I used to be able to. I guess I probably still could with some practice," she said. Then one of her eyes squinted suspiciously. "Why?"

The door opened behind them again, and Heath and Christy appeared, Heath carrying plates of buns and toppings and Christy carrying a large bowl. Pushing off the picnic table, Liza walked toward them.

"Can I help bring anything out? I'm going to get my drinks to put in the cooler."

"They're already in the refrigerator, but if you want to grab the corn that's on the counter, the butter and the salt and pepper, that would be appreciated."

"Sure thing," Liza said and passed them.

Inside, she grabbed the food and pulled a beer from the refrigerator. As she exited, she noticed the way the small family interacted with each other. Derrick playfully swiped at the back of Heath's head when he apparently said something deserving of it, then the way Christy and Derrick easily chatted with each other.

Despite barely knowing them, when she crossed the yard, she realized she felt completely comfortable with them. For the next few minutes, they were all in prep mode, Derrick pulling off the hamburgers, Christy and Heath spreading things out on the table in a well-rehearsed dance. Then they were all sitting.

Liza waited to take a plate and was glad she did, because all three bowed their heads. She did, too, and listened as Derrick said a brief prayer. "Dig in!" he said, and Heath was the first to the bowl of what turned out to be macaroni salad.

Christy smacked his hand. "How about you let our guest go first," she said, side-eyeing him.

Sheepishly, Heath handed the spoon to Liza. "Sorry."

"Thank you," Liza said.

She took the spoon, dropped some macaroni salad on her plate, then handed the spoon back to Heath. Heath accepted it and dug in.

They were all silent while they filled their plates, then settled in to eat. Liza took a bite of the burger and sighed. Realizing she'd done it out loud, she covered her chewing mouth and laughed. "Sorry. I love grilled burgers, but it's been a while."

"Well," Christy said. "From now on, you have an open invitation for every cookout."

"Thank you. And I'll be here," Liza said, and meant it.

"How goes the list?" Christy asked in between bites.

"Good. I think. Marked off three things. Only four more to go."

"What about the art show?" Derrick asked.

"What art show?" Christy sat back, and Liza realized Christy hadn't actually seen the list.

"One of the items is to have an art show. It's scheduled for the Maple Hill Art Center in September."

"Really?" Liza was a little taken aback by Christy's excitement. "Will they have a reception?"

Liza nodded. "I believe so. I'm actually going down next week to get my pieces and some of my furniture."

Christy paused. "By yourself?"

Liza shrugged. "Yes. I'm getting a moving truck from Derek. I'll just get someone to help me when I get down there. I thought maybe I could bribe Heath to help when I get back."

Heath looked up from his plate, then at his mom, then back at Liza and shrugged. "Sure." He went back to eating and the three adults smiled at each other.

"But you'll be driving all that way in that big truck, all by yourself?" Liza looked up at her, but noticed the comment wasn't actually directed at her. It was directed at Derrick. Before she could say anything, Christy said, "Didn't you say you owed her, Derrick?"

Eyes wide, Derrick gave Christy a hard look, and she returned it. Liza jumped in. "Yes. It's fine. I can handle the drive."

Wiping his mouth, Derrick turned to her.

"Christy is right. I do owe you. You are going down next Monday, right?" Liza squirmed against the hard bench and nodded. "I'd be happy to go down with you."

"Derrick, you really don't have to do that."

"Yes, he does!" Christy said. "I mean, unless you don't want him there for some reason."

Liza felt her cheeks warm. "That's not it."

"Good, then. It's settled."

As Christy looked down at her ear of corn and crunched the kernels off the cob, Derrick caught Liza's eye and winked. He mouthed, "Seriously, it's fine."

She started to tell him not to worry about it, but Heath broke in. "Can we play Whiffle Tag?"

"I guess that's up to Liza," Christy said.

Liza looked around the table. "What the heck is Whiffle Tag?"

All three laughed.

"It's a game we made up with Heath when he was young. It's kind of baseball, but not, with a whiffle ball."

"Want to play, Liza?"

Not wanting to be the odd person out, Liza shrugged. "Why not? You'll have to tell me how to play."

"After we clean up and our food rests a bit," Christy said.

Heath's shoulders sagged, and Liza silently thanked Christy as the food she'd eaten weighed on her stomach.

"I second that," Liza said.

"You ready for camp, Heath?" Derrick asked, which led to a discussion about the summer sports camp Heath attended every year. Liza just sat back and listened as the three of them fell into conversation about the camp, and things Heath was excited about and not excited about.

Finally, they all appeared to have gotten their fill of food, with Christy being the first to stand. She gathered bowls and plates, and Liza stood to help, but she shooed her away. "Heath can get that. Grab yourself another beer and hang out here and relax."

"You sure?" Liza asked. As easy as they'd conversed on the Fourth, Liza felt a twinge of nervousness at being outside, alone with Derrick, who had already moved to the grill and was scraping down the grate.

"Yeah. Derrick can keep you company. The deal is, he buys the meat and grills it and then he doesn't have to clean-up."

When Liza looked at him, he looked almost apologetic. "Don't take that as I don't think I should clean up. After cleaning up after people at the pub every evening, I hate doing dishes."

Settling back on the bench of the picnic table, she waved him off. "It's fine. I hate doing dishes, too. I used to volunteer to vacuum the entire house, clean the surfaces, and wash windows if Anna would do dishes."

He laughed. "That's some serious hate."

"Yeah. Mom used to try to make me do it. She gave up on that pretty quick."

"Understood. You don't strike me as someone who likes being made to do anything."

"Hello, pot. Meet kettle."

That made him laugh. He closed the lid of the grill and walked over to sit across from her, grabbing a beer from the cooler on his way.

He peered at the beer in her hand, and she showed it to him. He nodded and showed her his, and she nodded. They sat in silence for a moment, then he said, "I'm glad you came to watch the fireworks the other night."

"Me too." It was all she could manage. What was she supposed to say? That she couldn't stop thinking about him.

How would that conversation go? "I appreciate you inviting me."

He tipped his beer bottle. "You're welcome anytime."

Seeing an opening to address the trip to Florida, Liza said, "I know Christy put you on the spot with the whole trip to Florida thing. Not that I wouldn't like the help, but you really don't have to."

He waved her off. "Seriously, I should have offered in the first place. Besides, she's always telling me I need a break from the pub. At least this way, I feel like I'm accomplishing something."

"And what would that be?"

"Not owing you," he said and again with the wink.

Dear lord, that wink was going to be the death of her.

Liza chuckled as she swung her leg over the bench to face him. "Touché. Considering you'll have to meet my mother, I might owe you when it's all said and done."

The screen door slammed behind them, and Heath took off running into the field, a plastic bat and ball in one hand and two mats in the other. She watched as he walked heel to toe across the field and dropped the other mat.

"Are you all ready?" he yelled.

Liza looked at Derrick. "Am I ready?"

Derrick put his beer down and crossed around to her, extending his hand. "It's fun. I promise."

Slipping her hand into his, she felt it close around hers and the ease with which he pulled her to her feet. Her body tried to keep moving into his solid chest, but she leaned back to stop the forward motion. Then he was walking away, leaving her to catch her breath.

Placing her beer on the table, Liza shook it off and followed. Christy fell in beside her.

"All right!" Heath said, nearly bouncing with excitement. "This is how it works. We'll do two teams. It's usually me and mom against Uncle Derrick, so we play it different. But teams are more fun. Boys against girls. Batter bats, then has to run to the mat on the other side and back again before the other team tags the home base carrying the ball. The tree is out of bounds and an automatic point for the other team. That's so someone—Uncle Derrick— doesn't keep hitting it way out in the field. So, you don't want to hit it hard, but you want to hit it hard enough to give you time to get to the base and back. Your team member is the pitcher. The other team has to stand by those trees, frozen until the ball lands. Your team member tries to tag one of the other team members. If they do, both freeze for five seconds. If you tag someone, you yell 'Freeze' and both of them freeze and count. Once you tag someone, you have to run back to the home base and touch it before you can tag again. Got it?"

Apparently, the confusion Liza felt showed on her face because Christy stepped in and nudged her elbow. "How about we do a practice play?"

Liza breathed a sigh of relief. "That would be great." They broke off into their teams, with Liza at bat, and Christy pitching. Derrick and Heath jogged to the out- of-bounds border and waited. When Christy pitched, Liza held back on her swing and it connected, sending the ball just short of the line of trees. She took off running and watched as Heath sprinted for the ball, snatched it up and ran toward her.

Christy dashed past her, easily catching up with her son, who was headed her way and tapped him on the shoulder, despite his attempt to dodge her touch. He groaned as she yelled, "Freeze!" It wasn't until they started counting that Liza looked to her left to find Derrick already halfway between the two bases.

Christy passed her at a hard run to the home base as she tapped the second mat and turned. The boys yelled, "Five, one thousand!" then Derrick called to Heath. "Throw it!"

Up ahead, Christy tapped the base and headed straight for Derrick as Liza passed him. Focusing on the mat, Liza heard laughing behind her as Christy tried to tag Derrick. Then she saw him, barreling toward the base from behind her, his long legs pounding on the ground. She dug deep, willing her younger self to make an appearance, and sprinted forward.

Her body naturally dropped, her feet sliding across the grass and into the base a split second before Derrick.

For a second, she thought he was going to run into her leg and envisioned him in a heap, their game-play coming to an end, but he nimbly jumped over the base, then turned around and hunched over with his hands on his knees, breathing hard.

Behind them, Christy whooped and hollered, running up beside Liza as she stood and checked the side of her leg. Green grass stains streaked across her leg, but there was thankfully no blood.

Heath appeared. "Can we play for real now? I think she's got it."

Derrick held up one hand, took a deep breath, and put his hands on his hips. Then he walked by Liza and tapped her playfully with his shoulder. "Game on," he whispered in her ear, and the hairs raised on her neck.

"Game on!" Christy said. "Let's go!"

Liza couldn't help but laugh, immediately pinpointing Christy as the competitive one. Given Christy's laid-back nature, it kind of surprised Liza, but it also made her happy. She was playing now, and she fully intended to win. It was good to have a teammate who felt the same way.

By the time they finished the game, the sun was setting, and all of them were breathless and dehydrated. When

Christy hit the mat to give them the final winning point, she did a little jig and then promptly dropped on the grass. She sat up as Liza collapsed next to her.

"Heath, go get us some waters," Christy said as Derrick joined them.

Heath, unaffected by the strenuous activity, though definitely affected by the loss, jogged past them to the water cooler.

"That was fun," Liza said, still trying to catch her breath after chasing Derrick all over the yard. "And you can run!"

Derrick shrugged. "Lots of practice."

When Heath appeared with the bottles of water and dropped next to them, Christy side eyed him. "Where are your big boasts now? Heath kept going on and on about how they were going to beat us."

"Never underestimate two women," Derrick said to Heath. "Especially competitive ones." He winked at them and took a long drink of his water.

Underneath her legs, the sweat mixed with the blades of grass, and Liza knew if she didn't get up, she'd end up with itchy welts. Reaching over without thinking, she used Derrick's shoulder to brace herself and very ungracefully pushed herself to her feet. He reached out to steady her, his hand supporting the side of her waist. She grabbed his wrist and got her balance, then smiled down at him. "Thanks."

He dropped his hand. "No problem."

"I should go," Liza said. "Thanks so much, all of you. It was a great night."

Derrick scrambled to his feet, then hauled Christy up. "Hold up, and I'll follow you home. Sis," he said and kissed her cheek. Then he and Heath did a well-rehearsed high-five handshake, before Derrick tousled his nephew's hair.

Comfortably, Liza walked to Christy and gave her a hug. "Thanks again."

"Anytime. And I mean that."

She stuck her hand out to Heath, and he took it, giving it a shake. "Heath. It was nice hanging out with you tonight."

"It was. Thanks!"

While Derrick disappeared around the mobile home, Liza went inside, retrieved the rest of her drinks, and went out the front. Then she gave him a wave, climbed into her car and took a deep breath.

She looked in her rearview mirror as Derrick backed up and turned his truck around, then waited for her to do the same. As she drove by him and waved, she mentally checked herself. Damn, she was happy.

Chapter Eighteen

They were an hour into the trip, and she'd barely said more than a few words. Not a morning person, Derrick thought. Check. Every once in a while, he'd glance over at her, bunched up in the seat, sipping her coffee, and staring out the window.

It had surprised him she'd not only shown up to his house on time, despite the early start, but that she'd only brought a gym bag with her. Having only traveled with Christy, who appeared to pack nearly everything she owned and was always late, he'd expected the same from Liza. That hadn't been the case. He'd probably brought more than she had.

"Mind if I turn on the radio?"

His voice in the stretched-out silence sounded louder than normal, and she started a bit. "What? Oh, no. Music is fine." Then she turned back to the window.

Though he hated to admit it, her choice of the radio over conversation disappointed him. Maybe she'd perk up some after daylight was in full swing. Pushing the radio knob, he pressed the scan button and let it run through the stations. "Oh, that one," she said as she reached over and stopped the scan. A familiar pop tune came in clear, and she turned back to the window while her toes tapped on the floor mat.

"Really?" he asked, cringing as the song continued.

Her head turned slowly to him, her coffee cup at her lips. Then she started singing, a smile creeping up on either side of the cup lid.

"Very funny. Now this stupid song is going to be stuck in my head."

Her answer was a shrug. "Just this one, then you can listen to your drinking music."

"Drinking music? What is drinking music?"

"Country. That is what you were scanning for, right?"

"No. Though I do like country. I was scanning for anything, really. Except this. Anything except this."

Rolling her eyes, she reached down and hit the scan button. "Fine, you whiner. Pick a station."

Typically, he would have conceded, but not with that song. Even he had his limits. "How about we find something we both like?"

"I think our tastes might be a little different."

The scanning radio paused on a classic rock station. He reached out and stopped the scan. After a few seconds of the song, he noticed her lips were moving in her reflection in the side window. "Like this one, then?"

"It's fine."

"See. Compromise."

Liza laughed and looked at him again. "That was me giving up. Not compromising. There is a difference."

He nodded. "Good to know. So are you among the living yet?"

Shifting so she faced him instead of the window, she took another sip of her coffee. "Yes. Sorry. Mornings and I broke up years ago. It takes me an hour or two to motivate."

"I figured as much." Despite really wanting to hear the song, he turned the knob down until the music was simply a space filler. "I was afraid we'd be making the whole trip in silence."

Her eyebrow raised. "You don't like silence?"

"You do?"

She shrugged. "Sometimes. I guess I just got used to it."

"I never did get used to it. Christy and Heath lived with me until he was six." He chuckled at the memory of Christy's decision to move out.

"What?"

"Nothing. Just remembering. Back then, I wasn't quite the patient man you see before you today. In truth, I was kind of an ass."

Liza nodded and took another drink of her coffee. "I met that man once."

"Funny."

"I thought so."

"Anyhow, so one day, out of the blue, Christy storms into the kitchen and screams at me that it's time to get her own place. Because if she doesn't get her own place, she's going to kill me in my sleep. Then stormed out."

"What did you do?"

"No clue." When she was silent, he looked over at her and was greeted with an incredulous look. "Seriously. I have no idea. To this day, I have no idea. But she wasn't playing around. A week later, she had the property and had purchased the mobile home. A couple of months after that, she was out on her own."

Liza played with the top of her cup for a bit, and Derrick remained silent, sensing that she was struggling to share something with him. "It may not have had anything to do with you. Not really. I understand wanting to break away and be your own person."

Seeing a window to get to know her better, Derrick took a chance. "Is that what happened with you? Breaking away."

The snorting, yet cute, laugh surprised him. "I didn't really break away. I kind of exploded my way out. I decided I wanted to go to art school, so I made it happen. Turning my back on my mother and her money. And now, fifteen years later, here I am."

From clear across the cab, Derrick could hear the depression in her tone. "Well, if it makes you feel any better, I'm glad you're here."

Her head snapped around, and he braced himself, but she just smiled. "Thanks. You're not so bad yourself."

Then she turned back to the window, but not before he caught the way her eyes had turned slightly red. Not wanting to push his luck, he reached down and grabbed the volume knob. "A little music for a while?"

Her answer was simply a nod, and he obliged, letting the music fill the cab. It was going to take time to earn her trust. A feat he realized he was more than happy to tackle.

On and off, they talked about mundane topics, only stopping occasionally for bathroom and food breaks. Liza was grateful, as the conversation at the beginning had turned entirely too depressing and intimate for her liking. And despite Derrick being one of the few people she genuinely enjoyed being around, by the time they pulled into the hotel just an hour outside their destination, she'd found her limit to be somewhere around fourteen hours.

"You sure you want to stop?" he asked as he put the truck in park. "I'm good for a couple more hours."

"No. This is fine. We wouldn't get much done tonight, and it'll be more comfortable than sleeping at my apartment," she said as she hopped out of the truck. "Or sleeping at my mother's." She added the last part as she slammed the door.

Inside, she got two rooms, then returned to the truck and climbed back in. Handing him his key card, she pointed to the rear of the building. "Pull around back."

"I wish you'd let me pay for my room, at least," he grumbled as the truck rolled.

Her answer was an annoyed look, partially hidden in the cab's darkness. "That was the deal, remember?"

"I remember. I didn't really agree to it, but I remember."

Liza rolled her eyes. She'd been uncomfortable with his help as it was. Mostly because she wanted to avoid mixing her Ohio life and Florida life as much as possible. Funding the trip was the only way she could make it right with herself, considering he was taking multiple days away from his business to help her move.

"How about we pick this back up tomorrow? I'm tired tonight."

"Fine," he said as he pulled into the parking spot. "What time do you want to leave?"

"Eight?" she asked.

"Can you make it by eight?"

She shot him a hard look. "I'll be here." Then she hopped out of the truck again, grabbed her duffel bag, and disappeared inside. By the time he followed, the hallway to their rooms was empty.

As they walked into her apartment complex and up the stairs, Derrick took note of the surroundings. Liza stopped at an apartment door and fumbled for her keys when the door next to her apartment flung open. An older woman, wearing a muumuu and using a cane, stepped into the breezeway.

"What do you want with this apartment?" she asked, narrowing her eyes at Derrick.

Liza stepped between them. "It's just me, Mrs. Jeffers."

Mrs. Jeffers' eyes lit up, and she smiled then opened up her non-cane arm. "Liza! You are a sight for sore eyes." Liza moved forward and hugged her, then stepped back as Mrs. Jeffers took a step up to peer at Derrick. "And who is this strapping young lad?"

"This is Derrick. Derrick, my neighbor, Mrs. Jeffers." Mrs. Jeffers looked struck at Liza's introduction.

"Neighbor. Please."

Liza laughed. "And friend."

"That's better," she said, then went back to studying Derrick.

When he stuck his hand out to her, she took it, and Derrick felt the strength in that grip that told a different story than the cane and ambling walk. He liked her immediately. "It's very nice to meet you, ma'am."

"Well now, a gentleman to boot," she looked at Liza and winked. "'Bout time you found yourself a keeper."

"Mrs. Jeffers. We're just friends. We came to clean out the apartment."

Disappointment instantly dropped Mrs. Jeffers' smile into a pout. "I was hoping maybe you got tired of up North and was coming back." Then she smiled again. "But I'm happy for you. You make sure you write to me. Tell me all about life up there and how you're getting on."

"I will. And I'll be back in a year, anyway."

Mrs. Jeffers looked from Liza to Derrick, then back at Liza, a twinkle now added to the smile on her face. "We will see about that," she said. Then winked and reentered her apartment, closing the door behind her.

When Liza turned back to Derrick, she was shaking her head, a smile that reached her eyes brightening her face. A smile he hadn't seen before, relaxed and unreserved. Derrick took a step back, struck by his sudden attraction to her, the desire to see that smile more often. To be the one who made her smile that way.

"What?" she asked, the smile faltering.

He shook his head. "Nothing. She seems like a character," he said as she opened the door and stepped inside.

Liza flipped on the light, and he followed. Once he was inside, she closed the door.

"You have no idea. Don't let that cane fool you," she said as she walked all the way inside the apartment. "One time, someone did try to break in. I heard the jiggling of the doorknob, then what sounded like someone trying to bust the door down. I grabbed my phone and called the cops and moved to the kitchen to grab a knife. A few seconds later, the banging stopped, and there was yelling outside. Then Mrs. Jeffers knocked on my door, told me they were gone. When I opened it, she was standing there with a loaded shotgun."

"By the way she shook my hand, that doesn't surprise me in the least." Derrick stepped into the living room and scanned the area, mentally making a checklist of things he could see and whether it would all fit in the truck. He realized she didn't have much. A loveseat and chair. A small entertainment center, one of those cheaper particle board ones you could buy from the discount department store. A couple of side tables.

The kitchen was also equally bare, just a few regular appliances on the counters. Liza was already moving toward the hallway in the back. He followed. At the end of the hall, she flipped on the light and moved inside her bedroom. Again, just a few things—a double bed and a small dresser. Another side table with a lamp. She turned around and walked to the other door, opened it, stepped in, and turned on the light.

At the threshold, he paused, letting his brain reconcile the abundance of color in that room with the sparsity of the other rooms. He tentatively took a step in, his eyes sweeping over the paintings stacked against the walls and filling the room. "Wow," he said. "You did all of these?"

"Yes," she said as she moved around the room.

A painting of an elderly man sitting at a bar caught his eye. A glass of amber liquid perched at his lips. There was something about it, the way he sat, hunched over by life, the light dimmed in his eyes. The resigned way he held his drink. The detail in the painting blew him away, so realistic it almost looked like a photograph. As she moved paintings around, he continued to admire them.

"I figure, get these boxed up and loaded first. I know I'm taking these back. Then the rest," she said.

"That's fine." He turned to look at her. "Seriously, Liza. These are amazing."

Her answer was the shrug he'd now identified as her signature move as she continued to sort paintings. "They're okay. Thank you."

Realizing he would not get past the wall she'd put up around her art, he gave up and turned his attention to the task at hand. If they were really going to be back on the road by late afternoon, they had some serious work to do. "Okay, direct me," he said and was happy at least that got a smile out of her.

"Grab those packing boxes from the back of the truck, if you don't mind."

With an overexaggerated salute, he headed for the truck.

It had been a long time since he'd felt the kind of tired that could only be brought about by moving. Though, it had turned out to be more mental than physical this time. Luckily, Liza was able to get a few teens from nearby apartments to help load the truck, which definitely made the entire process move faster. Still, packing the truck took up most of the morning. Liza's system had been brutally slow and equally painful, almost to the point he was virtually unneeded until the actual loading of the truck started.

In her defense, she had told Christy she was fine without help. Except for having company, she'd been largely right.

As soon as they placed the last box inside of the truck and one last sweep of the apartment revealed no hidden items in danger of being left behind, Liza went to the office to turn in her key while Derrick started the truck.

When she reappeared, Derrick watched her slow at her apartment door, touch the door lightly with her fingertips, then take a deep breath and stride to the truck.

When she climbed into the cab, he could tell she'd been crying. Back and forth, his thoughts battled over whether he should say something. He finally landed on yes. She was his friend. "You okay?"

He expected a yes or, maybe, no answer at all. Instead, her body and face angled to the window, she said, "No. But I will be."

Liza watched out the window as St. Petersburg slipped past them. She was trying her hardest not to cry. Something she'd been doing a lot of lately, she realized. Also out of character for her. While she didn't want to admit it, it had been nice having Derrick along, making this last step just a little easier. The final nail in the coffin of her forced relocation. Even if it was only for a year.

"Turn up here, right?" Derrick asked, bringing her back to inside the cab.

Scanning her surroundings, she nodded. "Yes. At the light."

As the truck turned into her childhood subdivision, she straightened in the seat. There was a part of her that just wanted to keep driving, but another part of her really missed her mother.

Liza cringed when Derrick swung into the driveway, watching the brick column at the entrance slide dangerously close to the truck's bumper. Then they were pulling up to the front. Her mother was already on the front porch, waving happily at them. *Please let this go well*, Liza thought.

Once hugs were given and reintroductions were made, Deborah led them into the house. "If you had let me know earlier, I would have planned something, Liza."

Which was the exact reason Liza hadn't told her mother the plan until they were leaving Ohio. "It's okay, Mom. We need to start back this afternoon, anyway."

They rounded the corner into the dining room, where a serving tray of cold cuts and cheese was already displayed on the table with an assortment of breads. A large salad bowl surrounded by fixings sat next to it, and two other serving bowls of chips. There were three place settings waiting on them and a pitcher of iced tea. "Mom," Liza said. "You didn't have to do this."

Her mother shrugged. "Anna, Scott, and Chloe are coming up in a couple of days, so I figured I would get enough for them, too. With such short notice, they couldn't get away today."

Liza didn't take the bait as she sat down, pointing to the chair next to her for Derrick. She'd already talked to Anna, and Anna understood.

Beside her, Derrick eased down in his chair and said, "Looks good, Mrs. Blackburn. Thank you."

"Deborah, dear. Call me Deborah. Don't be shy. I'm sure you've worked up an appetite."

Except for the clink of serving utensils against the bowls, they were silent while they filled their plates. Liza realized she was starving as she flopped cold cuts on the bread. From the way Derrick piled on the meat and cheese, it was obvious he felt the same way.

After they'd settled into the meal, Deborah was the first to speak, "Did you get everything moved out of the apartment, then?"

Liza nodded as she finished chewing her sandwich. She swallowed and put it back on the plate, using the napkin in her lap to wipe her hands. "Yes. All done and keys turned in."

"Anything you plan to leave here?"

"No. I think I'll just take it all back to Ohio since it's already in the truck."

Deborah turned the conversation to Derrick. "It was very nice of you to help Liza out with this. It makes me feel better that she has someone up there looking out for her."

That charming smile spread across Derrick's face, and Liza inwardly rolled her eyes. "It's no problem at all, Mrs..." He corrected himself. "Deborah. We've enjoyed having Liza around."

Deborah's head cocked to the side. "We?"

"My sister, Christy, and my nephew, Heath. Liza has fit right in."

"Oh, I thought for a minute there was maybe a Mrs. Derrick."

Derrick laughed. "No, ma'am."

"You don't have a significant other, then?"

"Mom!" Liza exclaimed as she picked up her sandwich, shaking her head.

Innocently, Deborah asked, "What? I'm just trying to get to know the young man."

The chuckle was low, but Liza heard it. "It's fine. No, ma'am. No significant other. My businesses keep me busy."

"Really? Businesses, as in plural?"

"Yes. I own a pub and a landscaping business. Also, the truck rental service and a 24-hour gym in town."

At the information about the gym, Liza looked up at him. "A gym? I didn't know you owned a gym."

He winked at her. "You never asked."

"Well, it sounds like you are quite the entrepreneur."

"Yes, ma'am."

"Well now," Deborah said with a wide grin. "That explains this quick trip. My Neil, Liza's Daddy, owned his own business. A small accounting firm here in town. I'm well aware of how much time and effort goes into running a business."

Dear lord, please let this end, Liza thought as she took another bite of her sandwich. A glance at Derrick's plate told her he'd barely gotten to eat during the cross-examination. "It was always so hard to tear him away. I appreciate you helping Liza. Why you needed to move all that stuff to Ohio right now is beyond me." The last was directed at Liza, who was mid-bite.

Covering her mouth to finish chewing, Liza mumbled, "Because I needed my artwork."

For a brief second a flash of darkness passed over her mother's face, then disappeared just as quickly. "Oh, that's right. The silly list your grandmother left you. Well, sorry you got dragged away from your businesses to just pick up some paintings."

Liza tensed and looked to her plate, willing herself to calm at her mother's flippant dismissal of her artwork.

"I'm glad I did," Derrick said. "There's at least one in there I'd like to buy for the pub, if she'll sell it to me. The one with the man at that bar. Did you see that one?"

Silence. Silence so thick Liza could feel it settle into the empty space around her. She looked up, met her mother's unreadable eyes. Then she noticed the two red splotches forming on her mother's cheeks and realized it was the first time she'd ever seen her mother blush.

Then Deborah animatedly clapped her hands together and turned back to Derrick. "Look at me, just talking away. So rude. You haven't even had a chance to eat yet. Go ahead and eat your lunch. You'll need it for the drive back."

Derrick sat frozen for a good minute before tentatively picked up his sandwich. He took a bite, smiled through chewing, then focused on the plate. Liza looked back down at her nearly empty plate, picked up a chip, and popped it in her mouth, trying to hide the smile that refused to be held back. Derrick had no idea what he'd just done, but Liza allowed the small vindication wash through her and felt her shoulders relax.

A couple of hours later, she and Derrick had said their goodbyes to Deborah and were well on the way back to Ohio. They'd already agreed to alternate driving, so they could drive through the night and make it back home by early morning. Music drifted through the speakers, and Liza again watched the scenery outside the window, still reveling in her mother's embarrassment.

When the volume suddenly lowered, Liza looked over at Derrick, whose eyes were trained on the road. "Okay," he said. "What hornet's nest did I kick back there?"

"What do you mean?"

"The whole painting thing. What did I miss?"

Liza shifted in her seat to face him. "My mother hasn't seen my paintings."

"Okay, so it's new then?"

"No, Derrick. She hasn't seen any of them."

The way his head whipped toward her made her lean back. "Are you serious?"

"Yep. Neither has Anna."

He turned back to the road. "Wow. Not one of them? How does that happen?"

"They never asked. I never showed them."

The silence went on so long Liza thought the conversation was over until he added, "Wow."

Liza's answer was a shrug, then she reached over and turned up the radio, shifted back to the window, and said, "Yeah."

Chapter Nineteen

A s hot as July had been, it hadn't prepared Liza for the miserable, soul-sucking heat of August. It was like someone had cranked up the sauna too high and locked the doors. Her poor little air conditioner had been working overtime just to knock out enough humidity so she didn't want to walk around the cottage naked, wrapped in ice cubes.

She was putting the finishing touches on her latest painting, this time of the city park splash pad. Kids laughed and jumped, water droplets spraying from under their feet. Adults sat on nearby benches, talking while their charges ran and skipped through the cool spray.

While she was finishing it at home, the painting had taken a full day of sitting at the park, sketching quickly to get at least their outlines down. A few people stopped by, peering over her shoulder at the canvas. Some would watch as she made quick strokes, getting the framework done, while others simply glanced and wandered away.

One woman who watched for a good while—how long Liza wasn't sure—waited for Liza to pause and then handed her a business card, indicating she may be interested in the painting once it was complete.

Something about that encounter, having a total stranger not only show interest but possibly want to pay for a painting, kick-started something inside Liza. Focus on her art replaced all other things. Any time she had a free minute—which was a lot these days—she was either sketching or painting. By mid-August, she had four of the six paintings finished and properly stored in the corner of her bedroom until the show. It was nothing for her to look outside and find night had crept up on her without her realizing.

Which is exactly what happened as she put the last strokes on the canvas, then stood up and stepped back to study it. And, to her surprise, her first thought was not about how something was wrong with the painting or the people, but that it was actually pretty good. At first glance, her critical eye could find nothing wrong with it.

Liza stretched her neck from side to side, then planted her hands on the small of her back and arched backward, feeling the kinks loosen. A glance at the wall clock told her she'd been painting for over four hours. She looked over her shoulder through the window at the graying skyline, as the sun set.

Her stomach growled, reminding her she hadn't eaten since breakfast. She considered getting dressed and going to the pub for dinner. But she'd already been there so many times in the last few weeks that her bank account had reminded her she was not independently wealthy. While she had received her monthly stipend, the electric bill had been a shock thanks to the air conditioner.

As if channeling her mother, she firmly told herself she had food at the cottage and did not need to go to the pub. Setting her mind to staying in for the evening, she shook off the feeling of disappointment, then headed to her bedroom to change her clothes and scrub the paint from her hands. She hoped there would be another cookout before the month was up. While she and Christy had met for dinner a few times—and several drinks at the pub the week Heath was away—Christy hadn't hosted another get-together. It was because Liza loved the atmosphere and had nothing to do with Derrick, she told herself, rather unconvincingly.

Out of nowhere, a little voice in her head told her to have one, which set off an internal argument about her ability to host a cookout, considering she'd never touched a grill in her life. Even her parents hadn't owned one.

But if Derrick agreed to buy the meat and cook at Christy's, wouldn't he do the same for her? She marked it down in her mental checklist to consider it later as she headed to the kitchen, pulled lunchmeat and sandwich fixings from the refrigerator, then pressed play on her phone's playlist. The music filtered through a small wireless speaker on the counter. Lost in fixing her dinner and the music playing, she didn't hear the strange sounds from the front porch until she wandered into the living room.

She strained to listen, telling her phone to stop as she stepped closer to the door. A yelp, and was that scratching? Her muscles tensed as she considered the wild animals that lived in the woods behind the cottage. Another scratching sound and then a low-pitched howl. Jumping back, she rushed over and snatched the phone from the carrier before returning to the door.

Liza took a deep breath, then cautiously turned the doorknob and cracked the door just enough to see outside. Then she threw the door wide open and screamed, rushing to the blood-soaked animal draped halfway up the stairs. Hank looked up at her, a whine coming from his bloody muzzle. She dropped to her knees next to him, panicked eyes scanning the gashes up and down his body, his brown fur soaked a dark red.

Words caught in her throat as her hand trembled the length of his body, and her brain processed what to do next. "It's okay, boy," she said, fat tears already streaming down her cheeks. "It's okay."

Her body unfroze, and she jumped up and sprinted to the bathroom, dialing Derrick at the same time. As the pub phone rang, she grabbed as many towels as she could and sprinted back to the front porch.

His deep voice answered, "Hank's Pub."

"Derrick! Derrick! It's Hank! Something happened to him. There's so much blood!"

As she gently put towels over top of Hank's body, her knee dropping into a pool of blood seeping out from under him, a sob exploded deep in her throat.

"I'm on my way," Derrick said, his voice calm.

"Please hurry. He's dying!" she yelled, but the call had already disconnected. Dropping the phone on the porch, Liza turned all her attention to Hank. Searching out the worst of the wounds, she pressed down on them. She expected him to whine or to growl. Something. The lack of reaction scared her more.

She stroked his head with her free hand. "It's okay, boy. It's okay. I'm here."

A fresh wave of panic slid through her as the white towels on his body turned a light pink, then a splotchy red. Hank's eyes, usually bright and friendly, were dimmer. He was dying. She knew it.

Letting go of the towel, she ran back into the house and swiped her keys from the counter before running back outside again. Then she jumped the stairs to the ground below, turned around, and shoved her arms underneath him.

Crying out as her body strained against the weight, she managed to get him into her arms. Her eyes lasered in on her car as she took a step, the full weight of his hundred and twenty pounds pressing her to the earth. She took a step, and her knees buckled. Forcing herself upright, she took another step, then another, her body adjusting to the extra weight. One step after another, tears cascading down her face, she made it to the car and then realized she had no way to open the door.

At the obstacle, her legs gave out, and she crumpled to the ground, her body shielding his from the impact. A quiet whimper told her he was still alive and set off a fresh round of adrenaline as she reached up and opened the back door, then stuck her foot up on the inside and kicked it open.

"Please," she said as she struggled to her knees. "Please."

With a primal scream, she put all of her weight into lifting him and got the first part of his body inside when she heard fast-moving tires on gravel, followed by headlights that lit up the area. Derrick's truck locked up as it appeared and skidded to a stop behind her car, Derrick already out before it finished rocking.

Sobs racked her body as he ran toward her. "Help me," she said, more of plea than demand.

"I've got him," he said. "Go get in my truck."

Shock rocking her, she had a hard time processing what he said. Gently, he pulled her away from Hank and looked her in the eyes. "Liza, I'm here. Go get in my truck. I've got him."

Nodding, she rushed toward his truck and climbed into the passenger side. When she looked back, Derrick was already walking toward her, easily carrying his dog in his arms. Once she was situated, he scooted Hank in headfirst so that his head rested on her lap, then climbed into the driver's seat and backed out.

Any other time, Liza would have been terrified over the high rate of speed he was driving on the back roads, but as she felt Hank's breaths get shallower and shallower, she mentally urged him to drive faster. When they neared the end of the dirt road, he plucked his cellphone from the holder on the dash and handed it to her. "Find the name Bryan in there. As soon as we get service, call it for me."

Hands shaking, she scrolled through the contacts, found Bryan, and watched the signal bars. As soon as one appeared, she pressed call and handed it back to Derrick. It rang twice and then she heard a man answer.

"Bryan. It's Derrick. I'm headed to your clinic. It's Hank."

He paused.

"Five minutes. He's lost a lot of blood, man."

Handing the phone back to Liza, she hung up, then reached over and put it back on the holder. Looking down at Hank, she made eye contact with him and held his gaze as the truck barreled along the back roads.

When Derrick swung onto a gravel driveway snaking between two pastures, she held Hank a little tighter to protect him from the bouncing. A small building, situated next to a farmhouse, sat at the top of the hill. The truck pulled in and skidded to a stop just short of the building, which Liza could now see was a veterinary clinic.

The lights were already on, and a man wearing jeans and a t-shirt appeared at the open door as Derrick slammed the truck into park and jumped from the driver's seat. He turned and grabbed hold of Hank, gently dragging him across the bench seat until he could take his weight, then lifted the sagging bulk in his arms and ran with him to the door.

The man, who Liza assumed was Bryan, stepped back to let him in. He made eye contact with Liza, then disappeared inside, closing the door behind him.

Under the dimming evening light, Liza held out her hands, blood drying into the creases in her skin. Looking down, she saw blood smears covering her shirt and pants and more blood puddled on the seat next to her.

Realizing he'd left the driver's door open and the dome light on without it running, she gently exited the passenger side, walked around the front of the truck and shut the door, then returned to her seat.

The tears didn't come slowly. They exploded from her, racking her body until she leaned forward on the dash and buried her face in her folded arms. And just cried.

She was still that way when the driver's side door opened, and the dome light flipped on. An ashen-faced Derrick climbed into the truck, situated himself behind the wheel and then just sat there for a moment, his hands gripping the steering wheel. Silently, Liza reached over and placed her blood crusted hand over his.

He turned, a shimmer of tears in his bright blue eyes as the dome light again ebbed to dark. "It doesn't look good, but he's going to try," he managed, his voice cracking slightly as he took his other hand off the wheel and placed it over hers. "He's going to do everything he can."

Words caught in her swollen throat when she tried to speak. She cleared her throat and tried again. "What happened?"

Derrick shook his head. "I don't know. It's going to be a few hours. He'll call me when he knows something. Would you like to come to the house while we wait?"

She nodded, thankful that he asked. "I'll need to stop by the cottage. Get some clothes and lock up."

Starting the engine, he nodded. "You can take a shower at my house if you need to."

She looked down at her hands and nodded. "Thank you."

Back at the cottage, Liza stepped over the blood drying on her front porch and entered the open door. She'd worry about that tomorrow. In her bedroom, she pulled a change of clothes from her drawers and headed straight back to the truck, for fear news would come sooner than they'd expected and mindful of her cottage being a dead spot.

At his house, he opened the door and motioned for her to enter. She couldn't help but look around, taking in the rustic décor fitting for a farmhouse. As they moved through the foyer and into the living area, the photographs on the far wall caught her attention. Six in total, some color, some black and white, organized around a large one in the center. Each contained people from different periods in front of the farmhouse.

"You can use the bathroom upstairs," he said as he walked to the kitchen and flipped on the light. He turned and looked her up and down, his eyes sad. "Towels are in the hall closet."

Reminded she was covered in blood, Liza's attention moved away from the photos and back to the clothes in her hand. "Thank you."

"Thank you, Liza."

Tears welled up again as she just nodded, then headed to the stairs.

Inside the small bathroom, she started the shower, then peeled off her soiled clothes and dropped them on the linoleum in the corner. Stepping in, she stood under the spray and watched as blood washed down her legs, turning a bright pink before spiraling down the drain.

She found Derrick in the kitchen. He was painstakingly fixing a sandwich; an open beer, half-empty, sat next to the pile of bread, lunchmeat and cheese. His hair was wet from a shower, and he was wearing a pair of sweats and a t-shirt. When Liza entered, her dirty clothes hugged to her chest, he looked up and smiled apologetically. "Sorry. I'm a stress eater."

She returned the smile. "Me too."

"Want one?"

She nodded, and his eyes shifted to her clothes. "I left the washer open for you, if you'd like to use it."

"That would be great."

He pointed the knife covered in mayonnaise toward the door. "Turn right and go all the way to the end of the hall. The laundry room is right at the end. You want your sandwich any certain way?"

Liza shook her head. "I'm not picky. Thanks."

Once her clothes were washing, she returned to the kitchen where Derrick was already eating at the island. He pointed at the stool next to him and slid the paper plate, topped with a sandwich and chips, in front of it. "You want a beer?"

"Please," she said, taking a seat.

He hopped from the stool, pulled a beer from the refrigerator, opened it, and sat it next to her plate as he took his seat again. A small shiver ran up her spine when his elbow grazed hers, and she immediately felt guilty. Now is not the time for this, she thought. No time is the time for this, she corrected. Instinctively, she shifted her body to put more room between them.

In silence so thick she could occasionally hear the crunching from inside his mouth when he bit into a potato chip, they ate. Her brain just kept playing the scene on her front porch over and over. Had her inability to get him to the car wasted precious minutes? Would it have even mattered? Lord knows she would have never found the vet's office on her own. And was her devastation even warranted? He wasn't even her dog, and Derrick seemed to be holding it together.

It wasn't until a rough finger slid across her cheek that she realized she was crying again, her head jerking back in surprise.

"Sorry," Derrick said, embarrassed.

"It's fine. I'm just a little jumpy. It's fine," she said, wanting desperately to remove that embarrassment caused by her reaction.

They finished the rest of their food in silence, then Derrick took the paper plates and dropped them in the trash can. Both intermittently glanced at the phone on the wall. "It could be a while before he calls. Do you want to watch a movie or something?" he asked.

While she didn't think she'd pay attention to a movie, she also didn't want to sit and think anymore. Her head was hurting. And she definitely didn't want to get into a conversation with Derrick. The night was already messing with her and felt entirely too intimate for the circumstances. "That would be fine."

She followed him to the living room, where he waited for her to pick a seat. She went for the armchair, and he stretched out on the loveseat. As he picked up the remote, he said, "Any preference?"

"Not really. No horror," she quickly added.

He craned his head back to look at her. "Not a horror fan?"

"No. I'm a chicken," she said with a shrug, remembering the one time she'd snuck a viewing of Nightmare on Elm Street and woke up in the middle of the night to Freddie Kreuger standing over her bed.

"No horror, it is," he said and flipped on the television, scrolling through the channels.

As he tabbed down the channels, she couldn't help the little excited sound that escaped her. "Oh! *The Goonies*!"

He looked back at her again, grinning. "I could totally watch *The Goonies*."

Choosing the movie, he leaned back against the arm of the love seat, his hands behind his head. Out of the corner of her eye, she checked out his frame stretched across the love seat and wondered what it would be like to lay there with him, to feel his arm wrapped around her and feel his chest move as he breathed.

Taking a deep breath, she gave herself a mental smack again and turned back to the TV, adjusting so he was no longer in her peripheral vision.

They were halfway through the movie, a movie she'd seen countless times as a child, when the phone rang. She sat up straight as Derrick vaulted from the couch and rushed to the kitchen. She stood up and grabbed the remote, muting the sound, then turned and faced the kitchen, clutching her empty beer bottle against her chest.

From the other room, she heard Derrick say, "Thanks, man."

He appeared at the door frame, running his hand through his hair. "He thinks he'll be all right."

Liza broke down, all the pent-up emotions and exhaustion coming out in sobs. Derrick crossed to her with his arms open. Without hesitation, she wrapped hers around his neck and hugged him, their mutual happiness flowing through them. When they released a few seconds later, Liza could see tears forming in Derrick's eyes.

"He said he'll need some time to heal, but he thinks he's going to be okay. Still not a guarantee. He lost a lot of blood, but in his experience, he'll pull through."

"So, when can we see him?"

"If he does okay tonight, we can pick him up tomorrow. We'll have to keep him quiet. I can maybe turn the laundry room into a makeshift pen for him," Derrick said, suddenly lost in thought. "I can probably take a few days off."

"Let me keep him."

"What?"

"Let me keep him at the cottage. He's comfortable there, and I'm home all the time right now, anyway. Let me take care of him."

"Are you sure? That's going to be a lot of..."

"Positive," she said, cutting him off. "I want to."

"Okay, then," Derrick said. "We'll go get him tomorrow evening and take him to the cottage. We can go over tomorrow and get it ready, clean everything up. And I'll bring his food down."

"It's settled, then."

Looking at the clock, he asked, "Do you want me to take you home?"

She shook her head. "Not unless, of course, you want me to go."

"No. I'm not going to be able to sleep, anyway. Want to finish *The Goonies*?"

Liza nodded. "Yes, please. Let me switch my clothes over."

"Want another beer?"

"I'll take another beer. What about your clothes? Do you need them thrown in?"

He shook his head. "No offense, but I don't think we're at the you-handling-my-underwear stage yet."

She laughed. "Point taken."

"I'll get them after you've switched out your clothes." As Liza walked down the hall toward the laundry room, Derrick said her name. She turned her head. "Thank you, Liza. Seriously. I bottle fed Hank. He means a lot to me."

"I didn't realize it until tonight, but he means a lot to me, too."

With a nod, he continued into the kitchen while she headed to the laundry room, a lot lighter than the first time she'd made that trek.

The next day was a flurry of activity while Derrick helped Liza clean the blood off her porch and prepare the cottage for Hank's arrival. She made him a bed in her room and placed things on the couch to keep him from jumping until the vet said it would be okay. Derrick brought a large container full of dog food and put it in the corner of the living room at Liza's direction.

"You sure about this?" Derrick asked. "I don't know how this is going to go."

Liza laughed. He'd asked her at least twenty times if she was okay with the decision. "Seriously, I'm good."

"Okay. Let's go get our boy." He opened the door and stepped back, waving her through.

"Let's," she said with a wink and headed out, handing him the keys to lock up behind her.

Hank was a mess, but at least when they entered his tail beat the floor for a few minutes. There were stitches all over his body, hair shaved away in long streaks around them. As Derrick moved over him, Hank whined and tried to raise his head.

Derrick leaned closer and patted him gently on the head. "Lay still, boy. It's okay."

Bryan walked in smiling, carrying a large plastic contraption and a brown bag. "He's definitely a tough one," he said as he handed both to Derrick.

Turning to Liza, he put his hand and out, and she shook it. "You must be Liza."

Liza nodded, not missing the unreadable look the two men gave each other. "Derrick says Hank will be staying with you while he recovers. That right?"

Again, Liza nodded.

"Just keep him as quiet as possible, and use the cone if he tries to get at his stitches or if you aren't watching him."

"Hear that, Hank?" Derrick said. "You have to wear the cone of shame."

That's when Liza realized what the big plastic thing was. Having never had a dog, she wasn't familiar with the contraption. But she had seen pictures. Poor Hank.

Bryan continued. "There are two medicines in there. An antibiotic and a pain pill. How is he with taking pills?"

Derrick answered. "Depends on the pills. I have some of those pill pockets you gave me last time. We'll get them down him. No worries."

"Okay. So other than that, just monitor him. If you get concerned at all, he starts throwing up or gets really lethargic, call me immediately. Derrick can give you my personal phone number. They'll set you up out front to bring him back to have the stitches removed."

"So, what do you think it was?" Liza asked.

"Could have been coyotes, a wild dog pack? I'm not really sure."

She looked between them. "How do we make sure this doesn't happen again?"

Derrick stood, shoving his hands in jeans. "I've got some friends who can help me check around. And I'm taking the four-wheeler out this weekend. This is the first time anything like this has happened, so I'm not sure yet."

Derrick could tell none of that appeased her, but it was the only answer he had.

Liza finally walked over to Hank and kneeled in front of him. His tailed thumped again, and his tongue flicked out to lick her hand. She stroked his muzzle.

"I think someone is stealing your dog," Bryan said with a laugh.

Derrick laughed with him. "You think?"

"Come on. You can get checked out, and then we'll come back for him," Bryan said as he and Derrick headed toward the lobby.

As they walked out, she could have sworn she heard Bryan say, "Your dog isn't the only thing that woman is stealing."

Chapter Twenty

I t was reception day for her show, and Liza felt like she was going to throw-up. Throughout the morning and afternoon, she'd kept her anxiety at bay while she prepared. When she'd arrived that evening, a half-hour early for the reception she had nearly begged Margaret not to have, it hit her. What if no one showed? Worse, what if they did?

Margaret had met her at the door, ushering her to another room in the Center, before disappearing again. In it, antique armchairs sat against the wall, facing the grand piano. The two doors on either side of the room were closed.

She wondered what that room had been back when the Center was an actual house with a family. Did the Christmas tree sit in the window up front? Did they host parties, or did the women walk through after dinner like she'd seen in the movies?

What if she hadn't hung something right? Had she charged too much? Margaret had helped her price the pieces she'd agreed to sell, consistently increasing any sales price Liza came up with. Did she really want to sell them?

She abruptly stood, crossed to the mantel and studied the elegant, antique mirror hanging above. She caught her reflection, hair done up in a French twist, make-up on her eyes, lips, and cheeks. Subtle, but still looked too much in comparison with the makeup-free existence she'd been living.

She took a deep breath, stroked a stray piece of hair back into place, and told herself to calm down. This was a means to an end. Nothing more. Nothing less.

A knock on the door made her turn, and Margaret entered, her nervous energy palpable. "People are showing up!" She was excited, yet somehow still dignified in the way her palms connected lightly with each other.

Liza forced a smile. "Great."

"I'll get everyone situated in the dining room for light refreshments, then I'll come get you. Smile! It's going to be a grand night."

Liza nodded and kept the smile until Margaret slipped from behind the door and closed it. Then her smile faded.

Out of habit, she reached for her phone and remembered she'd left it in her car. Pulling her hands together, she interlocked her fingers and worked them back and forth as she moved to the bookshelf and focused on the titles.

Time crept slowly without the distraction of her phone, and she had to keep pushing the negative thoughts away. Voices of her professors telling her she wasn't ready. Voices of others telling her pursuing an art degree was a worthless dream.

Outside the door, she heard people arriving. Margaret's welcoming southeast Ohio lilt was the loudest as she guarded the door. Her ears perked up at Derrick's voice, and she noticed her anxiety calm slightly at his presence. Under the door, the light waxed and waned as people walked by, their whispered voices blending into each other. She looked at the window and considered for just a moment escaping through it. Then the door opened and snatched her attention away from that thought. It was Margaret, her smile beaming. "It's time!"

With one last deep breath, she followed Margaret out the door to what she was sure would be the worst moment of her life.

As she entered the room of semi-familiar faces, her breath caught at the sight of both her mother and Anna in the corner. Anna's smile was wide, while her mother's lips were set in that thin smile she reserved for moments she thought were a waste of her time.

Any confidence Liza had built up between the room and the reception shattered.

"Aunt Liza!" Chloe's voice rang above the controlled din, prompting them all to turn her way. She froze at the door, her eyes bouncing across the faces, the artery in her neck pounding with her heart. Then two little arms wrapped around her legs, and she looked down at Chloe's grin. Reaching down, she picked her up and squeezed her.

Anna appeared, their mother close on her heels. "Oh, Liza, you'll wrinkle your outfit," said Anna.

"We came to surprise you, Aunt Liza. Are you surprised?"

"I am, Love Bug," she said, making eye contact with Deborah. "Very surprised."

Margaret's voice boomed from behind her. "Welcome, everyone! I would like to introduce tonight's celebrated artist, Ms. Elizabeth Ann Blackburn, presenting her show "Art in Waiting.""

A "whoop, whoop, whoop" sounded from the back. Liza found Derrick, Christy, and Heath tucked in the back of the room, that toothy grin giving away Derrick's transgression. Then it faded. Liza looked back to find Margaret giving him a withering look.

Once Margaret was certain there would be no more outbursts, she continued. "Please feel free to enter the gallery whenever you're ready. Ms. Blackburn will be on hand to answer questions. If you wish to purchase any of the pieces, please let one of our ushers know, and they will place a sold sticker on it. Liza?"

Her face flushed when she realized she was expected to speak, a detail Margaret had omitted during their many meetings. Setting Chloe back on the floor, she straightened out the wrinkles in her dress and smiled. "Um," she started, mentally correcting herself for using the filler word. "Thank you all for coming tonight, and I hope you're not disappointed."

Silence, then a soft round of applause traveled through the room, followed by rustling as many of them moved toward the gallery. The commotion gave Liza a moment to address her family. She moved to hug Anna, then her mother. "How did you guys get here?"

"We flew in last night."

"I flew on a plane, Aunt Liza!" Chloe interrupted. Liza stooped down so she was eye level with her niece.

"And? Was it awesome?"

"So awesome!"

Anna's hands moved to Chloe's shoulders. "You can tell Aunt Liza all about the plane tomorrow. Tonight is her night, remember?"

Chloe smiled. "That's right. It's your night, Aunt Liza. But I can tell you tomorrow, right?"

"Sure can, honey."

"Come on. Let's go look," Anna said, taking Chloe's hand. As she passed Liza, she planted a kiss on her cheek. "I'm so proud of you."

As Anna and Chloe headed to the door, Deborah also leaned in to kiss her cheek. "Congratulations, dear."

"Thanks, Mom," she said and returned the kiss.

"Are you coming?" Deborah asked.

"In a few. I just need a minute."

Deborah nodded and followed Anna. A few more people stepped up to congratulate her. She shook their hands and smiled, trying desperately to put their faces with a name and coming up short. Then Derrick was beside her. "Mrs. Evans!" he said to one woman. "Don't you look beautiful this evening."

The elderly woman blushed and smiled, shooing Derrick with her wrinkled hands. Mrs. Evans. Board member. That's right. She'd met her a day she was volunteering. "Thank you, Mrs. Evans. Enjoy the show."

As people moved up, Derrick introduced them immediately, and if he knew she'd met them before, he'd work in the reference. Like, "Jacob, my man! How's the hardware store faring?" reminding Liza she'd met Jacob when they'd visited his store for wood to repair the shed. As they kept funneling past, she realized there were more people in attendance than she'd originally realized.

It surprised her, really. To see that many people interested in art. Though a small voice told her it wasn't the art that interested them as much as checking out Dot's granddaughter. When the last person walked by, Liza turned to follow.

Derrick grabbed her arm and gently pulled her to face him. His hand moved to her hair where he smoothed down the cowlick she assumed was up.

"Thank you," she said, feeling the heat of his hand on her head. The way her body relaxed against his touch terrified her. The last thing she needed was this kind of complication. And Derrick smelled like a huge complication. And of Old Spice. But that was neither here nor there.

"You're welcome. Now, get in there, and knock 'em dead," he said. And there was that warmth in her belly again.

With a nod, Liza turned and headed for the gallery, not sure if she was trying to get there or get away from Derrick. Inside, people were already milling around. Some were gathered in the corner, studying her painting of a man, a little girl, and a dog. It was one of her favorites; a memory of watching the three frolic in the park always came to mind. She'd snapped a picture with her phone and painted it that week, working on her own details and giving it an ethereal feel in the way the landscape disappeared into fluffy, white clouds. As if someone was watching the trio from another world.

She continued to scan the room, then a small crowd moved to the left and revealed her mother and Anna in the other corner. Her breath caught, and panic bubbled up as she realized they were studying the painting of the three of them many years ago. They were on a beach, all three smiling. Liza looked like she was about Chloe's age, Anna four years older. Both sported matching one-piece, floral bathing suits and stood on either side of their mother. Deborah wore a simple one-piece black bathing suit, a pink floral wrap around her waist and a floppy, laced black hat protecting her face from the sun.

She'd painted it entirely from memory, her first memory as far as she knew. Which meant it had a childlike quality to it, her mother and sister more detailed than she. She walked toward them, her hands wringing. As she moved, her eyes raked over the paintings. One already had a sold sticker on it, sending a shock of excitement through her. It was a simple landscape, the beach at night. Then sadness followed when she thought about not having the piece in her possession anymore.

Anna saw her approach, her hand still firmly clenching Chloe's, who already appeared thoroughly over the whole thing. Anna nudged their mother with her elbow. When she turned, Liza's steps faltered at the tears in her mother's eyes. As Liza closed the gap between them, Deborah opened one arm and closed it around Liza's shoulder.

"It's beautiful," she said, turning to the picture again.

Liza nodded, unable to speak without breaking loose the dam of tears threatening to rupture.

Deborah turned, eyeing the painting of Liza and her grandmother at the kitchen bar. "Is that you and mom?"

Liza nodded again. "The last time she came to my apartment before she died," she managed. "It's why I was late for her funeral. I stayed up all night painting it, so I overslept." The last part just slipped out so easily, she hadn't realized she'd actually said it until it was done. Nearly five months of silence, released.

Anna moved up beside them, her arm slipping around Liza's waist. "This is why you were late? Why didn't you say?"

"I didn't think it would matter."

Her sister and mother looked at her, then at the painting. Deborah opened her lips to speak, then closed them again. Anna just gave her a squeeze.

"Sorry to barge in on family time," Margaret's cheery voice announced from behind. "I have some people who want to meet you."

Liza hesitated, looking questioningly at her family. Deborah released her grip and smiled. "Yes. Go."

Anna squeezed her and let go. "Go have an amazing night. We'll still be here."

Straightening herself, Liza leaned into both and then followed Margaret. As she walked away, her mother said, "Liza. I'm so proud of you."

At any other time, those words from her mother may have made her cry. But she didn't have time for them to sink in because Margaret was already ushering her to a group of people in the far corner.

The rest of the evening was a blur as she spoke with guests about her art, her plans, how she is enjoying Maple Hill. A few times, she'd made eye contact with Derrick and Christy, receiving warm smiles from them both and an enthusiastic thumbs up from Christy. They eventually migrated to her family and seemed to be doing their best to entertain them.

By the time the last guests drifted toward the door, Liza was exhausted. Happy, but exhausted. Her mother walked up to her and initiated a hug. Though it caught her off guard, she returned it.

"We're going to go back to the hotel. Chloe is getting tired. Maybe, if it's not too late, you can stop by?"

"Sure. How long are you all staying?"

"Through tomorrow. We want to see the cottage. If that's okay with you."

"Of course, it is," Liza said. "I'll call you in a bit."

Anna walked up to her with Chloe in her arms, her head on her mother's shoulder. Liza pushed her niece's hair back from her eyes and kissed her forehead, then kissed Anna's cheek. "I'm so proud of you," Anna said.

"Thanks," Liza said. "And thanks for coming. I'll call when I'm done here."

Anna nodded, then followed her mother out the door.

Liza looked around the gallery, noticing the small dots on multiple paintings and photographs. Her heart soared that someone would actually want to pay for her work. Christy appeared, wrapping her in a bear hug. "This was so awesome!"

"Thank you," Liza said.

Derrick moved up behind her and hugged her as well. After spending nearly a month in each other's company and homes caring for Hank, any awkwardness they had felt was long gone. Even after Hank started to heal and was ready to be cut loose again, they had found some reason to eat dinner together or just simply hang out on her front porch or in his garden.

After sharing *The Goonies*, they'd continued with more favorites from the eighties with regular movie nights. Eventually, she'd grown so comfortable in his home, she rummaged through his refrigerator without asking first. They'd even gotten to the point that they both sat on the loveseat together, eating out of the same popcorn bowl.

When she wasn't with Derrick, she was with Christy. They, too, had hung out more, either meeting at the coffee shop before Christy's shift at the hotel or having dinner a couple of times a week. In only five months, she'd grown to consider them both family.

Even Maple Hill had grown on her, the realization sudden and powerful.

"You want to go out and celebrate?" Derrick asked, pulling her out of her own thoughts.

Liza shook her head. "Love to, but I'm going to go hang out with my family at the hotel for a little bit. Raincheck?"

"Yep," he said, then gave her a side hug.

Christy hugged her, too.

"Thank you, both. Seriously."

With a wink, Derrick headed for the door, followed closely by Christy, who turned to look over her shoulder at

Heath, who was meandering around the gallery. "Heath, you coming?"

He nodded. "In a minute."

Christy's eyebrow raised, and she looked at Liza and shrugged. "Don't be too long. I'm sure Liza would like to go."

With that, Christy and Derrick left. For a few minutes, Heath continued wandering around the gallery, pretending to look at her paintings. Then abruptly turned and walked toward Liza. He stopped, shifted from foot to foot, then took a deep breath.

"Liza?"

"What's up, Heath?"

He paused, shuffled his feet, and shoved his hands in his pockets. "I was wondering, would you look at my drawings sometime?"

Of all the things she thought he'd say, this was not one of them. "You draw?"

His answer was a nod. "Mostly comic book stuff."

"I'd love to look at them."

Those words triggered a grin bigger than she'd seen since they'd met. "Really?"

"Of course! We'll work out something. I'd love to see them."

From outside the room, Christy yelled, "Heath! Let's go!"

The smile faded, and his eyes rolled. "I'd better go."

Liza nodded. "Thanks for coming, Heath. It means more than you know," she said as he walked past and to the door.

Then he paused. "Liza. Don't tell my mom, okay? About the drawings."

While her face screwed up in confusion, she nodded, "Okay. If that's what you want."

With a wave, he ambled out.

Alone now, she turned in a circle, and an overwhelming sense of pride washed over her. She'd done it. Granted, it had been forced on her, but she'd done it, nonetheless. As she took a lap around the room, she counted six pieces sold. It wasn't a lot of money, but it marked the first time someone besides her grandmother had bought one of her pieces.

As she headed to the door, she turned and took one last look at the gallery, then flipped off the light.

"Thanks, Grandma," she said to the darkness. Then closed the door behind her.

By the time Liza made it to the hotel room, Chloe was already passed out in one of the two queen beds. Anna and

Liza sat on the other bed while their mother took one of the armchairs in the corner.

For several hours, Anna and Deborah grilled Liza about her life in Maple Hill. She filled them in on Hank's near miss. "You might get to meet him tomorrow."

"And he stays in the cottage at night, even though he's outside all day?" Deborah asked, unable to contain the horror in her voice.

Liza nodded.

"Doesn't he bring in dirt? And what about fleas?"

"No fleas, mom. Dirt, sometimes, but nothing I can't clean up. It's fine," Liza said, then stood up and went to the small refrigerator to pull out one of the bottles of water she'd brought with her. "Anyone else want something?"

Both of them shook their head.

As she sat back down, Anna looked hard at her. "You seem happy here."

Liza shrugged and took a drink of her water. When she finished, she said, "It's nice here. I understand why grandma loved it so much."

Deborah's eyes narrowed. "You're not considering staying here, are you?"

"Mom!" Anna said, then clamped her hand over her mouth when Chloe stirred. She lowered her voice. "When

Liza decides whether or not she wants to stay here, she'll tell us."

For a moment, mother and daughter had a stare- down and Liza realized some conversations had taken place before their visit. Then Deborah relaxed. "You're right. I'm sorry, Liza."

Confused over the shift in power that had just taken place, Liza just said, "It's fine. Like Anna said, you all will be the first to know if anything changes." She realized it hadn't been automatic to tell them she'd be returning home at the end of the year.

Anna smiled at her and patted her leg.

Wanting desperately to turn the conversation away from her, Liza asked Anna about Chloe, which set her off on a proud mom speech.

More than once, Liza caught her mother studying her from the corner of her eye. Whatever Anna thought, Liza knew better. Deborah wasn't quite finished yet.

Liza spent the better part of the next morning tidying up the cottage. It wasn't that bad, really, considering housekeeping wasn't necessarily her best trait. Still, she gave everything a once over.

When everyone arrived, they spent the first part of the visit ogling over how small the cottage was until Liza moved them to the front porch. Despite the cool nights, daytime was still warm, but everyone seemed comfortable as they sat in the porch chairs.

"Are you coming home for Christmas, Aunt Liza?"

Liza picked Chloe up and sat her on her lap, rocking gently in the chair. "Yep. I plan to come home through New Year's."

"Then you have to come back?" Chloe asked, her lips pouting.

"Yes. Then I have to come back."

"For how long?"

Liza felt two sets of eyes on her. "Not sure yet, Bug." She looked up at Anna, then Deborah, then back to Anna. Her sister had one eyebrow raised but didn't comment.

The sound of rustling in the bush off the side of the house startled them all, and Liza stood, knowing what was coming. Out of the overgrowth burst a mass of brown fur. Chloe's eyes went wide as Hank rounded the corner of the house, then her lips trembled.

Fear clouded Anna's face as she looked from the dog to her daughter and Deborah stood, backing up behind the chair.

"That's Hank. He won't hurt you."

As Hank reached the steps, he noticed the strangers and paused as if sensing their nervousness.

"That is a huge dog," Anna whispered.

Slowly, his tail wagging, Hank climbed the stairs and looked at Anna. "Just put your hand out so he can sniff it."

Doing as instructed, Hank stuck his head forward and sniffed Anna's hand. Liza looked down at Chloe, who had her head buried in her shoulder. "He won't hurt you, Chloe."

Her lips trembling, Chloe looked up at Liza. "Are you sure?"

Liza gave a sharp nod. "Positive. He's my friend. Here. Give me your hand."

Gently, Liza took Chloe's hand in hers and extended them both out to Hank. Hank sniffed, then his long pink tongue flicked out and licked Chloe's hand, making her giggle.

"Come here, Hank," Anna said, relaxing, and Hank moved into her, rubbing his body against her legs, his tail beating off of her leg.

"Can I play with him?" Chloe asked.

Looking at the size of Hank against Chloe, Liza said,

"Maybe not play. He's not used to little kids. He might jump on you and hurt you by accident. But you can throw a stick for him. Would you like that?"

Chloe nodded.

"Hank. Find a stick!" Liza commanded. Hank spun around and vaulted from the porch, disappearing around the side. A few seconds later, he returned, carrying a stick in his mouth.

Liza stood up as he ran back up the porch stairs and dropped the stick at her feet. As soon as she bent down to pick it up, Hank shot back down the stairs and waited in the yard. Liza handed the stick to Chloe and stood behind her. "Okay, just throw it as hard as you can that way," Liza said, pointing away from Hank.

Chloe grasped the stick and flung it. Hank shot after it, catching it before it hit the ground, and Chloe giggled. Hank returned to the stairs and dropped the stick again, this time at Chloe's feet. Chloe picked it up and tossed it again. Again, Hank caught it before it hit the ground and brought it back. Liza lost track of how long the two did this until Anna cleared her throat.

"We should probably get going," Anna said, her face reading motherly love.

"Yes, we should," Deborah echoed, and Liza realized her mother, her fingers gripping the back of the chair, still hadn't moved. For the first time, Liza realized the reason they'd never had a dog growing up. It hadn't been the hair or the fleas. Her mother was afraid of dogs.

"Aw, mom," Chloe whined and tossed the stick again.

"It's okay," Liza said. "Hank needs to go home, anyway. Hank, drop the stick." He did as commanded and walked up to Chloe, nuzzling her while Chloe hugged his neck. "Hank, time to go home," Liza said, and Hank took a last look around and then dashed off into the bush.

From behind her, Liza heard her mother breathe and then move around the chair. Liza opened the front door, and they all piled in, Chloe looking longingly at the place Hank had disappeared.

"Thanks a lot. You know she's going to be asking me for a dog, now, right?" Anna whispered.

Liza shrugged, then wiggled her eyebrows. "That's what aunts are for."

As they all said their goodbyes, then walked to the rented car, Liza hugged each of them once more. Standing in the driveway, she waved at them and fought back tears. She had an overwhelming feeling to just jump in the car and go with them. How had her grandmother done it all those years?

Her phone rang as she closed the front door behind her. When she looked at the caller ID, she smiled. "Are you spying on me?"

Derrick laughed. "I have no idea what you're talking about. Figured it might be hard having your family leave, so I was just checking on you."

"Thanks. It wasn't fun."

"Movie night?"

"Do I get to pick the movie?"

"Yep."

"Then, yes. I'll be up in a bit."

"Sounds good."

They disconnected, and Liza ran inside to shower and change clothes. She also put on a little mascara and a swipe of lip gloss.

When Liza's scrolling stopped on a new romantic comedy, Derrick made a grunting noise through a mouthful of popcorn from the other end of the loveseat.

"You said my choice," she said, clicking on it and entering the code to rent.

She leaned over, dug her hand into the popcorn bowl on his lap and returned to her side of the loveseat. As the opening credits rolled, she snuggled into her corner, curled her legs next to her, and threw the blanket from the back of the loveseat over them. Derrick, giving in, swung one leg up and stretched it out across the loveseat, his foot lightly resting against her shin. Neither seemed to notice.

As the two main characters bantered back and forth, Derrick couldn't help but steal glances at Liza, who was completely engrossed and unaware of the attention. It was nice to see her smile. When she'd arrived, Derrick could tell her family leaving had taken a toll. Then he had realized he knew virtually nothing about her personal life in Florida beyond the names of her immediate family and that her father had died when she was young. She'd worked at a college before coming to Maple Hill but doing what, he didn't know. What about friends? She never mentioned them. A boyfriend? He assumed no, but as the old saying goes, to assume is to make an ass out of you and me.

Briefly, he wondered if Christy even knew any of the personal information about her, but he highly doubted it. Christy's closed lips did not carry over to him. He knew far more about the people of Maple Hill than he ever wanted to know. But that was okay. They had been each other's confidantes for most of their lives. That it had carried over into adulthood shouldn't be a surprise.

No, Liza, he realized, was just less inclined to talk about herself. Sure, she might give some information here and there, but those deep facts, the feelings that go with them, she wasn't one to just blurt it out.

If he was telling the truth, it was one reason he enjoyed hanging out with her so much. There was no drama. No long-winded discussions. Just hanging out. It was the first time he remembered being this comfortable with someone of the opposite sex, his social life typically consisting of a football game party here and there. The occasional game of golf or an impromptu fishing trip with some buddies he only saw once every couple of years.

But now, sitting there with her, he found he wished she talked a little. She probably knew more about him than he knew about her, which, being a bartender, was rather unsettling. It wasn't like he didn't know how to listen.

She shifted and her braid fell to the side of her neck. Then she laughed at whatever had happened on the screen, and he thought how much he liked the sound of that laugh. So focused on just watching her face light up, he didn't realize she was looking at him until their eyes locked.

Her head cocked to one side, and in a vain attempt to cover the fact that he'd been watching her, he smiled and looked back at the television screen, shoving another handful of popcorn in his mouth. What was he doing?

Derrick forced himself to watch the movie, realizing he'd missed the main plot while creepily staring at Liza, but found himself laughing now and then anyway. And the main actress wasn't too bad on the eyes either.

At some point, he felt extra weight in the popcorn bowl sitting between his legs. Her eyes still glued to the television,

Liza rummaged around in the bowl and retreated again to her side, a pile of popcorn in her hand.

And again, he watched her, the way she smiled at the screen every time the main characters traded barbs or were caught in some compromising position obviously designed to bring them together in the end. He had never understood the draw of romantic comedies. They all ended the same—happy and with the main characters together. What was the point?

But watching her get so much joy from the antics on the screen, he started to understand. Not that he'd be randomly watching them on his own, but if it made her happy, then he'd happily watch them with her.

And that's when the lightbulb went off and burned through his body. He liked her. And not just as a friend. Not as a buddy. He could see the two of them watching movies together, only she'd be leaned against him instead of nestled into the other side of the loveseat. Her hand would be on his chest. His arm draped over her, his hand resting on her side.

When she'd hugged him the night of Hank's emergency, he'd felt the way she'd pressed against him and, just like now, his own body had reacted. He'd wanted to kiss her that night, to feel her arms wrapped around his neck, feel the heat of her skin on his. Just like he wanted to kiss her right now. Out of the corner of his eye, he saw the main characters move in closer, their mutual attraction coming to a head. His hand reached up to her neck and slipped behind her hair. She closed the small gap between them, her hand on his chest, and then gracefully lifted on her tiptoes, and their lips moved closer.

"Popcorn?" he said loudly, shoving the bowl toward Liza.

The frustrated scream that erupted from her made him yank the bowl back and hug it to his chest. Throwing the blanket off of her legs, she growled at him. "Really?!"

"What?" he yelled back at her, surprised by the sudden wave of fury.

"You just ruined the whole movie!" She sat back against the couch and crossed her arms.

Derrick had to work hard to stifle the laugh.

"Okay, all I did was ask if you wanted popcorn." Was this the moment when he realized she was slightly crazy? The moment that would wash away any possible attraction he had to her? He hoped so.

At that, she turned to face him, one leg under her and the other hanging off of the couch. "You watch football, right?"

He nodded slowly.

"Imagine, it's the fourth quarter, fourth down. Last play of the game, and your team is down by a point, and they have control of the ball. They break the huddle and line up. The ball is snapped, and the quarterback takes a step back. A man is open in the end-zone, the quarterback throws the ball. It flies through the air, the receiver is running, the opposing team keeping in step with him. Then the ball descends toward him. His hands are up. It looks like he's going to catch it. And boom, someone steps in front of the television. When you see it again, he's caught the ball, and your team is celebrating, but you missed that play."

He stared at her while his brain tried to piece together a connection between a football game and romantic comedy. Not to mention, he got a little excited that it sounded like she might be a football fan, considering she'd never mentioned a game. Or wanting to watch one. He almost asked, but one look at the seriousness in her face, the way she was tapping her foot on the hardwood floor, told him that was not the way to go.

Feeling like he was in class again, put on the spot by the teacher to answer some question that would ultimately get him laughed at by his peers, he said, "The kiss is like the catch?"

"Ding, ding, ding," she said, enunciating the sarcastic answer with a slow clap.

He wasn't so sure he liked her much at the moment, but at the same time, he was strangely turned on.

"The kiss. That is what we are waiting for."

Bewildered, he said, "But you already know it's going to happen."

The groan was loud and guttural. "I know we know it's going to happen! That's not the point. We've invested all that time watching those characters fall in love. The kiss is the touchdown!"

He thought he got it now. He thought it was silly, but he thought he got it. Setting the bowl down, he raised his hands in mock surrender. "Okay, okay. I'm sorry I ruined your movie. It won't happen again."

Liza took a deep, calming breath, then sighed. "It's fine. Sorry. I get very serious about my romantic comedies."

"You think?"

She laughed, and the tense mood evaporated. "I'm still mad, but maybe not that mad. It's just been a long day."

He saw that as an opening. "I'll bet you miss your family and friends."

Frustratingly, her answer was just a shrug as she stood up and stretched, her empty glass in hand.

Following her lead, he also stood, gathering the empty popcorn bowl and his own glass from the side table. Together they walked into the kitchen, her in the lead. As she headed to the sink to wash her glass, he threw out the invisible fishing line again. "Unless you don't."

This made her laugh. "Depends on the day," she finally said as she rinsed her glass and put it in the drainer. Then, she turned to face him and leaned against the sink. "That sounded mean. I do miss my family."

As he moved to the sink, she scooted over to give him room. He washed out the bowl and his glass, dropped them in the drainer, then turned and leaned against the sink, too. "Not your friends?"

She gave an uncomfortable smile. "You have to have friends to miss them."

"That can't be true."

Again, the shrug as she pushed off the sink. At first, he thought she was leaving, but instead, she scooted out the stool and sat down. "Unfortunately, it is. Don't get me wrong. I have lots of acquaintances. Three hundred and ninety-two, according to my Facebook friends list." The last part was said with a chuckle. "But friends, I don't know. I had them at one time. A group of people from college. But then, we just grew apart over time."

Afraid any interruption would stop her from talking, he simply moved to the empty stool and sat down next to her.

"They had families and careers. Many of them moved away, chasing whatever dream they were chasing. And I stayed where I was. And I do miss my family. Don't get me wrong. But it's been nice here, being just me. No baggage.

No preconceived notions. No black sheep label. But I do miss them," she said again, as if trying to convince herself. Then she shook her head. "Anyway, enough about me."

"Black sheep, how?" he asked, deciding to take the direct approach.

"Let's just say I don't really fit into the Blackburn ideals. As you know, my Dad owned his own accounting firm. He was really successful. My mom, at one time, was an attorney. She quit to take care of us, but she was apparently very good at it. My sister followed in her footsteps. She and her husband have their own practice. She was top of her class. Got all kinds of scholarships. Me? I went to art school, turned down a softball scholarship just because I didn't want to play anymore, racked up a bunch of student loans, and ended up working most of my young adult life as an administrative assistant. Then moved up to an executive assistant. Don't get me wrong! I rocked that job. It was just another mark on me. Liza, who couldn't finish anything. Liza, who always messed up. Liza, who was late to her grandmother's funeral and tripped down the aisle and ripped her dress."

He smiled at the memory of that day, though at the time, he had to admit even he had been judgmental. As a matter of fact, he'd made a very costly decision based on that one meeting. One he now somewhat regretted.

"If it helps, they did nothing but rave about your art at the show when you were off talking to people."

"Even my mom?" Liza asked, her lips thinning in disbelief.

"Especially your mom." He could tell she didn't believe him. "It's the truth. She just kept staring at it in awe, whispering to herself that she had no idea."

Liza glanced at the clock on the wall and stood, signaling the discussion was over. "I really should get back to the cottage. Hank will be wondering where I am. Thanks, Derrick."

"Even though I ruined the movie?"

"Even though you ruined the movie." She grinned and headed toward the door, giving him a brief wave before exiting.

Long after her car had pulled out of his driveway, he sat at the island, deep in thought, and realized he was falling for this woman, a new concept for him. It had been years since he'd even remotely considered committing to someone. What was the point? He was busy all the time. Then in blew Liza, and he had to decide now, was it worth it? If so, what next? Was there even an opportunity for a next?

Chapter Twenty-One

L iza sipped her coffee while Christy rummaged through her purse for her ringing cellphone. They'd opted to sit inside the coffee shop as the temperature had dropped below Liza's comfort zone. She had to admit, though, the changing leaves from green to orange, red, and brown, had been as beautiful as she'd hoped. There were already a couple of pictures on her phone to be painted at some point. By the time Christy produced her phone, it had stopped ringing.

"Seriously, how much stuff do you have in that bag?" Liza asked with a chuckle.

"You shush." Checking the screen, Christy rolled her eyes. "Sorry. It's Heath."

"No worries," Liza said. Not that it mattered. Christy had already redialed and had the phone to her ear.

"Hi. Whatcha need?" Christy listened, then sighed. "I can't, Heath. I need to be at work at 4:30. Can you catch a ride?" Silence. Liza watched as Christy's face screwed into a mix of frustration and guilt. "I know it's important. I can see if Uncle Eric can pick you up." Then she shook her head and let out another sigh. "Shoot. No. He has a meeting tonight." Silence. "I know, Heath!" Embarrassed, she lowered her voice. "I know. Just see if you can catch a ride. Let me know. Okay. Bye. Love you."

She disconnected and slumped back in her chair. "I am a horrible mother."

"You are so not a horrible mother."

Flustered now, Christy dropped her phone in her bag and put it back on the floor. "Some kind of meeting for class officers next year. It irritates me when they have these meetings right after school without notice. Do the people making these decisions not work? Hopefully, he can find a ride." Her face hardened into a frown as she sipped her coffee. Then she shook her head and tried to smile. "Anyway, you don't need to hear all of my mama drama."

"I'll go pick him up."

Christy paused, considered, then shook her head. "I can't ask you to do that."

"You didn't ask. I offered. I'm not doing anything else today that I can't easily rearrange. Or better yet, put off. I'll pick him up. We'll go get some dinner. It's no problem."

"Seriously?"

"Seriously."

Christy jumped up, rounded the table, and wrapped her arms around Liza. "Thank you! Thank you, thank you."

Liza patted her shoulder lightly. "Anytime."

Returning to her chair, Christy picked her bag back up and started digging through it. First, she pulled out her cellphone and sent a text. Liza assumed it was to Heath. Then she dropped the cellphone back in her bag and rummaged again. "I'll give you some money."

As Christy produced her wallet, Liza reached over and covered Christy's hand with her own. "I don't need you to give me money."

"But...," Christy started, but Liza gently squeezed her hand.

"Christy. I've got this. I want to do this. Relax and let me do this."

Christy exhaled sharply as she retook her seat and dropped her bag back to the floor. For a moment, Liza thought she might cry, but Christy took another deep breath, exhaled more slowly this time, then smiled. "Thank you."

Liza winked and sat back against her seat. As they sipped coffee, she studied her friend. Friend, Liza thought.

It was a foreign word to her as of late, and it took her by surprise how quickly it had happened. How quickly Christy had grown from stranger to someone in her life who she trusted. That she wanted to help. Then there was Derrick. She wasn't even sure what her thoughts were about him. Some days, they were simply friends, thrown together by proximity and a shared love of her grandmother. But other days, days when they were relaxing on his couch watching movies or sipping tea on her front porch, when his smile brightened his face as she walked into the pub, some days she thought maybe there could be more there.

Then there was the cottage, the feeling when she walked through the door, knowing it was hers. All she had to do was take it. The Art Center, all the ideas she'd had the past months for that place. The grants she'd already researched. The peace she felt standing in the gallery, hanging other people's artwork.

It was like pieces of a puzzle snapping into place. One by one, snap, snap, until the picture in her mind spelled home. She was home. Deep down in her gut, the place where disappointment and fear can't reach, where possibilities and dreams reside, something churned and fought to the surface. Everything she'd wanted, a life surrounded by art, friends, a home of her own, was right there for the taking. All she had to do was take it. And the first step was applying for the still open executive director job at the Art Center.

"Earth to Liza." Christy's hand waved in front of her face, snapping her back to the present.

"Sorry," Liza said with a laugh. "What did you say?"

"I said, how is your list going?"

"Good. I only have two more paintings to do, and they're already started. I just have the Snow Ball dance next month and then sleigh riding. If it snows."

"Farmer's Almanac says it's gonna, so you may luck out there."

"I'm not sure it'll be luck. I'm already cold. I can't see sitting in frozen stuff on purpose."

Christy grinned. "You'll love it. I promise."

"This Snow Ball dance, are you going to be there?"

"Yep. I've never missed it. We'll have fun! Oh, I meant to ask you, are you going back to Florida for Thanksgiving and Christmas?"

Liza shook her head. "Not Thanksgiving. I can only be gone for two weeks, and I want to save a few days in case I need them. I'm going a couple days before Christmas and back the day after New Year's. It works out, because this year, my sister goes to my brother-in-law's family for Thanksgiving. Mom, I guess, is just going to go with them."

Christy straightened and beamed. "Well, then you are officially invited to the Lowe Thanksgiving feast at Derrick's." Then she dropped back down and leaned in. "I mean, it's more of a meal than a feast, but there's typically only three of us. Seriously, though. We'd love to have you."

Her response was immediate. "Great. I'd love that. Just let me know what I can bring."

In her bag, Christy's phone vibrated, and she held up her finger, dug through and pulled it out. "Shoot. I have to go. I have some things I have to do before I go into work. I'll touch base with you about Thanksgiving. Are you absolutely sure about Heath?"

"I'm sure." Besides, Liza thought as Christy gathered her stuff and picked up her mug, *I have a resumé to work on*. "I'll text you when I've picked him up. I'll take him to your house after we eat."

"Perfect," Christy said. "Thank you again. Seriously."

"Stop," Liza said, waving Christy toward the door.

"Go. I've got this."

With a goodbye, Christy rushed out the door. Liza returned to the counter, ordered a refill, and sat back down. She pulled out her computer, sipped on her coffee while it booted up, then navigated to her personal resumé folder. Once the document loaded, she got to work.

Heath opened the passenger door of the car and maneuvered himself in, his bookbag dropping on his lap with a soft thud. Once he was settled, his seatbelt on, and the door closed, he said, "Hey, Liza. Thanks."

"No problem at all." Liza put the car in drive and drove through the school parking lot. "Besides, I figured it was a perfect time for you to show me your artwork."

"You still want to see it?"

Liza glanced over at him, then back to the window. "Of course."

"Cool."

"I was thinking pizza for dinner. You okay with that?"

"Always."

As Liza pulled onto the main road and brought the car up to speed, she asked, "How did your meeting go?"

"Fine," Heath answered as he rummaged through his backpack and pulled out a set of earbuds. "Do you mind if I listen to some music?"

Chuckling to herself, Liza flicked her hand. "Nope. Have at it."

Heath slouched down in his seat, pushed the ear buds in his ears, scrolled through his phone, and tapped it. The muffled sounds of fast-tempo music drifted from the earphones.

Liza glanced at him, then back to the road with a smile. No wonder Christy liked to talk so much when they were together. She'd be offended, except she still remembered what it was like to be a teenager. She wouldn't have had anything to say to her mother's strange friend either.

Pizza came first, which didn't surprise Liza in the least.

Food trumped everything for teenagers, especially teenage boys. She was glad she'd opted for a large as Heath gobbled down the slices. There would still be some left over for Christy when she got off work. Again, conversation was stilted with Liza asking benign questions about sports or school and receiving short, one-to-three word, answers. Eventually, she gave up and finished eating. As soon as they were done, Heath immediately cleared both plates and glasses and washed them in the sink, while Liza worked on putting up the pizza.

"Where is your aluminum foil?" Liza asked.

Heath pointed a wet hand to the drawer under the microwave. She opened it, pulled out the aluminum foil, wrapped the leftover pizza, and put it in the refrigerator.

The kitchen back in order, she turned to Heath. "Okay, let me see these sketches."

Heath wiped his hands on his jeans and disappeared down the hallway, which Liza assumed led to his bedroom, then returned with a sketchbook hugged to his chest. Liza sat back down at the table, and Heath took the seat across from her. After a long pause, he dropped the sketchbook on the table, slid it across to her, then sat back against the chair with his arms crossed.

When she flipped open the first couple of pages and the characters jumped out at her, her eyes widened. She was no expert in comic book art, but what she saw as she slowly flipped through the pages was excellent work. Even with her untrained eye, she saw some areas in which Heath could improve. Some attributes of the characters didn't fit quite right, but there was raw talent there.

"Wow, Heath," she said, looking up at him. "These are amazing."

A red hue darkened his cheeks. "Seriously?"

"Yes. Seriously. I mean, I'm not really a comic book artist." Then she paused, her memory giving her smack. She smiled.

"But I might know someone who is. Would you mind if I take a few pictures of these and reach out to him?"

Panic washed across his face. "I don't know."

"If not, that's fine. But seriously, you have a gift, I think. As far as I can tell, these are great. If I can get them to someone who actually does this, you might get some real feedback on them."

She waited while he processed it, then nodded. "I guess that'd be okay."

"Excellent!" Liza pulled out her phone and snapped a few pictures, then closed the book and slid it back to Heath. "Thank you for showing these to me." She glanced at the clock. "Well, I should probably head back to the cottage. You know, if you ever want to help out at the Art Center, I'm sure they'd love to have you."

"Really? I never thought about that," Heath said.

"That would be fun."

Liza gathered her coat and purse, then headed to the door. "Anytime. And I mean that, Heath. Anytime you need something, just call."

"Thanks," Heath said as he walked her to the door.

She paused and turned. "Oh, and Heath, show your mom those. She loves you. She might not appreciate it in the same way, but she loves you, and she'll love them because she loves you."

The irony in her own words struck deep. How many times had she actually tried to show her mother her artwork, her sketches? Never, she realized. She'd never actually asked her mother if she wanted to see her artwork. Not once. A cold wash of realization spread through her as she came to terms with the part she'd played in their rocky relationship. "Seriously, Heath. Show your mom."

He nodded. "Okay, I will. Thanks again, Liza."

With a wink, she headed out the door.

Chapter Twenty-Two

She fit. That's all it came down to. Despite only being four of them, they had demolished the turkey and fixings, all sitting back in their chairs and holding their stretched stomachs.

"This was amazing," Liza said, pushing her hair behind her ear and revealing the line of her neck. Derrick stared at it for a moment, his eyes traveling to her profile, the easy way her smile was setting on her face.

"Thanks!" Christy said, pulling Derrick's attention away from Liza. She was staring at him, her head cocked to one side, a smirk on her face. He told her to shut up with his eyes, then cleared his dishes.

"You'll have to teach me how to cook a turkey like that someday," Liza said as she followed Derrick's lead and picked up her own dishes.

Christy shook her head, reached over the table, and placed her hand on Liza's arm to stop her. "Nope. You're the guest." Then she turned to Heath, who was finishing up another pile of mashed potatoes. "That's what I have a teenager for."

Heath glanced at the clock on the wall and groaned. "Mom, the game is about to start."

Derrick interrupted from in front of the sink where he was already washing. "Then I guess you should get on it then and stop shoveling food in your mouth."

As he stood up, Heath scooped up two more heaping spoonfuls of the mashed potatoes and shoved them into his mouth. Christy caught Liza's attention and pointed to the living room. Wiping her mouth with her napkin, Liza stood and followed her.

"I feel bad about not helping to cook or clean-up," Liza said as they moved toward the couches.

"Don't," Christy answered, taking the armchair. "It's good for them."

As Liza settled onto the loveseat, she leaned against the arm and shifted toward Christy, her hand propping up her head. "Well, I appreciate it. It was all really good."

"You're welcome anytime. When are you leaving for Christmas, again?"

"Day before Christmas Eve and back the day after New Year's. I was thinking, though, would you guys want to come to the cottage for a little pre-Christmas dinner?"

"Sure! Just give me the dates as early as possible so I can ask off of work."

Liza pulled out her phone and scrolled to December. "I'm pretty open right now, so whatever works for you."

"Thursdays will be better for Derrick. I know that much. What about the Thursday after next?"

As Liza put it in her calendar, she said, "Works for me."

When she finished, she put her phone face down on the side table.

"We'll work out the details later, food and such. Just tell me what you need me to bring."

"Nope. This is a thank you from me. Just bring any drinks you want and yourselves. Also, I have a few presents for each of you."

Christy's eyes lit up. "And we have something for you." Her grin was wide and over-exaggerated, making Liza laugh.

"I don't know whether to be excited or scared," Liza said suspiciously.

"You'll love it. And if you don't, pretend you do," Christy winked, then she looked over her shoulder at the sound of voices and clanking dishes coming from the kitchen, then back at Liza. "By the way, thank you for telling Heath to show me his drawings. They're so good. I don't know why he didn't want to show me." Just a twinge of hurt came out in that last sentence.

Breathing out a sigh of relief, Liza said, "First, don't take it personally. Showing someone your art is a big deal, and it can be hard sometimes. Second, I am so very glad he told you. I've been figuring out a way to talk to you about his Christmas gift without breaking his confidence for weeks. After he showed me his sketches, I reconnected with an old college friend who happens to work in the industry. I sent him a picture, and he's willing to mentor Heath. It will kind of be a talk on the phone, send him his sketches, get feed back thing. He's in California right now. Even so, he said Heath has a lot of natural talent and would love to work with him."

Christy's eyes teared up. "Are you serious?"

"It's okay, right? If I give Heath that information as a present?"

"Okay? Oh, Liza. You're going to make me cry. He'll be so excited."

Christy moved from the chair to hug Liza over the arm when Derrick walked into the room with Heath close on his heels. "Do we need to go back to the kitchen?"

Pulling away from Liza, Christy laughed, discreetly wiped her eyes, then turned on Derrick. "Shush and come on."

Derrick took the space next to Liza on the loveseat, and Heath plopped down on the floor, remote in hand in front of him. He turned on the television and flipped through to two sportscasters talking about the upcoming match between the two teams. All but Liza were dialed in, and she could feel the building excitement in the room. She had no idea who they were rooting for, or if she felt so inclined, who she would root for, but it didn't matter. She was happy to just sit with them. Her friends.

A side glance at Derrick changed the narrative in her head just a little. *Or more?* she thought, then snuggled back against the loveseat to watch.

Chapter Twenty-Three

Flashbacks to standing in the corner of her high school dances rapid-fired as Liza took a seat at a corner table. Around her, the townspeople chatted and laughed, all decked out in semi-formal attire, flashy dresses that twinkled under the lighting, hair perfectly set in wedding- worthy styles, and so much jewelry. All of which drew even more attention to her outsider status as she sat alone in a simple black dress. She reminded herself to strangle Christy for not giving her a heads up.

The chair beside her scooted back, and she startled to the side before looking up. Derrick smiled down at her, and she found she was a little relieved at the sight of his suit. A simple, black suit over a blue shirt, likely to be seen at any church service or wedding, made her feel less underdressed. His hair, usually indented from a ball cap, had been slicked back. It wasn't a look she typically found attractive, but somehow, he pulled it off. He plopped down beside her, resting his elbows on the table while he also observed the party-goers.

"Little much, huh?" A grin tugged at the corner of his mouth.

Liza chuckled. "Maybe a little. It is beautiful though."

He sat back, crossing his arms, and turned to face her. "It is. It didn't used to be this fancy. It started in a barn and was more like a square dance."

"What happened?"

He grinned, held his hand in the air, and rubbed his fingers together to indicate money.

"So, why are you here?"

"I'm on the board."

Liza's lips pressed together as she held back a smile. He really just could not help himself. She'd met a lot of workaholics in her life, but Derrick was by far the worst of them. No wonder he wasn't taken.

Despite her attempt to hide her reaction, Derrick cocked his head to the side and asked, "What?"

"Nothing," she said, shaking her head.

A squealing speaker at the front of the hall stole their attention before he could speak. The din of voices slowed and then petered out as a tuxedoed Bill took the small stage. He tapped once on a cordless microphone, then smiled, patiently waiting for the final hold-outs to silence themselves.

When it was quiet, he brought the microphone to his mouth. "Ladies and Gentlemen, thank you all for attending our 15th Annual Snow Ball Celebration! Thank you all for your hard work this year raising money for our Winter Wonderland." Applause erupted. He let it linger for a moment before waving everyone to silence again. "Are you ready to hear the numbers?"

Liza jumped at the amplified shout, then again when screams and cheers broke out.

Bill smiled again. "Drum roll, please!" All around her, feet tapped in double time to create the effect. And stopped just as suddenly when he cut it off again with his hand. "This year, we raised ten thousand, three hundred, and thirty-nine dollars for the Winter Wonderland!"

Despite the room being sparsely occupied for its size, the celebration expanded through the space like a raucous crowd at a Friday night football game. Liza couldn't help but clap and cheer with them.

A rush of belonging took her by surprise as she turned to find Derrick looking at her. Staring at her, really. She couldn't take her eyes off of his as heat built in her stomach and spread through her body. He leaned forward and her body reacted, pulling her in. Her hand moved toward his as the space between them closed.

A jostle broke the spell as someone dropped into the chair on the other side of her. "Sorry I'm late!" Christy shouted as she plopped her purse on the table and pulled up on the strapless, sequined dress. "Did I miss the announcement?"

Liza's mind still reeling from the unexpected moment with Derrick, she asked, "What?"

"The announcement. Did I miss it?" Christy paused and looked hard at Liza. "What's wrong with you?"

The slow burn in her face flamed. She needed to get out of there and calm herself. "I'll be back," she shouted a little too loudly as she jumped up and rushed to the bathroom.

Luckily, the bathroom was a one-seater, and most importantly, the door locked. Standing in front of the sink, she checked her face in the mirror and thankfully found it absent of redness. Her hands planted on the sink, she leaned in for a closer look. Satisfied her skin color had returned to normal, she straightened.

A rap on the door reminded Liza she was taking up valuable space at an event. Checking herself one last time in the mirror, she opened the door and smiled sheepishly at the less than enthused woman on the other side, then headed back to the ballroom.

As she entered, she noticed the empty chair where Derrick had been and scanned the room, finally spotting him near the front with a group of people she assumed was the board.

She sat down next to Christy, who side-eyed her but didn't press further. Instead, she just handed her a full glass of wine. "I drank the rest of your other one," she said matter-of-factly, no apology in her tone.

Before Liza could respond, she was cutoff by someone announcing the start of the Snow Ball. "Explain to me how this works again," Liza said.

"When the music starts, each board member picks someone out of the audience to dance with. Then that person picks someone. Then that person picks someone. Until everyone that is able to dance is on the dance floor." Hearing how it worked again didn't help the butterflies fluttering around her stomach at the thought of having to dance with not just one, but maybe multiple strangers. "Don't look so terrified. They don't bite," Christy said as she sipped her own wine. "Well, except Harold over there. The guy dressed in the baby blue tuxedo. Same tuxedo, by the way, he's dressed in since this thing turned fancy ten years ago. He might bite. But everyone else is fine."

Liza's gaze landed on Harold talking to three women in the corner of the room, who all looked like they were politely trying to escape. When he turned, Liza let out a laugh at the gold chains draped over thick bushy chest hair where a shirt should be. His gray hair was slicked back with so much oil it reflected off the lights above. She leaned over to look at his shoes, and even from that distance, she could tell they were alligator—or at least faux alligator. She sat back up, took a sip of her wine, and shook her head. "I can believe that."

Christy nodded at her to solidify her opinion. They slipped into easy conversation, Christy talking about Heath and work, and Liza filling her in on the status of the list.

When the conversation stalled, Liza swirled the wine in her cup and took a deep breath. "I've applied for the executive director job at the art gallery."

In shock, Christy spun in her chair and targeted all of her attention on Liza. "What? Are you serious? Does this mean what I think it means? Because if it does, I'm going to get stupid excited here in a minute."

"I think so, yes. I've decided to stay in Maple Hill after the year ends. If I get the job."

Christy let out a high-pitched squeal, then latched onto Liza's neck and squeezed her hard. Liza allowed it, even returning the hug, but as soon as Christy released her, she immediately looked around the room to see if anyone had noticed. They hadn't, all too wrapped up in each other. Even Derrick, who was at the front of the room in deep conversation with another man about twenty years his senior, didn't appear to notice.

"I'd like to keep this quiet, at least until I'm hired."

Christy clamped her lips shut and made a locking motion with her fingers before dropping the serious facade and clapping quietly. "This is going to be awesome."

Liza's heart warmed at Christy's excitement. She just hoped she got the job, now that she'd told Christy. It was key to her staying.

Christy leaned in close to whisper, "When you decide to tell everyone, let me know because I fully intend to throw a party."

Liza whispered back. "You just want a reason to drink."

"Right on, sista," she said and downed her glass of wine. For all her bravado, Liza already knew that wine would probably be Christy's last drink of the night.

As for her, she was going to need just a little more liquid courage if she was expected to dance with strangers.

Derrick watched Liza walk from the hallway back into the room. Maybe it was his imagination, but it appeared she was disappointed by his empty seat. As her eyes moved across the room, he turned his attention back to Jesse and another tale about the big fish he'd caught over the summer.

Derrick nodded and smiled, but his eyes kept darting to the other side of the room. At first, it looked like she and Christy were just in normal conversation when Christy suddenly smiled, then reached out and hugged Liza hard.

Not one for gossip, he typically avoided knowing things for his own sanity. In this situation, though, he found he wanted to know what had happened between them.

As a matter of fact, he wanted to know everything about Liza. And it irritated him that whatever secret she'd told had been to Christy first. All of which took him by surprise, just like the moment the two of them had shared before she had run off. The moment they'd shared where he'd come very close to leaning in and kissing her.

Life had a tendency to throw curveballs. Of all people, Derrick understood that and was usually ready for them. Not this time, though. This time he'd been caught off guard, and he didn't like it. Not one bit.

Music started, and he followed the board members as they spread out, looking over their shoulders and waiting for Bill's nod. When they received it, they fanned out and chose their first dance partners. He glanced toward Liza and Christy to find Liza's chair empty, so he moved across to Mrs. Waters.

At eighty-three, Mrs. Waters was already pushing herself to her feet as he approached. Even if she hadn't been his intended target, she was now. Taking her hand gently, he bowed, and she attempted a half-curtsy, using her cane to balance herself. Then he presented his elbow, and they walked onto the dance floor. Not too far though, in case she needed to sit down.

Like a ballroom dance, he took her hand in his and then put his other hand high on the back of her rib cage. She did the same, the cane bouncing off his side as they slowly turned in a circle.

He talked to her for a few minutes, yelling loudly so his voice cut through the background noise to her hearing aide. She smiled at him, patting his shoulder like she used to when he was a kid. As they rotated, he noticed Liza had returned to her seat.

Then the buzzer sounded. Mrs. Waters turned to the crowd and waved at Mr. Waters to join her, causing everyone in their line of sight to smile as the older man wobbled to swap places with Derrick. He gave his hand a firm shake; then the two moved in, their dancing much closer and more relaxed than hers and Derrick's.

Free, Derrick turned and saw Liza being led out to the dance floor by Martin Lansing and red, hot fury erupted through him. He was so focused on Liza's grin at Martin, he didn't notice Christy staring at him until they made eye contact. Her eyebrow shot up and her sneer widened into a knowing grin. Derrick glared at her and spun around, looking for the next person.

As he moved his way through the crowded dance floor, Derrick tried to keep tabs on Liza who, to his surprise, seemed to be comfortable doing her part and asking other people to dance.

When the buzzer sounded, he looked out and saw only a few stragglers left at the tables, then zoned in on Liza, who was also looking around. He moved through the crowd of dancers and moved up beside her.

"May I?" he asked.

Her smiled beamed as she easily slipped her hand into his and moved into him. Her cheeks were flushed, her eyes twinkling under the lights, and he knew if he didn't say something, he'd actually kiss her this time. "Are you having fun?"

"Surprisingly, yes! I've met so many people, and everyone's been so nice. I never thought I'd have this much fun asking people to dance."

As they turned, he noticed their bodies gravitating toward each other.

"You look really nice tonight."

That just made her beautiful smile widen even more.

"Just nice?" she asked, teasing.

"You look breathtaking." The electricity between them zapped as she stared at it him for a moment, her smile faltering at the seriousness of his tone.

She blushed. "Thank you. You look very handsome yourself." As she spoke, her eyes left his and glanced everywhere around the room except at him. He took a chance, moving his hand further around the small of her back to bring her close, feeling for any ounce of resistance on her part.

There was none, and she leaned closer, pressing against him. Then she turned her head and rested her cheek on his chest, and he was undone. Four words hung at the tip of his tongue. *I wish you'd stay.* But he didn't say them. Instead, he simply held her closer, enjoying the way she gave into him, the way she felt in his arms, that their bodies seemed to just fit.

When the last note of the song settled around them, he felt her release her grip and wanted desperately to pull her back. But he didn't. Instead, he met her smile.

"Thanks," she said.

With that, she walked away through the crowd.

"Oh, you are in so much trouble."

He didn't have to look to see who owned the voice. "Christy, don't start."

Turning in the opposite direction, he disappeared into the crowd of dancers and out the back door. He needed some cold air.

Chapter Twenty-Four

The two paintings she'd spent two months perfecting leaned against the living room wall, both draped with a white sheet. On the counter were various appetizers—cheese and crackers, olives—probably too much for just the four of them. A part of her wished she hadn't offered to host the little impromptu Christmas party. Given it was her idea, obligation was a powerful motivator, no matter how strong that obligation actually was.

She finished laying everything out and checked the ham in the oven, the smell of which wafted through the house and made her instantly homesick. There was something about the holidays and the smell of cooking that always made her want to be at home.

Outside, Hank barked, signaling his presence and the approaching vehicles. She opened the door, and he trotted past. She laughed. "You know you're not supposed to be in here yet," she said.

His answer was to crawl onto his blanket on the couch and curl into a ball. With a shrug, she waved at Christy and Heath as their car rolled to a stop. Behind her, Derrick's truck pulled in.

The sizzle of a pot overflowing caught her attention, and she left the door open for them while she ran to check the stove. At the stove, she removed the overflowing pot of green beans from the burner, gave them a stir, turned the heat down, and put it back on the burner.

From the living room she heard Derrick ask, "What are you doing in here, Hank?"

Liza stepped out of the kitchen and wiped her hands on a towel. "Leave him be."

"You spoil him, you know that?" Derrick said with no seriousness in his tone.

Liza shrugged, then looked over her shoulder at Christy and Heath as they entered, each carrying a dish.

"Where can I put this?" Christy asked. Liza stepped to the side and pointed at the kitchen table. Christy and Heath put their dishes down. "Cookies and pie," she said as she kissed Liza on the cheek.

"All I brought was a bottle of wine," Derrick said, holding it up before putting it on the counter.

"I told you guys not to bring anything, but thank you. I love your cookies. And wine. Everybody hungry?"

Derrick walked to the living room with Heath and Hank. "Always. And it smells good."

"Smells can be deceiving." Liza moved back to the stove and stirred the contents of the pans. Again, she opened the oven and peeked at the ham. Off to the side of the sink, she lifted towels off rising rolls to check them and then put the towel back on.

As she closed it, Christy appeared beside her. "Anything I can do to help?"

Straightening, Liza set the small egg timer for fifteen minutes, then tossed the towel she'd been holding onto the full dish drainer. "I don't think so. It'll be ready in about a fifteen, twenty minutes."

They both leaned against the counter and watched Heath and Derrick play with Hank, his nails clicking on the hardwood floor. The noise filled the small space. "Keep it up, and I'll make you go outside." Christy's authoritative tone was undermined by her laughter.

Derrick held up his hands and stepped back. "It was all Heath's fault."

"It was not!" Heath yelled, and Hank barked, his whole butt wagging with his tail.

"You ready to go home?" Christy asked as the noise in the other room lessened.

"I am, actually. I'd be lying if I didn't say I was a little homesick. It's hard not to be right now. Christmas is always a big deal. Mom hires someone to decorate the house outside, and we spend all week decorating the inside."

"Sounds nice," Christy said, then snapped her head around at the sound of Heath wrestling with Hank. "Heath! Take it outside!"

"It's cold outside, mom."

"Then stop it," she barked, then turned back to Liza. Derrick moved around the table and sat between the women, eyebrows raised.

"Figured I probably should sit down so I don't get yelled at, too," he said.

Liza laughed. Christy did not. "Stop encouraging him."

"I didn't. I swear," he paused and gave that mischievous grin. "Okay. Maybe a little." He reached for an appetizer and popped it into his mouth. After he chewed, he turned to Liza. "When are you leaving?"

"I fly out the day before Christmas Eve."

"Back when?"

"Fly back on the second."

"Day after New Year's? Oh, that'll be a fun trip," Christy interjected while slapping Derrick's hand. "Save some for the rest of us."

Ignoring their banter, Liza rolled her eyes. "I know. I'm not looking forward to it."

"Liza, do you care if I play my game for a while?" Heath asked.

"Not at all," Liza said before Christy could comment. She knew Christy would have said no, but honestly felt bad for Heath being the only kid. It had to be boring. "Why don't you take it to my bedroom? I'll yell at you when dinner is ready."

He jumped up and dashed from the room. When Liza looked at Christy, she was met with a thin-lipped glare. Liza shrugged. "My house. My rules." Then grinned at her friend.

Just as Christy started to speak, the egg timer dinged, and Liza jumped up.

"Ohhh! Saved by the ding," Derrick said, resulting in a smack to his arm from Christy.

Opening the stove, Liza pulled the ham out to rest, then put the rolls in. "Dinner will be ready soon."

"Smells amazing," Derrick said as Liza set the egg timer again and returned to her seat.

She'd barely sat down when Christy launched her attack, "We need to talk about you spoiling my son."

"Nope," Liza said. "I plan to do a lot of that in the coming years if he'll let me. He's a cool kid."

Christy's eyes widened as she looked from Derrick to Liza, then back to Derrick. Across from her, Derrick stopped mid-drink of his iced tea and then put it back to the table. Liza mentally kicked herself. She hadn't wanted Derrick to know yet. She hadn't even told her family. And from the look on his face, it was clear Christy hadn't told him, which Liza found surprising. From what she could gather, the two told each other everything.

"What was that now?" Derrick asked, looking between them.

Well, there was no point in lying to him. It wasn't like he would talk to her family before she would. Besides, he had a right to know, considering she would be his neighbor. "I've decided to stay in Maple Hill after the year. That is, if I'm hired on at the Art Center. Their board meeting is tonight, actually."

"Seriously?"

Liza nodded. Derrick shot his sister a glaring look. "From your lack of reaction, it appears you've been holding out on me."

"Don't be mad at Christy. I asked her not to say anything. I haven't even told my family yet. Besides, if I don't get the job, the whole plan could change."

He nodded and reached for another appetizer while Christy's head was turned. Derrick's mind was spinning. His feelings for Liza had been fairly easy to keep at bay when he thought she was leaving. Now what was he supposed to do? This wasn't good. Not that her staying was bad, but did he really want to pursue a relationship with her? Because he already knew she could never be just a fling for him. Not only had he realized she would never allow it, he could also never allow it. He liked her too much for that. Maybe a break from each other would help set everything straight again.

"Derrick," Christy said, breaking through his swirling thoughts. "Did you hear me?"

"No. Sorry. What?"

"I said, you could drive Liza to the airport and pick her up, couldn't you?"

He mentally went through his schedule for the upcoming week and then nodded. "Sure. I don't see why not?" Apparently, the two women had held an entire conversation while he had been processing.

"See? Problem solved. I don't blame you for not wanting to leave your car," Christy said as the egg timer dinged again.

"You sure?" Liza asked as she stood and returned to the stove.

She opened the oven, and when she bent over to pull out the pan of bread, Derrick felt a twinge at the shape of her body. Crap. "Yep," he said. "Sure can. Looks like it's about dinner time. I'll go check on Heath."

He scooted back from the table and disappeared into Liza's bedroom, where he found Heath draped across the bed on his stomach playing a handheld game. Derrick realized escaping to Liza's bedroom had not been the smartest choice, as his eyes fell on different items in her room: her dainty tennis shoes peeking out from under the bed, her tank top draped over the dresser, her beauty products on the nightstand—all of which had an unnerving effect on him.

This was ridiculous. It was like her announcement had opened the floodgates to any feelings he'd had for her. Hoping to break the spell, he smacked Heath's leg. "Hey, kid. Dinner is ready."

Heath's finger snapped up, telling Derrick to hold, and returned to his device. Without missing a beat, Derrick reached over Heath and snatched the game out of his hand, hitting the off button.

"Hey!" Heath yelled, then, realizing his mistake, lowered his voice. "I was playing a game, Uncle Derrick."

"Yep. And I said dinner was ready. Come on."

Flopping off the bed, a sulky Heath followed Derrick into the dining room, where Liza and Christy had already laid out the spread. As they took their seats, Christy side- eyed

Heath. Heath glanced at his mother, then at the food. "It looks great, Liza. Thank you."

Christy beamed, and Derrick tousled his hair, eliciting a frustrated "Hey!" as Heath tried to rearrange his floppy locks.

"Thanks, Heath." Liza took her seat between Derrick and Christy. "You want to say grace?"

Heath glanced at Christy, who nodded. Sticking out his hands to either side, he waited for Derrick and Christy to take his. Liza did the same, clasping Derrick and Christy's. As her hand slipped into his, Derrick tensed, feeling the warmth of her soft palm fit snuggly into his. As Heath started the brief prayer, giving thanks for the food and each other, he forced his mind to listen, and on the amen, he released her hand a little too quickly.

Liza didn't seem to notice and immediately dug into the food, slopping it onto her plate. Christy, however, noticed. Obvious by her smirk and raised eyebrows. He glared at her and reached for the mashed potatoes as they all finished filling their plates and fell into silence while they ate.

"I can't eat another bite," Derrick said, leaning back in his chair as he pushed his plate back. "That was amazing, Liza. Thank you."

Liza, who also pushed her plate back, grinned. "Thank you. I wasn't sure if I could pull it off, if I'm being honest."

"Well, you did," Christy said. She stood and started gathering plates, smacking Liza's hand away when she tried to protest. "You cooked. We clean. Sit there, and take a load off."

"I seriously can..."

"Sit," Derrick said, as he, too, stacked plates.

Throwing her hands up in surrender, Liza moved to the couch and sipped on her drink while the other three started clearing the table. A wet nose poked at her arm, and she looked down at Hank, who dropped his block-head on her lap. She laughed and stroked his head, watching as his eyes fluttered closed. "You've completely stolen my dog," Derrick said, stepping into the living room, the dish towel still over his shoulder. "You okay?"

"What? Oh, yes. I'm fine," Liza said, forcing a smile. "Just a little homesick, I think."

With a nod, he returned to the kitchen, where they made quick work of cleaning up.

As they entered, Liza stood up. "Ready for presents?"

"Yep!" Christy said, matching Liza's excitement.

"Me first!" Liza yelled and jumped up. While the three of them found seats, Liza pushed the chairs out of the way and pulled out the two covered paintings and the small, neatly wrapped gift. As she passed them out, she said, "Don't peek until I say go."

Christy looked excited, Derrick confused, and Heath wary as she sat down on the couch where she could see all of their reactions. For just a moment, self-doubt crept in, and she second-guessed her gifts. But she quickly pushed it back down. "Okay, go."

Christy and Derrick lifted the covers from the paintings, and Heath unwrapped his gift. Immediately, Christy burst into tears. Derrick just sat back, his mouth hanging open in awe. And Heath looked confused as he stared at the comic book.

"Liza. This is beautiful," Christy whispered. Derrick leaned over to look at her painting, a collage of pictures of her and Heath. She stood up and crossed the living room. Liza stood to meet her, and they hugged.

When they released, Liza looked at Heath. "There is something inside the comic book, Heath."

He flipped through the pages until the envelope fell out. Setting the comic book on the table, he opened it and read the sheet of paper. His eyes widened, and he looked at the comic book again. Then back at the paper, then the comic book, and finally, his eyes shifted to Liza. "Are you serious?"

Liza nodded. "Yep. I'll introduce you through a video chat after the holidays. But yes, if you want it."

"Mom!" Heath yelled. "She's going to introduce me to the guy who inked this comic book." His grin wide, he handed his mother the comic book. While she flipped through it, he awkwardly stood, then took a quick step toward Liza, gave a half hug, and returned to his seat just as quickly. "Thanks, Liza!"

"You're welcome."

Liza looked over to Derrick, and her smile faded at the blank expression on his face. Christy crossed around to see the painting—a collage of the pictures she'd seen hanging on the farmhouse wall. Generations of their family, the black and white photos painted in color from Liza's imagination. And in the center, a painting of Liza, Derrick, and Heath. Christy's hand went to her mouth and a small sob escaped.

"Did I mess up?" Liza asked, panic in her voice. "I'm sorry."

"What?" Christy asked. "No! No, Liza. It's gorgeous. It's just...it's gorgeous."

Liza looked at Derrick, who moved the painting to the side and stood up. He crossed the room in two steps and hugged her tightly. "Thank you," he whispered in her ear.

Of all the reactions she'd expected, the depth of their response had not been it. His hug lingered. It lingered too long, well past appropriate for friends. And Liza gave into it, smelling the faint cologne on his shirt, feeling the way his arms wrapped completely around her, enveloping her. She leaned into it, suddenly oblivious to the others in the room. It was just her and Derrick. All it would take was for her to look up. Look up and lean in. Somehow, deep down, she knew that.

"Okay!" Heath yelled. The moment shattered along with their embrace. "Our turn. Get your coat on, Liza!"

"My coat?" Liza asked, taking two steps back from Derrick and avoiding eye contact with him.

"Yep! Hurry!" Heath took off for the front door.

"Okay, Heath," Christy said with a laugh. "Give her a minute."

Confused, Liza pulled her coat from the hook in the corner while the other three put on theirs, then she followed them out. In a line, they all walked around the house and toward the shed in the back. Why would they be going to the shed? Her steps hitched the closer they got, and she didn't realize she'd slowed down until Derrick reached back and took her hand. "Come on," he said with a chuckle.

At the shed, Derrick pulled out a key and unlocked it. He reached in and flipped on the light, then stepped back so Liza could walk in. She paused at the door, taking in the small one-room shed they'd converted into a studio. Looking over her shoulder, she made eye contact with Derrick. "Are you serious?"

Christy clapped her hands together. "Are you happy with it?"

"Happy? When in the world did you all do this?" Liza asked as her hands ran over the counter space for painting. A small utility sink sat in the corner. Paints and canvases waited for her against the wall.

"Anytime you weren't home," Derrick said.

"Yeah. Getting you out of your cottage is not the easiest thing in the world," Christy said.

"How did you know I wouldn't come out here?"

"Because you're a chicken," Derrick said.

Tears formed as she turned around in the room. Then she walked to them and pulled them all into a hug. "Best Christmas present ever. Thank you, guys."

"Well, considering your news earlier, now this makes sense," Derrick said.

They all laughed and headed back. As they rounded the corner, Liza heard the phone ringing. She picked up the pace and rushed inside, grabbing the phone before it could switch to voicemail.

"Hello," she said.

"Liza. It's Margaret." Liza held up a finger to the group walking in and mouthed *Margaret*, then stepped into her bedroom.

"Hi, Margaret," she said, her heartbeat quickening as she waited for the news.

"I just wanted to let you know the board would be thrilled to have you come on as executive director."

Liza kept her yell of excitement contained. "That is so great to hear. I'm very excited."

"And so am I. Can you start January fifth?"

"January fifth is perfect. Thank you." Out of the corner of her eye, she saw Christy staring at her from the living room, her hands clasped together at her chest. She gave her a thumbs up and Christy mimed an excited dance. "Enjoy your Christmas, Liza," Margaret said. "I look forward to working with you."

"Same to you, Margaret." Then the call disconnected.

Liza had barely turned around before Christy let out the excited scream she'd been holding back. Liza joined in, meeting Christy to give her a hug. Still at the front door, Heath and Derrick looked at each other.

"I guess this means she's staying," Heath said with a laugh.

Derrick looked at Liza and grinned. "I guess it does."

Chapter Twenty-Five

As the plane touched down, Liza found it hard to believe it had been five months since she had last stepped foot on Florida soil. Inexplicably, the homesickness that had gotten easier over the months made a comeback with a vengeance. The thought that she still had to wait through the landing process and make it out of the terminal before she could see her family was almost too much to bear.

Anna would be waiting on her, and hopefully Chloe, too. She missed their faces and the way Chloe's little arms wrapped around her neck in a big hug, something Liza knew would fade quickly as the years passed. Where earlier her decision to stay in Ohio had been made, now every part of her second-guessed it.

It seemed to take forever for the plane to land and for the other passengers to disembark. As she stood in the line of travelers, some looking wearier than others, her toe tapped impatiently on the aisle. Finally, she was nodding a thank you to the flight attendant and freely walking through the terminal—power-walking really, her rolling suitcase struggling to keep up with her without overturning.

She'd barely cleared the terminal door when a child's voice yelled across the crowd. "Aunt Liza!" As Chloe appeared, running as hard as her little legs could carry her, Liza dropped to one knee, opened her arms, and caught her as she barreled into her embrace.

"Chloe!" she yelled, matching Chloe's pitch, and squeezed her tight. "I have missed you so much, Bug."

"Me too!" Then she wiggled out of Liza's grip, grasped her hand, and pulled her.

"Hold on," Liza said with a laugh as she struggled to get to her feet, her legs annoyed from sitting on the cramped plane. Once she was standing and had reclaimed control of her bag, she let Chloe lead her just a few feet to Anna, who held a big "Welcome Home Liza" sign over her head.

When they embraced, Liza fought back tears. Anna stepped back, her hands firmly on her shoulders, and looked her over. "Well, it looks like you're no worse for wear, living in the artic."

Liza laughed. "Please tell me it's still warm here."

"Warm is relative, but yes. Compared to where you live, it's warm." Then she draped her arm over Liza's shoulders, her other hand grasping Chloe's, and steered Liza toward the doors. "Come on. Mom is waiting for us."

As they reached the parking lot, Deborah grinned and waved from the car. The trunk popped open, and Liza dropped in her suitcase as Anna and Chloe climbed into the back seat. Liza sat down and leaned over, she and her mother genuinely hugging.

"I'm glad you're home, Liza," Deborah said.

"Me too, Mom. Me, too," Liza said as they pulled away.

At the house, Liza disappeared to the upstairs bedroom to change her clothes and freshen up. She sent a quick text to Christy and Derrick to let them know she'd arrived safely.

Christy sent back a "Great! Have fun! Miss ya already" which made Liza smile. Derrick managed a thumbs up. She laughed and shoved her phone back into her pocket.

As she walked down the stairs, she heard Deborah, Anna, and Chloe in the kitchen. Their laughter rang through the house and just twisted the homesickness deeper into her heart. What was she thinking, considering staying in Ohio? Granted, when she was there, she was the happiest she'd felt in a long time. Especially now that she had gotten the job. A job that was perfect for her.

She rounded the corner and pushed the thoughts back.

Tonight was for spending time with her family, not second-guessing her life decisions. She could do that tomorrow.

While they ate dinner, Liza talked about Ohio, and Anna filled her in on her law practice and all things Chloe. When they finished eating, Deborah volunteered to give Chloe her bath while Liza and Anna moved to the front porch.

"You've decided to stay in Ohio, haven't you?"

Liza flipped her gaze to Anna, then to the setting sun. "Yes."

"Thought so."

"What do you think about it?"

Anna looked at her. "I think you need to do what makes you happy. But I can't say I want to see you move that far away."

"I don't know. There, I'm happy. Like, really happy. Like everything is right for the first time in my life. But then I come back here, and this is home, too, and I suddenly don't want to leave again."

Shifting in her chair so she could fully face Liza, Anna said, "That's normal. I felt that way when I moved away. And that was three hours away."

"I didn't know that. I thought you were ready to get away."

"I was. But it didn't make it any easier." Liza nodded. "What did you do?"

"Put my big girl panties on and dealt with it." Anna laughed and took a drink.

"But it's so far away," Liza said.

"Not that far by plane." Silence stretched out between them. "Can I be honest for a minute?"

Liza shot her a look. "Since when do you ask permission?"

"True. Okay. So, obviously, I don't want you to leave. And obviously, I'll miss you. But you need to do what's right for you. And this Liza," she said, making a circular motion with her finger framing Liza's face, "this Liza is happy. And Liza, you haven't been happy in a really long time. I see that fire in your eyes again. Like you're on the path, finally, that you're supposed to be on. And honey, the only thing I want more than for you to stay here is for you to be happy."

Liza burst into tears and Anna immediately rose to her feet and scooted onto the bench beside her, her arm draping over her shoulder. "But what about, Mom?"

"Mom will be fine," Deborah said as she stepped out onto the front porch. "Your sister is right. All of it. I didn't realize how unhappy you were until I saw you happy again." Liza stood, and for the first time since she could remember, she nearly ran into her mother's arms and hugged her hard. It felt good, freeing, to have that hug again. Typically the person to avoid mushy moments, Deborah didn't let go this time until Liza did, and when they parted, she brushed a stray hair out of Liza's eye and smiled at her. Then she kissed her cheek.

Deborah stepped past her and took one of the seats, and Liza followed, sitting down next to her. She looked from Anna to Deborah and back again. "I love you guys."

"Me too," said Anna.

"Me three," Deborah said, and they all laughed at the memory of when they were just the three amigos, depending solely on each other just to get by. Off in the horizon, the sun took its final dip, and Liza realized the night was perfect.

"So, that Derrick boy. He's a cutie," Deborah said nonchalantly.

At first there was silence, then Liza and Anna simultaneously broke out in laughter.

Chapter Twenty-Six

"How did it go?" Derrick asked as his truck pulled out of the airport parking lot. As promised, he'd been there to pick her up. She hated to admit, even to herself, how much she'd missed him. Not that her mother's near constant mentioning of his name had helped matters.

"It went good. Really good, actually. I needed that."

"I'll bet. Did you tell them about moving here?"

"I did," Liza pushed her hair out of her face, just as her stomach growled. She grabbed it and laughed. "Sorry. I didn't eat this morning."

"Want to stop somewhere?"

"Yes, please."

"I could eat, too. How did they react?"

"Surprisingly, really well. Apparently, I seem happy."

He looked over at her and smiled. "You weren't happy before?"

"Apparently not."

"Well, if it helps, we're glad you're staying."

Liza felt her cheeks warm and turned her head to hide the blush. "Thanks."

Derrick steered the truck onto the offramp. "Any preference?"

Recovered, she turned back to him. "Nope. Wherever is fine."

At that, he groaned. "Seriously? You're one of those?"

"One of those what?"

"'Everything's fine' people."

"You asked if I had any preference. Right now, the only preference I have is food."

"With how many exceptions?" he asked as the light turned green, and he turned onto the main drag.

"None. Your pick."

"Okay," he said and turned the truck into the one fast-food restaurant she hated with a passion. It took everything in her, but she clamped her mouth shut. After all that, there was no way she was going to say anything to him.

He parked and looked at her. "Okay?"

She swallowed back the no and just nodded yes as he moved to get out of the truck.

"You sure?"

"Yep," she said, finally opening her door. Her eyes scanned the surrounding restaurants, and she wondered if she could make it to one of those on foot. No. She'd told him no exceptions. She would just suffer through it.

Then he laughed and climbed back into his truck.

"What?" she asked, standing just outside of the passenger side.

"Get back in the truck," he said, still laughing. "We aren't eating here. You hate this place."

"What!" Out of the corner of her eye, she saw two customers glance at them. With a growl, she crawled back into the truck and glared at him. "How do you know that?"

Still laughing, he put the truck in drive and shrugged. "I've been paying attention. You were seriously going to force yourself to eat food you hate, rather than admit you were wrong, weren't you?"

"I wasn't wrong. I just didn't think about this place. Any other place would have been fine." In a fake huff, she crossed her arms across her chest and pouted her best pout. "I hate you, by the way."

His laughter grew louder as he pulled into another restaurant parking lot and put the truck in park. "Now, is this place okay?"

"It's fine," she said. When his head cocked to the side and his eyebrows raised, she laughed. "For real. It's fine."

"Come on. Let's get some food into you before your head spins." With that, he climbed out of the truck and crossed around to her door, but she was already out and walking toward the restaurant, her body taking over control when the smell of food hit her.

Chapter Twenty-Seven

Her office. It wasn't something that she thought she would ever have. It was tiny, just a little hole in the upstairs corner of the two-story house that served as the Art Center. The extent of its décor was a mahogany desk and chairs. The white painted walls were spattered with faded spaces in the shape of picture frames. It wasn't much, but it was hers.

She hoped she'd be able to do with the space what she wanted. It might be her office, but it was going to get depressing if it stayed like it was. Putting her box on the desk, she pulled out the few items she'd purchased over the weekend—a pen holder and pens to fill it, a notebook, a file organizer, and a mouse pad.

At a soft knock on the door frame, Liza looked up to find a grinning Margaret. "Hey. You getting settled in?"

Stepping away from the desk, she looked around as Margaret stepped into the room. "I haven't really started yet, but I'm excited. Thank you again for this opportunity."

Crossing the room, Margaret sat in one of the two seats across from the desk. Taking her cue, Liza sat in her desk chair and rolled to the side so she could see around the monstrous and ancient computer monitor.

"The board is excited to have you. Even if we hadn't already heard so much about you from your grandmother, your resumé was stellar. We look forward to seeing what you can do about getting some grants in here."

Liza grinned. There was a lot she couldn't yet talk about, but grants weren't one of them. She'd spent most of the previous week researching options for the Center. "I've already found several. I just have to get all the details. Some will have matching dollars, so I need to get into the financials and see where we stand."

"We're broke, is where we stand," Margaret said with a laugh. "But hopefully you can change that. Just get the information. I'll help you navigate the donor waters."

"Thank you. I have a lot of ideas."

"I hope so." Margaret looked around the office. "And do what you need with this office to make it yours." Then she pointed to the monitor. "And please order yourself a computer that isn't from the dark ages."

A breath of relief escaped Liza. "That is the best news I've heard all day. This thing is ancient."

"James was a great executive director, very good with the donors. But he was not technologically savvy. At all."

"I kind of figured that, from the state of the Center's website and social media pages. That's honestly the first thing I plan to do—update those. Frankly, if you don't have a presence digitally, you don't have a presence at all anymore. I also need a list of the classes currently scheduled and contact information for those teachers. I'd like to get in touch with them."

Margaret beamed. "I'll have that to you by the end of the day." Before Liza could get out a thank you, Margaret was slapping her knees and standing. "Welp, I'll leave you to it. You have my number if you need anything. Don't hesitate to call."

Liza stood with her. "Thank you again, Margaret."

"Don't thank me yet. You haven't met Eleanor." Before Liza could ask about Eleanor, Margaret was out the door. Sitting back in her chair, she leaned back and just took a moment to soak everything in.

Her phone dinged, and she picked it up, tabbing to the text notification from Christy. "Congrats girlie! Woo- hoo! Love ya!"

Liza grinned and sent her back a thank you, then silenced her phone. Pressing the button on the computer's tower, she waited as it creaked its way through the booting process. When the little green flashing line popped up, her mouth dropped open. This would not work. Not at all.

Reaching into her bag, she pulled out her laptop, connected it to the internet, and shoved the other computer's monitor and keyboard out of the way. Taking a sip of her coffee, she settled in to create a Facebook page for the Center.

Chapter Twenty-Eight

Of all the things her grandmother had instructed her to do, sleigh riding had been near the bottom of the list. They were nearly into March, and she'd really thought she might escape that task. But mother nature had other plans, in the form of a snowstorm that dumped nearly four inches of snow overnight. And it was beautiful, there was no denying that. Granted, she'd ultimately enjoyed all of the activities, but standing atop Derrick's hill, peering down at the fresh blanket of snow, a shiver of nerves ran up her spine.

They had all laughed at her when she'd appeared from Derrick's bathroom. The balloon of Derrick's snowsuit encapsulated her entire body, making her walk more of a wobble. Christy had provided the snow boots. Even Heath had reluctantly joined them. The gloves and hat were also

Derrick's. A testament to their Ohio roots, they were all dressed in just jeans, coats and snow boots.

The hill behind the farmhouse was a sloping drop-off that entered the woods. From their vantage point, Liza could see the corner of her cottage. On the other side, there was nothing but trees.

Derrick appeared beside her, a wooden sleigh propped in the snow next to him. "You ready for this?" he asked, and they both startled when Heath ran screaming past them, body-flopped onto a body-length sleigh, and shot down the hill. His sleigh went airborne for a second when he hit a mound, kicking up snow when it landed. Her eyes darted to the row of trees near the base of the hill and then back to Heath as he sped toward them. She hadn't realized she'd been holding her breath until he rolled off, landing safely in the blanket of snow, and she exhaled.

She turned to Derrick with a nervous laugh. "I was ready for this. I don't know if I am now."

Dropping the sleigh in the snow, he held onto it. "Hop on. It'll be fun. I promise."

Hoping he was right, Liza straddled the sleigh then, using Derrick's arm for support, lowered herself down. A yelp escaped her when the sleigh shifted, and she grabbed his arm with both hands. Below her, the hill looked much steeper from her seated position. Too steep.

"You can do it!" Christy yelled.

She shot her a thin smile. Off to the side and dragging his sleigh, a grinning Heath was nearly back to the top of the hill.

"I'm going to count to three," Derrick said. "Don't forget to roll off at the bottom."

Liza gripped the rope and nodded as Derrick said, "One, two, three," then gave the sled a gentle push. At first the descent was slow, fresh snow crackling under the sled, then the nose tipped, and she was gliding down the hill. Laughter bubbled up as wind stung her cheeks, then a "Woo-hoo!" as it picked up a little more speed. When she reached the bottom, she rolled off into the snow, then stood and looked up at the hill. She raised her arms in triumph as Derrick and Christy clapped for her.

Breathless and smiling so hard her cheeks hurt, Liza trudged up the snowy embankment dragging the sled behind her. When she reached the top, Christy clapped again.

"So?" Derrick asked as he reached for the sled.

She handed him the rope and flopped down on the snow. "That was awesome!" Then she looked around. "Where's Heath?"

"I don't know. He said he needed to run inside for a minute. Here," Christy said, extending her hand for Derrick to hand her the rope. "I haven't done this in forever."

An eyebrow raised, Derrick put the rope in her hand and stepped back. Liza watched as Christy placed it on the flat part of the hill, sat down, and then started scooching forward until the sleigh hit the downslope and took off, Christy's screams of enjoyment echoing across the valley.

With Christy off, Derrick turned to Liza. "I know it's not on your list, but you want to make a snow angel?"

"Yes!" She had forgotten all about snow angels, something she'd only seen on TV.

She reached up and grasped his outstretched hand, then followed him to an untouched place in the snow.

"Hold both of my hands," he said, and she took them. "Now just lay back flat." Slowly he lowered her until she was flat on her back, the cold snow nipping at the back of her uncovered neck. "Now make a windmill motion with your legs and arms."

Recalling what she'd seen in the movies, she pumped her legs and arms a few times. "Now what?"

He extended his hands again and hauled her to her feet. "Now look."

She turned to see the impression of an angel in the snow and grinned at him. He smiled back, his gloved hand reaching up to her cheek. Frozen, she waited for his touch, feeling that heat radiate through again despite the frigid temperatures.

"You have some snow on your cheek," he said and gently brushed it off, leaving a fiery trail where his hand had touched. Even when his glove lowered, he didn't step away and the space between them grew more solid with each passing second. She tilted forward. As did he. Another inch. He followed. Then they were there, lips nearly touching.

"Liza! Try this!" Heath yelled as he ran toward them, his plastic sled carried under his arm.

Startled, they jumped apart as he reached them, oblivious that he'd interrupted something. Liza glanced over as Christy topped the hill. Heath shoved the sled at Liza. "Here! Do what I did. Run and jump on it!"

Liza took the sled, giving Derrick a questioning look.

He just laughed and stepped back.

"Heath, I don't know..." she started, but then stopped. Why not? If she was going to do this thing, she might as well enjoy it. And the way Heath did it had looked fun. "Okay, fine. What's the worst that could happen?"

Sled in hand, she stood in front of the same section of hill Heath had started on earlier. "I just run and jump on it?"

"Yep!" Heath said, nearly bouncing with uncharacteristic excitement. Had she noticed the white film on the bottom of the sleigh, she would have known the source of his excitement. But she didn't notice it. Instead, she just ran forward and jumped on it, hitting the same track Heath had made earlier.

Immediately she knew something was wrong. When the sleigh hit the packed snow, it shot down the hill like a bullet. She tried to scream as the snow-covered ground blurred, but it was cut short by cold air attacking her lungs. Trees flashed in front of her, and her brain tried to tell her to roll off, but she froze, her hands gripping the edge of the sled. The last thing she remembered was the hard, brown bark of a tree, then pain, then nothing.

Christy was the first one through the hospital room door, followed closely by Derrick. Rushing to Liza's hospital bed, Christy nearly vaulted onto the mattress, her eyes still red from crying. She leaned in and hugged Liza firmly, but not with her usual squeeze. Liza looked over her shoulder at Derrick, who had taken up residence in the far corner.

Christy released the hug and leaned back. "I seriously thought you were dead."

Forcing a smile, Liza gently shook her head. "Just some stitches and a concussion. I'll live."

"I'm so sorry!" Christy cried, tears erupting from her eyes and cascading down her cheeks.

"For what? It was an accident."

From the corner, Derrick said, "Not exactly." He motioned for someone in the hallway to enter, and Christy's face hardened in barely concealed rage.

Head down, his ball cap clutched to his chest, Heath sheepishly entered the room, paused at the door, then walked to the bed. Christy stood up and moved to the side, delivering a withering look to her son. "Go on," she snapped. "Tell her."

A lone tear slid down his cheek, and he angrily wiped it away before taking a deep breath and exhaling slowly through trembling lips. "I'm sorry, Liza. It was. My fault. I waxed the bottom of my sleigh."

Well, that explained the luge like ride she'd taken. Reaching out, she waited for him to take her hand. "Did you mean for me to get hurt, Heath?"

Refusing to make eye contact, he shook his head. "No. I just thought it was funny. I'm sorry."

Liza patted his hand and grimaced as pain radiated through her entire body. Something told her it was going to hurt worse before it got better.

Christy appeared next to Heath, taking hold of his shoulders. "We've talked, and unless you're uncomfortable with it, Derrick is going to take you home with him tonight to keep watch. I have to work the evening shift, and I don't have any sick time left this month. The doctors said someone needs to keep an eye on you tonight. That way you can go home when you're ready, and it's not so far of a drive. You okay with that?"

Liza glanced at Derrick, who gave a curt nod. Her gut reaction was to decline and just go home to rest. But she'd be lying if she didn't admit having a head injury made her nervous. "That's fine, if it's okay with you, Derrick."

Again, with the nod. She was starting to think he was angry with her about something, the way he stood in the corner with his arms crossed like that, just nodding. A sharp pain in her head halted any desire to find out. Let him be mad if that's his problem. They could hash it out later.

"Okay, then. We're going to head out." Christy let go of her grip on Heath, leaned down, kissed Liza's cheek, then ushered Heath toward the door. As she passed Derrick, Christy placed one hand on his shoulder, paused for a moment, then walked out.

Alone now, they stared at each other, neither speaking. Then he pushed off the wall and dropped his arms. "I'm going to go get a coffee. I'll be back."

Before she could respond, he disappeared. Alone now, Liza ran through the events of the day and realized the sleigh ride had completed her list. She dropped her head back on the bed and winced as the sudden movement resulted in a wave of nausea and fresh pain. It should have been a day of celebration. A gathering at the cottage, clinking champagne glasses with at least Christy and hopefully Derrick. All she had to do was make it through the rest of the year, and her life would be back on track again.

Any wallowing she'd planned to do was cut short when the doctor walked into the room. She went over Liza's diagnosis and after care, informing her medicine had been called into the hospital pharmacy, then left as quickly as she had entered.

It wasn't long before a young man appeared pushing a wheelchair. "I don't need that," Liza said, sure she could handle the walk out of the hospital.

"Sorry, ma'am," the young man said as he popped the folded chair open and locked it in place. "Hospital policy." As soon as she stood, her head took a swim, and she swayed. A strong hand wrapped around her upper arm to steady her. She looked up to thank the young man but found Derrick's stern face instead. "I think she'll take the wheelchair."

Weak now and just ready to lie down somewhere, Liza nodded, and they both supported her as she turned around and dropped into the wheelchair. Then they were on the move.

They'd driven a good fifteen minutes before Liza finally asked, "Are you mad at me or something?"

Genuine shock lit up Derrick's face as he turned to look at her, then back at the road. "Mad at you? Why would I be mad at you?"

"I was just wondering. You seem angry."

"No, I'm not mad at you. Heath, yes. You, no."

She adjusted and sucked in her breath, her words coming out clipped and breathy. "Don't be too hard on him. He didn't mean for that to happen. Besides, if I'd rolled off, it wouldn't have been a big deal." Her breath sucked in again as the truck wheel on her side bounced into a hole and back out again.

"Sorry." His glance only lasted a second. "Not much I can do about the potholes."

"It's fine." Closing her eyes, she leaned her forehead against the cool window, then straightened again, figuring it wasn't a good idea. She was supposed to stay awake anyway and had already felt herself drifting off in just those few moments. "So, what's going on with you then, if you're not mad?"

"Honestly? You scared the shit out of me, Liza." At her name, she glanced at him and met his eyes. "I really thought you were dead."

"Well, I'm not." It was all she could come up with, and thankfully, he'd looked back to the road. It made her nervous anyway, driving on the patchy roads with snowdrifts on either side of them and pitch blackness ahead of them. That morning, she'd thought the entire scene beautiful, but driving in it now, only white on the outside and silence on the inside, was unsettling.

"I'm glad," he said out of the blue, and it took her a moment to process that he was commenting on her last statement. Then his hand slipped across the bench seat and landed on hers, covering it easily, his warmth warming her skin. He gave her hand a gentle squeeze, then returned to the steering wheel.

It was enough to send a shiver through her, followed by a sudden rush of heat that traveled through her body. She fought the urge to slide across the seat and lean into him, to let his arm drape across her shoulder.

But she wasn't going to do that. It was a moment of concern, that's all. They'd spent a lot of time together over the past months. It was understandable that he'd been worried. She would have been, too.

"Me too," she followed and then looked out the window. "Me too."

When they made it to the farm, he hopped out and hurried around to the passenger door before she could get out. As they made their way up the sidewalk, he held onto her arm. She allowed it all the way to the front door and inside.

But once inside, she patted his hand. "I'm good now. Thanks."

Without hesitation, his grip released, and he took a step back to shed his coat, hanging it on the coat rack in the corner. She, however, had only managed to get one arm out, the brace on the other giving her fits.

A guttural growl escaped her, then she laughed and held her cloaked arm out to him. "Do you mind?"

"Not at all."

Derrick slowly peeled off her coat and hung it next to his on the rack.

"Can we agree that anything I try to do for you in the next twenty-four hours is simply a friend helping a friend and not a commentary on your gender?"

She snorted, then cringed at the pain that shot through her body.

"Deal?" he asked.

"Deal."

He paused to see if she was going to change her mind, then put out his arm for her to take. And she did, as she felt the effects of removing her coat throughout her bruised body.

At the loveseat, she used his arm for support as she lowered herself down. A couple of winces and whines later, she was settled. He disappeared and returned with a blanket and pillow.

She took it from him, stretched her legs out, and propped her head on the pillow. "I thought I was supposed to stay awake."

"No. I'm supposed to wake you up every twenty minutes," he said as he scrolled his phone and started setting alarms.

"Derrick, you can't really be expected to..." He shot her an annoyed look, and she clamped her lips shut. "Okay. Fine."

After he finished setting the alarms on his phone, he reached down and tapped her feet. "Scooch a little."

After she pulled her feet back a few inches, he sat down in the space and covered his legs with the rest of the blanket. "You good?"

She nodded. They'd been on that love seat watching movies how many times? Five? Ten? She'd lost count. Her eyes roamed over his profile as he turned on the television and started scrolling. Handsome. He was handsome. A hottie as Anna would say. And available. So what was she waiting for?

And then a wave of nausea washed over her, and she remembered why she was there. All thoughts of anything but a platonic night in were washed away with it.

Chapter Twenty-Nine

I t felt odd being in Derrick's house without him, spooky even, like her painting—now hanging in place of the old pictures—was watching her. Making sure she acted appropriately, despite the overwhelming urge she had to snoop. Seriously, who wouldn't? It had been four days since the sled accident. And while Margaret had insisted she take a week off to recover, boredom had set in the day before. She'd asked Derrick if she could use his internet to search out grant opportunities, and he'd obliged by dropping a key off at the cottage on his way to the pub.

A few hours later, she was sitting on his loveseat and trying to focus on the search results cascading down her laptop screen. Half the battle of securing grant funding was just finding the grants. As she clicked and read, clicked and read, she jotted notes down in a red spiral notebook.

She was so focused, the vibration of her phone against the polished oak coffee table made her jump. Pushing her laptop off her lap and onto the loveseat, she stretched over and used her fingertips to coax the phone closer. Then she picked it up and answered it without looking at the caller ID.

"This is Liza," she said, picking the laptop back up and placing it on her lap.

"You snoop through my drawers yet?"

Though she laughed out a, "No," her cheeks burned for having considered it.

"How's your search going?"

"Going okay. Hey, you don't by chance have a laptop charger, do you? I forgot to bring mine."

"Check the lower right drawer of my desk in the library. It's where I keep all of my cords."

"You have a cord drawer, after all?"

"Doesn't everybody? Feel free to use what you need. Drinks. Snacks. Random cords. Whatever."

Closing the lid on her laptop, she sat it on the table and stood, giving her back a stretch.

As she made her way to the library, Derrick asked, "Want to come to the pub for dinner?"

She flipped on the light and stepped in, instinctively breathing in the rich smell of leather and old books. "Maybe. We'll see how far I get. Why? What's the special?"

"Chicken Pot Pie."

Her nose wrinkled in disgust.

"I heard that nose wrinkle from here."

Admiring the rows of beautifully bound books again, she laughed. "You don't know me that well."

"Apparently, I do. So?"

As she crossed to the desk, she opened the bottom drawer, revealing a tangled mob of cords. She grabbed a handful, and the whole tangle came with it. "Maybe. If I can find the cord in all this. Wow."

Dropping it all on top of the desk, she started sorting through them, painstakingly unraveling one that looked promising only to find it was a printer cord circa 1980. "Why do you have all of this stuff?"

"Might need it. So?"

"Fine. I'll be there."

In the background, Liza heard the buzzer announcing a customer. "Gotta go. Customer. See you this evening."

"Sounds good," she said, her fingers still untangling. The call disconnected, and she placed her phone on the desk while she pulled loose a cord, examined it, and fist- pumped the air in celebration. She dropped the cord next to her phone and grabbed the remaining ball of cords to drop it in the desk drawer when her eye caught something.

It was half-buried under other paperwork, but she had looked at that flowing penmanship so many times, just the few visible letters caught her attention.

Depositing the cords in the drawer, she pushed it closed with her leg then looked around the room. Gently, she pushed back the paperwork on top of it to reveal a letter, similar to hers but with Derrick's name on the front. Hesitantly, she picked it up and flipped it over, the open flap calling her name. She pulled out the letter, then stopped. This wasn't right. Whatever was in that letter was personal to Derrick. She had no right reading it. Why wouldn't her grandmother include him? He'd been as important to her as she and Anna.

Despite those thoughts, her hands refused to stop pulling it from the envelope. They unfolded it, and she started to read her grandmother's words to Derrick. The way she loved Derrick, Christy, and Heath like her own and how blessed she'd been to have them all in her life. Liza smiled, a fat tear sliding down her cheek, a sad smile on her lips.

Until she reached halfway through the letter and saw her name. Holding her breath, she read. Silent partner in the pub. Take care of Liza. If you do, the pub is yours without further payment. Or you can pay it off, if you don't wish to agree. And under no circumstances, tell Liza about the deal.

She read it again, shock freezing any emotion she may have felt as the words sunk in. She dropped the letter onto the desk, not bothering to put it back in its envelope, and marched out.

Liza paced her living room while Anna's line rang. When her voicemail answered, Liza groaned. After the beep, she left a brief, "Call me as soon as you can." Then dropped the phone on the table and cursed her inability to send a text message.

The anger had dissipated, leaving behind just a sick feeling. For nearly a year, she'd hung out with him. Had learned to trust him. And a part of her she hadn't fully accepted yet thought there might even be the possibility of a relationship. She had thought he felt the same way. Now she would never know. Liza wished she'd never seen that letter.

The phone rang. She snatched it up and answered.

"Hey," Derrick said. "I thought you were coming to eat dinner. Everything okay?"

No, everything is definitely not okay! Not okay at all. That's what she wanted to say, but she just said, "Everything's fine. I just got busy. Listen, can I call you later?"

"Sure," he said, and she could hear the mix of confusion and surprise in his voice. She hated that she recognized it. "You sure you're okay?"

"Yeah. Something just came up. I'll talk to you later."

"Okay, then. Call me if you need anything." He'd barely gotten the sentence out before she hung up.

The phone clenched in her hand, she breathed in and then exhaled slowly twice. Thankfully, before she had time to work herself up again, the phone rang. This time, she checked the caller ID first. Seeing that it was Anna, she answered. "Hey."

"Hey yourself. Everything okay?"

"Nope." Liza walked to the couch and flopped down. "Not at all."

"Okay?"

"The whole thing with Derrick was orchestrated by Grandma."

"What do you mean?"

"I mean, she left him a letter, too. His pub in exchange for helping me for the year."

There was silence followed by a door closing, as Anna moved to another room. "Okay? What do you mean his pub for helping you?"

"Just what I said. She apparently helped bankroll his pub. If I came here, and he helped me for the year, then he gets the pub free and clear. If not, then it reverts to their original agreement that upon her death, he pays the balance in full to avoid issues with heirs."

Again, Anna was silent for a moment. "Okay? I'm not seeing the problem here."

Liza dropped onto the couch and let out a sigh. "I thought he was helping me because he wanted to help me. I thought there was something there. Oh my gosh, Anna. Are you really going to make me spell it out for you?" she asked, the hardness in her voice sharper than she intended.

"Whoa, now," Anna snapped, the big sister tone coming out.

"Sorry, I am just...I don't know what I am. Sorry."

"It's fine. Did something happen between you two?"

"No. Not really," Liza said. "Not yet, anyway." A tear slid down her cheek. Angrily, she wiped it away. She refused to cry over him.

"Now it makes sense. You're in love with him!"

Liza rolled her eyes. "I wouldn't say in love."

"Whatever. There's something. Am I being supportive sister or brutally honest sister here?"

Despite wanting to opt for the easy route, Liza said, "Brutally honest, please. I called for your advice."

"Then, Liza, you're a thirty-four-year-old woman. Go talk to the man."

Liza shook her head. "No. I'm not doing that. At least not until the year is up. The letter specifically told him not to tell me. What if he had to sign an NDA? I don't want to cause him to lose his pub."

There was silence, then a sigh. "Okay, fine. Given what Grandma did with yours, that is a reasonable assumption. Now, why do you care?"

"Because regardless of the reason, he and Christy have been a huge help to me. I just apparently got the signals wrong."

"So, you are in love with him."

"Stop that. I'm not in love with him. That doesn't mean I want to destroy him."

"Okay. Keep telling yourself that as long as you need to."

Liza let out an irritated huff. "I change my mind. Supportive sister."

Anna laughed. "Fine. You have, what? Two months?"

"Sixty-four days."

"Then just focus on work. I mean, if you're still planning to stay, that is."

"Yes. I'm still staying. That job is a dream job for me. I'm not going anywhere."

"Okay, then. Focus on work. Do your thing. Wait until the year is up and see what happens."

Liza tried to imagine the next two months without interacting with Derrick and frowned. There was no way she could be around him and pretend she hadn't seen the letter. "I can do that."

"I'm coming!" Anna yelled, then said, "Geez. Five minutes, people. Five minutes. I have to go. I love you."

"Love you, too."

"Let me know if you need vengeful sister."

It was Liza's turn to laugh. They said their goodbyes and Liza hung up. Suddenly, Maple Hill seemed a lot lonelier.

Chapter Thirty

Derrick looked up from the bar when the buzzer sounded. It wasn't until the disappointment at seeing Christy stroll in settled on him that he realized he'd been hoping for Liza. And that irritated him, almost as much as her sudden disappearance. At least from his orbit. She was still in Maple Hill. He knew that much. And still in the cottage. He saw her lights through the leafless trees on his way home. Part of him would be glad when those trees were full again so he could stop looking through them.

Christy plopped down on a bar stool and dropped her oversized bag on the counter. "Hey, big brother. Do you think you could pick up Heath from baseball practice this afternoon? I got called in this evening."

"Sure," he said, pushing Liza from his mind and back to restocking. "What time?"

"Six."

"That's no problem. He played well last game."

"Yes, he did. Must be all that whiffle tag." She grinned and stood back up.

"Speaking of, have you by chance talked to Liza lately?"

Christy pursed her lips, and her eyes shifted up as she considered. "Actually, I haven't now that you mention it. Between work and baseball conditioning, there hasn't been much free time. She did talk to Heath a few weeks ago about that comic book guy, but other than that, no. Why? You haven't talked to her?"

Derrick shook his head. "No, but never mind. I was just wondering. I thought maybe I'd done something."

"I'll check in on her."

"You don't have to do that."

Christy waved him off. "I need to talk to her, anyway. I guess I also need to talk to you." She grinned that toothy smile that meant she was about to ask Derrick to do something he would not like. "I want to host a staying party for Liza the night before her year ends, and I want to do it at the farm."

Derrick wrinkled his nose. Not at the party, but at hosting at the house. "Can't you do it here?"

"I could, but I'd rather do it at the farm. It won't be that many people, and I'll handle everything, including cleaning for the party and clean-up after."

"Why the farm?"

She shrugged and slung her bag over her shoulder. "Since when do I need a reason to use my family's home?"

Narrowing his eyes, he sighed. "Fine. Whatever."

As if she hadn't already known he'd give in, she clapped excitedly. "I'll let you know the plan, and I'll check in on her, too. Because now that you've made me stop and think about it, it is weird that I haven't talked to her."

"Whatever, but don't mention me."

Christy rolled her eyes. "Suit yourself, brother. Okay, I have to go. Thanks for getting Heath."

"No thanks needed."

As she sauntered out, Derrick returned to stocking, doing his best to not think about Liza.

Christy knocked on Liza's office door, then strode in without waiting for an invite.

"So, what's going on between you and my brother?" she asked as she plunked down in the wooden chair on the other side of the desk. "More importantly, what's going on between you and me?"

With a deep breath, Liza pushed back from her computer and rolled to the side so she could see Christy. Guilt set in. As did irritation over her direct questions. It took her a moment to process which emotion was stronger. "I have no idea what you mean, Christy."

Christy leaned forward, propping her elbows on the desk. "Don't give me that pile of poo. I haven't talked to you in weeks and, I just learned, neither has Derrick. You're acting weird right now, and I want to know why."

"It's nothing. I've just been busy learning this job, and I've been painting in the evenings. It's a lot."

Christy's eyes narrowed, then she relaxed against the chair. "Okay, then. I mean, I don't believe you, but okay. Keep your secrets. Can you do me one favor, though?" She didn't wait for Liza's answer. "If, for whatever reason, you want nothing to do with my brother, can you not lump me in there?"

Evidently, guilt was where she was going to land. "Christy, it's not really something I want to talk about right now. And it's nothing bad. It really is mostly this job," she lied. "That's all. I'm trying to build programs and secure grants. Plus, learn the town."

"We're still cool?"

Liza nodded, though she wasn't entirely sure. She couldn't help but wonder how much Christy knew, though instinct told her it had to be nothing. Still, it was best to keep her distance for now, if nothing else, to avoid letting the truth slip. "We are good."

"Good. And you and Derrick?"

"Good there, too. Just busy."

"Well, great. Because I'm throwing you a party the night before your year is over, and your attendance is required."

"Christy, you don't need..."

"I thought you said we're cool?"

"I did."

"Then you know I fully plan to celebrate you staying. So, plan to be there. Mark it on your calendar. Whatever you executive director-types do. It will be at the farm."

Forcing a grin, Liza nodded. "Okay, then. I'll mark that evening off."

"Perfect." She checked the clock on her phone and jumped. "I gotta go. I'll be late." She headed to the door and turned. "Good, right?"

"Yes. Good."

With a wave, Christy disappeared.

Derrick had finished stocking and was moving to the kitchen when his cellphone vibrated. He dug it from his pocket and answered. "This is Derrick."

"I don't know what you did, big brother, but whatever it was, you need to make it right."

"What are you talking about?"

"Liza. She's mad at you," she said, elongating the word mad.

"What did she say?"

"She didn't have to say. Me, I'm good. You, not so much. What did you do?"

"Christy. I have no idea. Seriously. The last time we talked, she was at my house, and everything was fine. Then that evening, it wasn't fine anymore. That's all I know."

"Have you tried to call her?"

"Yes. And text her. I've asked to stop by. It's always the same thing. She's busy. She's not home. I finally stopped because it was venturing into stalkerish. I don't know."

"I'm headed into work. I'll figure it out. Don't worry. Gotta run. Bye."

"I wasn't," he said, but the line was already dead. It didn't matter because it was a lie, anyway. He had been worried.

More worried than he would ever admit to another human. Worried enough that it was already shifting to anger. After the last year, he deserved better than the cold shoulder, didn't he? Did he?

He had no idea what he'd done, and she had opened no doors to discuss it. If he were a better man, he might have pushed the issue, showed up on her doorstep, forced at least some kind of discussion.

He wasn't a better man. Instead, he'd just simply taken the hint. Though it made absolutely no sense to him. One minute, they'd been inching ever so close to that line between friendship and relationship, and the next, she was again a virtual stranger.

With a shake of his head, he brushed it off. If that was how she wanted it, fine. He had work to do.

Chapter Thirty-One

*S*eriously, who throws a staying party?, Liza thought as she stepped out of her car. Christy, that's who, and from the look of the floating heads moving around the front room of the farmhouse, she'd invited nearly every person Liza had met the past year.

What was she thinking? Agreeing to a party at Derrick's house, of all places. Not that she had been asked, but she could have put up more of a fight. She was just not ready for this. She wasn't ready to be back in that house or back around Derrick.

As of midnight, the entire ordeal would be behind her. Derrick would get his pub paid off. She would get her inheritance and the cottage and start making it her own.

All would work out for everyone. She just had to make it to midnight.

"Are you going to stand out here all night or what?" Christy's voice from the front door brought her attention back to the party.

Whatever she thought about the party, it didn't matter now. There was no way she was going to disappoint Christy. Though she wondered if the location of the party was a setup.

And while she hadn't mentioned the rift between her and Derrick, Liza knew Christy had noticed. It would have been impossible not to notice, as much time as she and Derrick had spent together over the last year. Not to mention, the two of them talked about nearly everything. There was no way Christy didn't know. Unless, of course, Derrick didn't care. That possibility hadn't entered her mind until she walked up the stairs.

In his library, Derrick tried to tune out the sound of the party below. Which he'd done a pretty good job of until he heard the roar announcing Liza's arrival. It hurt more than he would ever admit, knowing she was just down the stairs from him.

Paperwork. He needed to focus on the mounds of paperwork on his desk. It was time for the annual purge and organize.

Taking a deep breath, he focused on the first pile. On top was a stack of mail he hadn't opened from when? A week ago? Two? Didn't matter, the envelopes were just for his records. He knew what was in them and paid online.

Pulling the first stack, his eye caught it—the neat handwriting of Dot. Slowly he put down the stack in his hand and picked up the letter. Then he picked up the envelope underneath. He remembered folding the letter and putting it back. And it shouldn't have been near the top of the stack. Not by a long shot. It all clicked—Liza in the house alone, needing a cord.

"Seriously?" he asked the empty room, his full attention now focused on the party downstairs.

Pushing back from his desk, he snatched up the letter and hurried to the stairs. Liza was in mid-conversation with Margaret about the next month's art installation when Derrick stepped up to them. "Hi, Margaret."

"Hi, Derrick. You have a beautiful home."

"Thank you," he said, cutting her off, his eyes snapping to Liza. "Liza, can I have a word with you? In private?"

Flustered at the interruption and his proximity, Liza took a step back and shook her head. "Derrick, we were kind of in the middle of something."

"Don't be silly," Margaret said, swiping at the air to wave her away. "You go and enjoy your party. We can talk about this Monday." Then she gave them the most overdramatic wink Liza had ever seen in real life, causing that blush to rear its ugly head again. Effectively fanning the anger bubbling up in its wake.

As soon as Margaret was out of earshot, she turned on Derrick. "What?" she hissed.

Ten minutes earlier, being talked to that way would have been the last straw for Derrick. But if at the heart of all this was the contents of that letter, he'd take it at least until he'd had a chance to explain.

"Outside," he said and nodded to the front porch.

When she didn't move, his eyes locked onto hers. "Please. Five minutes."

"Fine. Five minutes," Liza said and followed him to the front door. Once outside, he moved off to the corner of the porch, out of the line of sight of the party-goers.

Following his lead, she too stepped out of sight, her arms wrapping around her body against the sudden change in temperature. She should have remembered to grab her jacket. Better yet, she should have said no. This was not a conversation she wanted to have with him tonight. Or ever, really. Given time to think about it, she would be perfectly happy to never discuss it. He would get what he wanted. She would have what she needs. They could move on with their lives and let it be over. Short of saying all of that, she couldn't think of anything else to say, so Liza just looked at him.

Derrick waited for her to speak, then realizing she wasn't going to, he sighed, ran a hand through his hair, and presented the letter. "This was laying open on my desk."

Her expression was unreadable. Well, he pretended it was unreadable. There was no shock. No surprise. Just what appeared to be disinterest. Finally, she said, "Okay?"

A rush of irritation ran through Derrick. "Okay?"

Couldn't this just be over yet? Liza thought. "Yes. I saw it. I don't know what else you want me to say."

"Is this why you've been acting so weird?"

Liza's hackles rose. "I have not been acting weird. I just decided it was best to put some distance between us."

"Because of this letter?"

"Because of a lot of things."

"But mainly this letter."

She huffed. "Yes, okay! Because of that. Of course, because of that. Seriously, Derrick. I understand why you did what you did. I mean, she manipulated me into moving here, after all. But that doesn't change that all of this time, I thought you were helping me, spending time with me because you actually liked helping me and spending time with me. So, yes, because of that."

Then he grinned. That boyish grin that only a couple of months earlier would have made her heart flutter and her body react like a teenager. Now, all it did was spark her anger.

"I'm going back inside. Now you know. Tomorrow is a year. If asked, I will testify to how much of a help you were to me and that you never told me. As of midnight, you're off the hook."

She turned to walk away when his voice, soft and serious, stopped her. "I paid it off."

Turning, she looked at him warily. "What?"

"The remaining balance. I paid it off. I made that decision at the reception after the funeral. In full. It's what I was doing at Bill's that day you were there. I was never helping you or spending time with you because of this."

"What are you talking about?" Her arms crossed against her chest again.

Now he squirmed. "You know how we first met, right? The funeral."

"Yes."

"Well, I kind of made a snap judgment about you, and let's just say it didn't really make me want to be tied down to you for an entire year."

She blushed. "Well, okay then." She turned to leave, but he reached out and gently took her arm.

"It was a stupid snap judgment, but I'm not sorry. Liza, please look at me."

Against the voice in her head telling her to run, she turned. He was so close to her, his body just inches from hers, those blue eyes looking down at her.

"I'm not sorry that I didn't take it. Because had I taken it, I would have felt guilty for not telling you. Why didn't you just ask me about it?"

"Because I wasn't sure if you had to sign something saying you wouldn't tell me. I didn't want you to lose your pub. So, the last year, it had nothing to do with the letter?" she asked again, just to be sure, hope replacing the evaporating anger.

"Nothing. Liza, I'm assuming I'm not alone in thinking there is more here than just friends, right?"

"No," she managed.

His head cocked to the side. "No, as in there isn't more, or no, as in I'm not alone? I just want to be clear here."

With a laugh, she nudged his chest lightly with her hand. "Not alone." He reached up and covered it, keeping her hand in place.

"That is good to hear. So, I have a proposal. How about we start over?" Derrick released her hand and took a step back, extending his hand to shake. "Hi, I'm Derrick. I was wondering if you would like to go out on a date with me?"

She grimaced and shook her head. "Seriously, that was creepy. I would have run the other way. How about we start maybe not that far back?"

"Fine, when do you want to start?"

With one step, she closed the distance between them again, so close she heard his breath catch. "When do you usually kiss a woman the first time?"

"Well," he said, his hand moving up her arm to her neck. "Date three?"

Liza slipped her arms around his neck as she lifted on her tiptoes, her lips a breath away from his. "Date three it is then."

Without hesitation, he closed the gap, his lips taking hers. Slow at first, searching. Her breath caught. Nerves rapid-fired through her body as his other hand wrapped around her waist and pulled her into him. Their bodies molded together. Months of pent-up attraction poured into the kiss, their hands grasping skin and clothing as they found their rhythm.

"Oh, my gosh!" Christy yelled from the open door, and Liza and Derrick jerked apart.

"Really, sis?" Derrick asked, breathless as he moved to the side, his arm still around Liza's waist.

Christy crossed the porch in two bounds and hugged them. "It's about time you two stopped being idiots! I love you both!"

"I love you, too. Now go back inside so I can keep kissing Liza, please."

Liza's blush deepened. Christy beamed, then tiptoed back to the door, closing it while still peeking through the crack.

Alone again, Derrick turned to Liza and grinned. "Where were we?"

"You were about to walk me inside," she said, planting her palm on his chest. The fog cleared, and her attention snapped back to the party inside. People who could walk out and see them.

With a groan, he kissed her forehead and sighed. "Fine," he said as he presented his elbow. "Your party awaits, madame."

As they walked toward the door, she lifted and whispered in his ear. "I haven't told you what the fourth date means yet."

He stumbled at the threshold, then straightened as she stepped in front of him and walked inside. She looked over her shoulder, then reached back for his hand. He took it, his thumb lightly caressing the inside of her palm, sending shivers through her body.

She smiled and led him in. As the door closed behind them, she was home.

Also By Michelle Leigh Miller

The Evelyn Series

Finding Evelyn

Reconstructing Evelyn

Evelyn

If you enjoyed The Cottage in Maple Hill and would like to be notified of new releases, sign up for her newsletter at michelleleighmiller.com. She can also be found on Facebook and Instagram.

Made in the USA
Middletown, DE
11 October 2024

62237077R00209